A Dance with Murder

Also by Elizabeth Coleman

A Routine Infidelity
Losing the Plot

A Dance with Murder

Elizabeth Coleman

PANTERA PRESS | SPARKING IMAGINATION, CONVERSATION & CHANGE

PANTERA PRESS

This is a work of fiction. Names, characters, organisations, dialogue and incidents are either products of the author's imagination or are used fictitiously, and any resemblance to actual people, living or dead, firms, events or locales is coincidental.

First published in 2024 by Pantera Press Pty Limited.
www.PanteraPress.com

Text Copyright © Elizabeth Coleman, 2024
Elizabeth Coleman has asserted her moral rights to be identified as the author of this work.

Design and Typography Copyright © Pantera Press Pty Limited, 2024
® Pantera Press, three-slashes colophon device, *sparking imagination, conversation & change* are registered trademarks of Pantera Press Pty Limited. Lost the Plot is a trademark of Pantera Press Pty Limited.

This book is copyright, and all rights are reserved.
We welcome your support of the author's rights, so please only buy authorised editions.

Without the publisher's prior written permission, and without limiting the rights reserved under copyright, none of this book may be scanned, reproduced, stored in, uploaded to or introduced into a retrieval or distribution system, including the internet, or transmitted, copied or made available in any form or by any means (including digital, electronic, mechanical, photocopying, sound or audio recording, and text-to-voice). This book is sold subject to the condition that it shall not, by way of trade or otherwise, be lent, re-sold, hired out, or otherwise circulated in any form of binding or cover other than that in which it is published and without a similar condition being imposed on the subsequent recipient.

Please send all permission queries to:
Pantera Press, P.O. Box 1989, Neutral Bay, NSW, Australia 2089 or info@PanteraPress.com

A Cataloguing-in-Publication entry for this book is available from the National Library of Australia.
ISBN 978-0-6457578-8-0 (Paperback)
ISBN 978-0-6457578-7-3 (eBook)

Cover Design: Elysia Clapin
Cover Images: (all via Canva.com) Ballerina Dancer Illustration by *levaLi from pixabay*, Splash of Paint by *Marks Of Hue*, Schnauzer Giant Clipart by *dmytrobosnak*
Publisher: Katherine Hassett
Project Editor: Kirsty van der Veer
Editor: Lauren Finger
Proofreader: Bronwyn Sweeney
Typesetting: Kirby Jones
Printed and bound in Australia by McPherson's Printing Group

The paper this book is printed on is certified against the Forest Stewardship Council® Standards. McPherson's Printing Group holds FSC® chain of custody certification SA-COC-005379. FSC® promotes environmentally responsible, socially beneficial and economically viable management of the world's forests.

*Marianne, Jackie, Stephanie and David, this one's for you.
Thank you.*

Dogs never bite me. Just humans.
Marilyn Monroe

Chapter One

Ted

Ted Bristol surreptitiously glanced at her watch. She was now thirty-seven minutes into her Tinder date with Jarrod Beasley, and he still hadn't asked her a single question about herself. Not that she could tell him the truth if he did. She obliged him with a rapt smile as he rabbited on about how he'd made the courageous move from chartered accountant to life coach. According to Jarrod, he was a feminist with an excellent sense of humour, and even though he had washboard abs from his daily workouts, his true priority was his spiritual fitness.

Ted looked down at her miniature schnauzer, Miss Marple, who was sprawled at her feet, and she could've sworn she saw her eyes roll.

It was a crisp spring night, and all around them the joint was jumping. They were at Trax, a dog-friendly outdoor restaurant sandwiched between the murky Yarra River and Flinders Street Station, lit up golden against the night sky. Ted could see pedestrians crossing the nearby Princes Bridge and diners across the water at Southbank, as the tall spire of the Victorian Arts Centre jutted up behind them and disappeared into the dark clouds. The whole precinct was buzzing, but she forced her attention back to Jarrod, subtly studying his squarish freckled face and his small blue eyes for signs of malevolence.

Saturday night last week, an ethereal ballerina called Giselle had turned up at Edwina Bristol Investigations (EBI), desperate for Ted's help. She'd recently been forced to deactivate her Insta account after an anonymous stalker had slid into her DMs with love messages from multiple untraceable accounts. But leaving Instagram hadn't worked. Handwritten notes had started turning up in her letterbox and even under her back doormat, and earlier last Saturday night, things had escalated. When Giselle had returned to her car after *Don Quixote* rehearsals at the Australian Ballet, she'd found a bloody lamb's heart on her bonnet. An archer's arrow was plunged through the heart, with a handwritten note:

See what you're doing to me?

The implicit menace in the blood-spattered note was chilling, and Ted wasn't surprised that poor Giselle was terrified. After Ted had calmed her and helped her to focus, Giselle had pointed her finger at Jarrod Beasley. Apparently, they'd gone on a Tinder date about six weeks ago, and when Giselle declined a second date, Jarrod had bombarded her with passive-aggressive texts, like:

How can you claim to be a fully evolved human if you're closed off to other humans?

'The guy's a narcissist,' Ted had told her.

'I suppose you're right,' Giselle had agreed. She was wearing a floaty dress in a smoky pink. A dark curl had escaped from her bun and was hanging atop her translucent face. 'I called him to try and discuss it, but that just seemed to make things worse.'

Ted was astonished, although she was careful not to show it.

'You called him? It's never a good idea to engage with a stalker, Giselle.'

'I know, it was stupid. I'm sorry.'

'Don't *you* apologise. There's only one person who should be apologising.'

When Ted thought of the men who wanted to own women and chose to terrorise them if they couldn't have them, and the men who tried to manipulate women into doubting themselves and took pleasure in making them feel violated in their daily life, it filled her with rage. Of course, women were capable of stalking too, but that wasn't the case in most instances, and certainly not in this one. It was a guy who'd left the bloody lamb's heart on Giselle's windscreen; she'd seen photographic evidence. The stalker had used a wi-fi jammer to disable all the CCTV in the vicinity, but luckily a passer-by had spotted something suss, and he'd snapped some pics from behind a tree.

Now, at Trax a week later, Ted reminded herself to take a step back and not jump to conclusions about Jarrod – even though he'd just told her he was home alone last Saturday night, which equalled no alibi, *and* he was a perfect physical match.

The shots showed a guy who could unhelpfully be described as 'of average height and build'. He was wearing a nondescript hoodie that obscured his face, and his jeans were equally nondescript. But in a stroke of good luck, his distinctive sneakers were captured in stark relief by a streetlight. Within twenty-four hours, Ted had identified the sneakers as Cariuma Gerry Lopez red canvas sneakers with a white 'lightning' stripe.

Did Jarrod own a pair? Once he let her get a word in, she was planning to ask. Not that a yes would be definitive, but hopefully it would be the first incriminating clue of many. She was hoping she could somehow get a sample of his handwriting, although she doubted that would prove conclusive. The writing in the notes slanted backwards, and the t's had a flamboyant loop, both of which were no doubt designed to disguise the stalker's regular writing.

Jarrod leaned across the table, and his eyes stared intensely into hers. He smiled, and his teeth were almost freakishly white. 'Why don't we skip the meaningless small talk?'

I'm not talking, Ted thought.

'I'm all about getting to the true essence of a human,' Jarrod said. 'I've got three questions I like to ask my life-coaching clients, in no particular order. I call it my Three-Step Self-Discovery Test.'

'Wow,' Ted said, when she was really thinking, *How much longer do I have to humour this guy before I can start my interrogations? Would another six seconds suffice?* 'Okay, I'm up for it. What are the questions?'

Jarrod paused, presumably to build the anticipation.

'First question: What's the most courageous thing you've ever done?'

That was easy, Ted thought. Emotionally, it was finally admitting to her dad that she blamed herself for her mum's death. Physically, it was defending herself against a violent embezzler twice her size who'd been intent on killing her and Miss Marple. Not that she'd share those things with Jarrod. And as it happened, she didn't have to.

'For me,' said Jarrod, 'it was making a difficult decision to do the right thing.'

Ted stifled a snort. Of course, she should have known Jarrod would only be interested in his answer.

'It was before I became a life coach. I was head accountant for a celebrity chef, and the guy was a crook. He wanted me to cook the books while he was cooking the food.' Jarrod paused so Ted could absorb his clever word play. She tried to look appropriately appreciative. 'And I'm not talking peanuts, the guy wanted to hide *big bucks*. So, I dobbed him in to the cops, even though I was scared for my safety. I didn't know if I'd end up in concrete shoes.'

No, Cariumas, Ted thought.

'He never went to jail, so I don't know what happened from the cops' end, but at least I know I did the right thing. And I'm still here.' He smiled at her as if to say, *Lucky for you.*

Ted wondered what the point of this story was. Was she supposed to applaud?

He took a swig of his wine. 'He's still a celebrity chef, and everyone thinks he's Mr Nice Guy, but he's bad news. You'll know his name, but there's no point asking. I'm not going to say.'

Ted couldn't rouse any curiosity. She suspected Jarrod had fabricated the story and, besides, she had no interest in celebrity chefs. Every time you went online, some random was telling you how to sauté spinach.

Just then, a large alsatian passing their table bared its fangs, and Miss Marple emitted a low growl. Jarrod glanced down at her as if he'd forgotten she was there.

'The little guy must be scared of that German shepherd.'

'She's female,' Ted reminded him pleasantly, 'and she's not scared.' This was the blackest mark against Jarrod yet. Since when would a dog called Miss Marple be male? And Miss Marple wasn't scared of anything. 'She's just warning him to keep his distance.'

But Jarrod was nodding at a waitress who'd appeared with their meals.

'Cheers,' Jarrod said as she deposited a lump of lamb shanks in front of him.

The shocking sight of the bloody lamb's heart on Giselle's windscreen flashed into Ted's mind, but she pushed the ugly image away. She braced herself for Jarrod's second 'self-discovery' question, but he seemed to have shelved that subject for now.

'You're a beautiful lady.'

Ted attempted a flirtatious smile. 'Thank you.'

Jarrod leaned across the table to look into her eyes. 'I hope you let yourself own the power your beauty gives you.'

Was this guy for real? Ted didn't derive power from her looks, she derived it from being a kickarse PI who'd recently solved her first murder. Not that it served her to share that with Jarrod.

'I try to,' she lied.

'And I love your dress.'

'Thanks.'

She'd bought this black silk halter-neck online from Zara especially for this covert job. She doubted she'd ever wear it again, but it was on sale, so that was a win. And at least it was tax deductible. Jarrod's approval was vindicating her decision to ditch her usual outfit of jeans with a T-shirt and/or hoodie and sneakers. That would never have worked with a guy like him. He'd said in his Tinder profile that he was looking for a woman 'who takes care of herself', which everyone knew was code for 'skinny and glamorous'. So, Ted had even applied some lipstick she'd bought from Chemist Warehouse and used a bit extra to rub into her cheeks. But that was as far as she was prepared to go.

'You're tiny,' Jarrod said.

Typical. In spite of his BS about being a feminist, Jarrod clearly wanted a doll. No wonder he'd been attracted to a ballerina. He'd probably wanted to pop her on top of a jewellery box (and a few other things) and watch her daintily twirl around.

Letting this probable stalker set the agenda was driving Ted crazy. It was time to start the investigating. 'So ... Have you met many other women on Tinder?'

Jarrod laughed. 'Are we going there already?'

'I guess we are.' Ted giggled.

Jarrod leaned back against his chair and revelled in her attention. His mousy-brown hair was shaved at the sides and floppy on top. Ted couldn't help noticing that the floppy bit hadn't budged, despite the stiff spring breeze. That must be some Trump-grade hairspray.

'I've met a few. I was seeing a model for a while, not that her career was relevant. I was attracted to her self-actualisation.'

Ha! Ted thought. *I'd be willing to bet her self-actualisation looked hot in a bikini.*

'And I dated a ballerina.'

Ted straightened. 'A ballerina? Wow.'

'She's a pro, she's in the Australian Ballet.'

'Oh my God, really? What's her name?'

'Giselle Tereiti.'

'Giselle? Beautiful name. And what happened with you guys?'

'It didn't work out. She wanted to take things to the next level, but she wasn't evolved enough for me. So, I cut off contact. It was the kindest thing.'

Ted nodded. Why would Jarrod need to lie if he wasn't Giselle's stalker? The evidence seemed to be adding up. All her synapses were screaming, *It's him!* She clutched at something else to say.

'How are your lamb shanks?'

'They're excellent,' Jarrod said. 'And I know my meat, my old man's a butcher.'

Ted watched him expertly dissect the lamb. 'Your dad's a butcher?'

'Yeah, and I'm proud to own my humble origin story.'

So, Jarrod had lied about breaking up with Giselle, he had no alibi for last Saturday night, *and* he'd also been around offal his entire life – it made sense that he'd use a lamb's heart to intimidate. For Ted the deal was now sealed, but she glanced down at Miss Marple for affirmation. Miss Marple's acutely intelligent eyes narrowed, and she wagged her grey tail to the left in a classic canine expression of negativity. So they were on the same page, as always.

While Ted was contemplating what to do next, Jarrod reached over and took her hand. It happened so fast that it took her a second to react, and before she could do anything—

'Ted!'

The voice was familiar, but out of context. Ted was still trying to place it when she turned to see Usma Ali, her warband leader from Swordcraft, the medieval battle game, where she usually spent her Saturday nights. Usma was at the tail end of a group leaving the packed restaurant. Ted hadn't noticed her in the crowd.

'Usma, hey!'

'Hey, Ted. Hey, Miss Marple. Why aren't you at Swordcraft?'

'Look who's talking.'

'My sister's birthday,' Usma said. She looked down at Ted and Jarrod's clasped hands and grinned. 'I'm guessing this isn't your brother.'

Ted laughed weakly. What if Usma blew her cover and outed her as a PI? Jarrod thought she was a real estate agent. But luckily Jarrod maintained his tradition of only being interested in himself.

'I'm definitely *not* her brother.'

He squeezed Ted's hand and she wanted to puke. Usma knew her as a fierce warrior in their all-female Ice Elves warband, who left a trail of 'dead' combatants in her wake. She wasn't the type who'd dump her warband for the sake of some guy, especially a guy like him.

'This is Jarrod. Jarrod, this is my mate, Usma.'

Usma gave Ted a sly little smile. 'Well, I'll leave you to enjoy each other's company.'

But I'm not enjoying it, Ted wanted to shout. *This is strictly work. I'm trying to take a toxic stalker off the streets.* But, instead, she was forced to say, 'Awesome. See you at Swordcraft next week.'

'Yeah, see ya then.'

Usma gave Ted another cheeky grin and sauntered off. Ted thought Jarrod would ask about Swordcraft, but it didn't involve him, so why would he? She tried to disentangle her hand, but he was already squeezing it again.

'Have I told you I'm developing a wellness app?'

Ted wanted to suffocate herself in her risotto. As she tried in vain to formulate an escape plan, Miss Marple trotted over to the water bowl that Trax left out for canine patrons. Ted watched distractedly as her dog lapped from the water. But when Miss Marple turned away from the bowl, she suddenly yelped. Ted felt a little kick of alarm.

'Miss Marple?'

Miss Marple limped back to the table, her fluffy tail hanging bleakly between her legs.

'Miss Marple! What's happened? Are you okay?'

Ted pulled her hand from Jarrod's and crouched down beside her dog, who was now sitting with her front right paw lifted plaintively in the air. Ted gently took the paw in her hand, and Miss Marple yelped again.

'I'm sorry. I didn't mean to make it worse.' Ted straightened and grabbed her handbag.

'What's wrong with him?' Jarrod asked.

'She's a *she*, and I don't know,' Ted snapped. She could feel herself freaking out as she took in the mournful expression on Miss Marple's fluffy little white face and the vulnerable way her injured paw was dangling in the air. 'She must have twisted her leg or something. I hope she hasn't done an ACL. I'll have to take her to the emergency vet.'

'What, now? Can't you do it tomorrow?'

'She's in pain!' Ted threw some cash down on the table. 'Sorry about this—'

'Are you serious? At least give me your number before you go.'

Ted paused for a millisecond, but she was too concerned about Miss Marple to argue the point, and it was smart to have the stalker's contact details. They exchanged numbers, and then Ted scooped up Miss Marple and carried her out of the restaurant, weaving her way through the revellers and over the pedestrian bridge to Southbank.

Despite the circumstances, it felt lovely to cuddle her dog in her arms. Miss Marple was aloof by nature, and although she'd recently learned to accommodate occasional displays of affection, it wasn't an easy transition for her. Ted knew the feeling.

The second they were over the pedestrian bridge, Miss Marple started trying to wriggle free of Ted's embrace. Ted wasn't surprised, she must have reached her PDA threshold.

'You shouldn't walk, you'll make your leg worse.'

But Miss Marple wouldn't take no for an answer, so Ted gently deposited her on the ground. To her amazement, Miss Marple started trotting along without the tiniest hint of a limp. Ted looked down at her, stunned, and Miss Marple looked back at her as if to say, *You wanted to get out of there, didn't you?*

Ted laughed. Miss Marple was the best.

Chapter Two

Ted was still frothing when she and Miss Marple arrived at her small SUV in the bowels of the Victorian Arts Centre carpark. She flung open the back door with an obsequious flourish.

'Madam.'

Miss Marple leaped onto the seat, and Ted clipped her harness into the seatbelt lock.

'You'll find the chilled champagne in the bar fridge beside you, and this switch makes the disco ball rotate.'

Miss Marple seemed to appreciate the gag.

Ted slid behind the steering wheel. She felt elated, and she knew that wasn't just down to Miss Marple's excellent ruse. She was elated because she'd already ID'd Giselle's stalker – and that meant she could soon deliver Jarrod to the cops and things would get back to normal with Spike. Well, the new normal. Whatever that turned out to be. She felt a rush of longing. Yikes.

Her phone rang, bringing her back to planet Earth. She checked the dash. Speak of the devil, it was Giselle. Ted was glad she could ease her client's mind. She pressed Accept on the steering wheel as she exited the carpark.

'Giselle, hey—'

'He's been in my house!'

Ted's heart skidded to a stop. 'What? Who?'

Giselle's voice was shrill. 'Who do you think? Jarrod!'

Jarrod? But how was that possible? Ted's brain was twisting itself into a pretzel as she turned left onto Southbank Boulevarde.

'Hang on a sec – what are you saying?'

'He left another anonymous note and some flowers in my living room, *tonight*. I only dashed out for dinner for a couple of hours. He must have been watching the house! He broke in through the laundry window. There's glass all over the floor! And blood!'

'Blood?! Are you okay?'

'I'm fine!' Giselle shrieked unconvincingly down the line. 'No-one was home. The blood's the stalker's – he must have cut himself when he smashed the window.'

Oh my God. Ted's head was spinning. Jarrod couldn't have done this – he'd been with her. She was still trying to catch her breath as she pulled off the road.

'What does the note say? Don't touch it, just tell me what it says.'

'It says …' Giselle's breath sounded ragged. 'It says … *I'm sorry about the lamb's heart, I hope I didn't frighten you.*'

The nerve of the guy. Flames of rage licked at Ted's vital organs. Two cars beeped behind her, and she realised she was parked in a clearway.

'Just because I didn't want to go out with him again.' Giselle was weeping now. 'What's wrong with him?'

There was no point stalling. Ted ripped off the bandaid.

'It wasn't Jarrod.'

'What?!'

'I'm sorry, Giselle. It wasn't him. I've been with him for the past two hours. Jarrod's not your stalker.'

There was silence from the other end of the phone, until Giselle made a small mewling sound.

'Then who is?'

Someone who has no qualms about violating your home, Ted thought. This was exactly the kind of escalation she'd warned Giselle about when she'd urged her to go to the cops. But Giselle had refused to involve the police, and she'd insisted on a non-disclosure agreement so Ted couldn't involve them either. For Giselle's own safety, Ted had to make her see sense.

'Giselle, this is break and enter! Who knows what he would have done to you if you were there. I can't state this strongly enough – you *have to* go to the police.'

'No. I don't want it getting back to my ex. Spike's a detective, remember? I thought you said you knew him.'

Ted squirmed. She wondered when she should reveal to Giselle that she knew Spike a lot better than she'd let on. She decided that time wasn't now.

'Er yeah, I know him a bit—'

'Well, he already thinks I'm a flake, and he'd freak out about the kids.'

'But your kids are safe. Aren't they staying with him?'

'Yes, and they're sleeping at his mum's tonight. I told him rehearsals are getting intense, so they're with him for a couple of weeks.'

'Okay, good,' Ted said. 'So, *they're* safe, but what about *you*? I don't want to alarm you, but this could escalate even further. And he's your kids' father, you can't keep him out of the loop forever.'

There was a small silence on the other end, and Ted suspected she'd found a chink in Giselle's armour. Another car beeped behind her.

'All right,' Giselle acquiesced, 'let's give it a week. If you haven't found my stalker by next Saturday, I'll tell my ex.'

'You promise?'

'I promise.'

'Okay, deal.'

Phew. Ted felt a load lift, although she hoped the agreement would prove academic. She was sure she could nail this snake within a week – she just needed a clue about who he was.

She careered across two lanes of traffic and flicked on her right blinker. 'Sit tight and don't touch anything, I'm coming straight over.'

'Okay ...'

'And in the meantime, I need you to think hard about who else it could be. Rack your brain, all right?'

'I will.' Giselle sniffled and hung up.

The arrow in front of Ted flashed green. She turned right onto St Kilda Road, away from the box-like National Gallery of Victoria and the Arts Centre next door that was always teeming with eclectic patrons. She was still reeling. While she'd been wasting her time with Jarrod Beasley, the real stalker had struck undetected because – of course – Giselle's security cameras weren't being installed until Monday.

Ted lowered the left rear window, and Miss Marple stood on her back paws and stuck out her head. In the mirror, Ted could see her miniature schnauzer's floppy ears flapping in the night breeze.

When she thought about it, Jarrod lying about breaking it off with Giselle was only evidence of an immature, bruised ego. And it seemed he was telling the truth about being at home alone last Saturday night. Why had she been so quick to jump to conclusions?

As if she didn't know. She'd wanted this case over with so she could start things with Spike. Ted felt appalled with herself. So now she was putting romance ahead of her investigations? *Get it together.*

Twenty minutes later, she pulled up outside Giselle's house.

It was an Aussie classic, a ubiquitous 1970s brick box. An apricot-coloured cat was curled in a plush ball on the front porch. Cats were Miss Marple's Kryptonite, so Ted took a pig's ear from the glove box and reached over to the back seat. Miss Marple hadn't noticed the cat – her eyes were fixed like lasers on the pig's ear.

'You stay here, I won't be long.'

But Miss Marple wasn't listening, she was already gobbling the ear.

Ted climbed out of the car. As she headed through Giselle's front gate and started up the path, she felt her step falter. This was the home where Giselle and Spike had been (presumably) blissful newlyweds, and where they'd conceived their three little girls. The thought put Ted on edge, but she told herself to snap out of it.

Giselle appeared at the front door. She was wearing jeans and a fitted top that accentuated her flawless skin, and her long dark hair was flowing in waves around her shoulders.

'Ted, thank God!'

'How are you doing? Are you okay?'

'Of course I'm not.' Giselle said as if it was a dumb question, and Ted had to admit she had a point. She led Ted through the surprisingly untidy house, into a living room filled with glitter, dolls, tutus, My Little Ponies and such.

It looks like a packet of marshmallows exploded in here, Ted thought. But then she noticed a tiny Western Bulldogs AFL jersey, a soccer ball and a toy truck among all the princess stuff. So, one of Giselle's little girls was less into sparkles and pink, and more like Ted had been as a kid.

'There they are,' Giselle said shrilly. She was pointing to a large bunch of Oriental lilies as though they might jump up and strangle her.

Ted sprinted to the coffee table and looked down at the note, written in the same hand as the earlier one, with those same large looping t's.

I'm sorry about the lamb's heart, I hope I didn't frighten you.
Psycho!

Ted took photos of the scene from several angles and did the same in the laundry, where droplets of blood were spattered on the floor with the shattered window glass. It wasn't a lot of blood, enough for the stalker to have cut his hand. Which gave Ted a clue to look for, if only she could work out where to look.

They retreated to the kitchen, and Giselle said out of nowhere, 'If it wasn't Jarrod, it must have been Tommy.'

'Tommy?'

'Yes, Tommy Braithwaite.'

Ted was surprised by the certainty in Giselle's voice.

'Who's Tommy Braithwaite? You've never mentioned a Tommy Braithwaite.'

'Why would I? He wears drawstring pants.'

Er, what? Ted couldn't make hide nor hair out of that, but now didn't seem the time to pursue it. Giselle was leaning against the kitchen bench, drained of colour. She looked as if the slightest breeze could topple her over.

'I think you need to sit,' Ted said.

Giselle nodded wanly and sank onto a dining chair. Ted put on the kettle and made tea. She set down a Peppa Pig mug in front of Giselle and removed a fake feather boa from a chair and sat.

'Tell me about this Tommy Braithwaite.'

Giselle sighed worriedly. 'He works at Mother Earth, where I buy my organic groceries.'

'Okay. And what makes you think it could be him?'

'He's into wellness, and he's always making suggestions about the best bone broths. Sometimes I order online, and he does the deliveries, so he knows this address. And he's a bit *too* friendly, you know? He asks about ballet way too much.'

Ted considered Giselle. With her air of fragility, she was probably a magnet for dudes with a saviour complex.

'Have there been any specific incidents of concern?'

'Yes. A couple of weeks ago he turned up here after my groceries had been delivered, because I'd forgotten to order my cinnamon toothpaste. *I* didn't even know I'd forgotten! He knows my order off by heart. Is it just me, or is that a bit creepy?'

Ted was still trying to process the cinnamon toothpaste.

'Ted?'

'Ah, yeah. That does seem a bit creepy. And does Tommy fit the physical description of the guy in the photos?'

'Yeah. He's the same height and build as Jarrod.'

Ted wanted to throw her hands in the air. Why was she only hearing about him now?

'I wish you'd mentioned Tommy sooner.'

'But *you* convinced me it was Jarrod.'

Ted thought that was a bit rich, considering she'd pressed Giselle for other names, and Giselle had only come up with Jarrod's. She reminded herself that her client was under a lot of stress.

'Plus,' Giselle added, 'like I said, he wears sustainable drawstring pants. And he's got dreadlocks. He's kind of alternative.'

'You mean he's a hippie?'

'Yeah. And I didn't think hippies did things like this.'

'Don't count on it,' Ted said. She knew from experience that people were all kinds of weird, so why should hippies be any different? 'His dreadlocks could have been hidden by the hood, and the guy with the lamb's heart was wearing Cariumas, remember? They're a sustainable brand, that'd fit with his ethos.' Ted could feel her nerve ends prickling with adrenaline. 'I'll pay Tommy a visit at Mother Earth on Monday morning and see if he's got cuts on his hands.'

Giselle stared plaintively at Ted across the table. 'I hope it's him. I don't know how much more I can take … It's so scary dealing with this all alone.'

'You're not alone,' Ted comforted her. 'I'm in your corner.'

'I meant without my husband,' Giselle said. 'But I had to end it, the marriage wasn't working.' She fixed Ted with her hooded steel-grey eyes and sighed fretfully. 'What is it with the world? Why is it so hard to sustain relationships?'

Ted had no idea, having spent the bulk of her adult life actively avoiding relationships that had any hope of going the distance.

Chapter Three

It was almost midnight when Ted turned right from Burnley Street into Victoria Street in inner-city Richmond. She stopped briefly at a pocket-sized park, Williams Reserve, so Miss Marple could do her thing. The tree-lined park was eerie in the darkness, but Ted was too preoccupied to be spooked.

She knew she couldn't blame Giselle entirely for pinning the stalking on Jarrod Beasley so quickly.

'It's my fault too,' she said to Miss Marple. 'I should have pushed Giselle harder to come up with other potential names.'

Miss Marple looked at her as if to say, *Don't beat yourself up*. But that was easy for her to say. To Ted's knowledge, Miss Marple had never allowed her personal feelings to intrude on a case.

Ted had stayed at Giselle's place to clean up the glass and drops of blood, and she'd waited until an emergency window repair was underway and Giselle's brother James had arrived to spend the night. Before she left, she'd briefly canvassed the street, but as she'd expected, no-one had seen the break-in. Giselle's laundry window wasn't visible from the street and, besides, it was a Saturday night and most of her elderly neighbours had been glued to *Death in Paradise* on the ABC.

Miss Marple finished her ablutions and they made their way out of the tiny park and back to the car. As Victoria Street widened into a boulevard, the monolithic Ikea store and Victoria Gardens Shopping Centre appeared ahead. Ted's apartment building was on the left, across the road from Victoria Gardens, near the iconic Skipping Girl Vinegar sign that was sadly no longer illuminated. It wasn't until she'd almost arrived at the building that she noticed a dirty old ute parked out the front. Her heart leaped. As she got closer, she could see a guy's broad shoulders outlined in the driver's seat, and a mop of curly, crazy hair hitting the ute's ceiling.

Spike!

A huge fit Māori man, shambolic smart-arse Spike Tereiti was the standout warrior in the 'Sons of Thor' Viking warband, and Ted's mock nemesis at Swordcraft. He was also a homicide detective and, inconveniently, Giselle's ex! Somehow, Ted and Spike had recently ended up solving a murder together. And after Swordcraft last Saturday night, Ted had *almost* taken him home.

Something had suddenly changed within her and Ted wasn't sure what it was, until she realised she was smiling. But she had to be professional. Was it wise, or even ethical, to engage with Spike in the circumstances? She decided to keep driving around the corner and enter her carpark through the rear. But Spike's car door had just opened, and he was unfolding his gargantuan body out of the ute. And now he was waving. He'd seen her. Ted had no choice but to pull over.

She brought her small SUV to a stop behind the ute, opening Miss Marple's door from the inside so she could regain her flimsy composure while her dog greeted Spike. Miss Marple bolted over to him, jumping up and down excitedly while he crouched to pat her.

'Miss Marple! Great to see you.'

Spike treated Miss Marple with a respect not often afforded to miniature schnauzers, and because of that he'd gained entry into the tiny circle of humans whom she considered her equal.

Ted climbed out of the car and attempted her usual swagger, which had a high degree of difficulty in the strappy sandals she was wearing. Spike straightened and smiled down at her. It had only been a week, but she'd forgotten how wide his smile was. It was almost too wide for his face, but it worked. She felt all fluttery in her chest, so she dialled up the kickarse.

'What are *you* doing here?'

Spike laughed his warm gravelly laugh. 'Friendly as ever. I'm staying at Mitch's place in Collingwood tonight.'

'Yeah?' Ted pointed behind her. 'Collingwood's that way.'

Spike laughed again, and his brown eyes travelled over her. 'You look nice.'

For a second Ted was robbed of speech, so she pretended to cough. She rallied quickly.

'What do you want?'

'You didn't come to Swordcraft tonight.'

'Didn't I? Thanks for letting me know.'

Ha! Ted was enjoying this already. If she couldn't strike Spike with her foam sword like she did at Swordcraft, why not land a few blows with banter instead?

Spike grinned.

'Do you try to be a pain in the arse, or does it come naturally? Rhetorical question.'

Ted laughed, but the moment was cruelled by a stab of guilt. Two minutes after she'd accepted Giselle's case, she'd discovered the man she'd almost taken home just an hour before was Giselle's ex-husband. What were the odds? This complicated matters, but high-stakes cases rarely came EBI's way, and Ted had figured she could still take the gig as long as she came clean – *ish*. She'd told Giselle she knew Spike from Swordcraft, making it sound as if he was a vague acquaintance, which would have been true six months ago. And what was six months, in the scheme of things?

Giselle hadn't seemed too perturbed that Ted knew Spike, but she'd been stunned that a tiny woman like Ted would do battle with burly guys like him.

'My size can be a tactical advantage,' Ted had assured her.

'If you say so,' Giselle had replied dubiously. 'Regardless, I *really* don't want Spike to know about this.'

And so here Ted was a week later, complicit in a serious secret that Spike had every right to know. It was why she'd been so one-eyed about nailing Jarrod, so she could close the case before Spike found out she was lying to him.

'To tell the truth …' Spike said.

'To tell the truth, what?'

He hesitated. Ted was prepping for the next mock insult, but he turned the tables on her by being sincere.

'I guess I wanted to make sure you didn't stay away from Swordcraft 'cause you're still mad at me about Maven. I tried my best.'

Ted felt a little clutch in her chest as she adjusted to the change in direction. 'I know you did.' She knew it wasn't Spike's fault that his homicide boss, Chief Inspector Craig Maven, had refused to publicly credit EBI for the murder she'd solved recently, even if she'd wanted to blame Spike at the time. 'I'm not mad at you.'

'Cool. So I haven't blown it then? You'll be back at Swordcraft?'

'Yeah, I'll be back at Swordcraft next Saturday, and I'll beat the crap out of *you*.'

Spike laughed loudly. 'In your dreams. It's like swotting a fly.'

Ted snorted, but privately she wondered whether she *would* be back next Saturday. Or would she still be trying to catch the stalker? What if she hadn't nailed Tommy Braithwaite or anyone else by then? According to their deal, Giselle would have to tell Spike about the stalker and Ted's involvement. He'd probably be too furious with her to talk to her, maybe ever again. She felt sick.

'But I tell you what,' Spike was saying, oblivious, 'after I've thrashed you, I'll shout you a consolation drink at the pub.'

Ted heard the unspoken bit at the end: *And we'll go home together and start something.* It made her feel a little flutter of panic. She liked to think she'd conquered the intimacy issues that had messed with her life since her mum died, but, really, who was she kidding?

'I know you've been through a lot with your mum and everything,' Spike said as if he were some kind of mind reader. His teasing tone had disappeared, he was gentle and empathetic. 'If you're not up for getting involved with anyone for a while, I can wait. I guess I just want to know … if there's anyone, will it be me?'

Ted stopped in her tracks. He liked her that much? She was touched by Spike's willingness to make himself vulnerable, and she knew the least she could do was respond in kind.

'I've always had lousy taste in men, so yeah, it'll be you.' She'd have to work on her vulnerability.

But Spike was undeterred. 'Excellent.'

Ted was transfixed by his smile again. She wanted to throw herself into his arms, and that made her want to run a mile. Luckily, Miss Marple's snout was pressing against her knee.

'Sorry, Miss Marple. I hear you.' Ted turned back to Spike. 'She's tired, it's been a long day.'

Spike nodded understandingly. Ted could tell he was hoping she'd invite him up, but she could also tell that he knew she wouldn't. They said their goodbyes and he climbed back into his dirty ute. As the ute pulled away from the kerb, she could already feel herself missing him. Which felt both scary and strangely nice. She climbed back into her car with Miss Marple and they drove to the underground carpark, then they caught the lift up to the fourteenth floor and headed down the corridor to 1421, Ted's small apartment. They went straight into the tiled kitchen, and Ted gave Miss Marple a late-night snack of kibble.

She took the last Corona from her fridge and plonked herself down on a fold-up chair in her living room. The apartment was still in a mess after her former 'friend with benefits', Joel, repossessed the sofa he'd loaned her, and a violent embezzler had ransacked the place in a fruitless search for hidden evidence. Both on the same day! Ted supposed she should buy a sofa, but she hadn't got around to it yet. Which was crazy, considering Ikea was literally across the road. She glanced briefly out her floor-to-ceiling windows and saw the Swedish megastore framed before the neon city skyline. She had too much other stuff to do, she'd order a new sofa online. Sometime. A rack of washing had been hanging out on the balcony for a couple of days, and she made a mental note to bring it inside.

She drank half the beer and realised she didn't want the rest. She went into her bedroom with Miss Marple, who flopped into her own bed on the floor next to Ted's and promptly fell asleep in a flurry of little snores. Ted brushed her teeth and climbed into bed. It had been such a huge day, she was expecting to fall straight to sleep. But, instead, she found herself consumed by wistful thoughts of Spike and his mop of messy hair squashed under his Sons of Thor Viking helmet. She thought about her Swordcraft Ice Elf outfit of plastic elf ears and her long ice-blue skirt and pauldron. It was so much fun going mano-a-womano against Spike with their foam swords. They feinted, weaved and blocked while swapping smart-arse sledges, all while hundreds of goblins, elves, Vikings, knights and other fantasy characters lay 'deceased' on the battlefield all around them.

Last weekend, the momentum of their battle had kept building and building, until Spike had given an almighty thrust and she'd met his sword with hers. The battle had climaxed as they'd both struck each other under their armour, and then they'd fallen to the ground and lain on their backs beside each other, panting, as the crowd cheered. It was awesome.

Ted threw back the doona. She was hardly going to fall asleep thinking about stuff like this! But it was weird how she and Spike's playful sledging on the Swordcraft battlefield had somehow evolved into something else. Or at least, it had been about to, before Giselle materialised. And then Ted had allowed her feelings for Spike to compromise her professionalism. She'd always prided herself on casting her net wide but in this instance her focus had been way too narrow. Had she made a mistake, taking Spike's ex-wife's case? But a successful outcome on a stalking investigation was bound to bring in a lot of new business. Sadly, there was no shortage of creeps targeting vulnerable women.

Ted's brain took a sudden detour, and she found herself thinking of her beloved older sister Roberta, 'Bob', whose vulnerability had been targeted by creeps more times than Ted could count. At least poor Bob had never been stalked, although she'd recently been caught up in a crazy catfishing scam that had almost cost her her life. Ted's blood still ran cold when she thought about what could have happened if she and Miss Marple hadn't arrived on the scene with seconds to spare.

Bob was seeing someone new now, and she'd already laid her heart bare again. That's who Bob was, and that was why Ted loved her, but it was also why she worried herself sick. If only Bob would learn to take a step back and protect herself just a little bit. But she was crazy about this new guy, Raj. Ted had never seen her sister so happy.

It terrified her.

Chapter Four

Bob

Bob Bristol carried a bucket of bearded irises out of her tiny florist, Blooming Beautiful, and set them down in her rear courtyard amid tubs of anthurium, snowballs, lilac, eucalyptus, waratah, flannel flower, dogwood and alstroemeria. As she paused to absorb the glorious array of colours and scents, she thought how lucky she was that after all these years, her flowers still filled her heart.

'Last lot,' a voice said behind her.

Bob turned to see Raj Dalal's legs emerging from the shop beneath a large bucket of blossom branches. His jeans were ironed, and Bob wondered why she found that so absurdly touching.

'There's a spot just here,' she said.

She managed to make some space between two tubs of tulips near the back door. She'd exiled the higher pollen-count culprits like the chrysanthemum daisies to the rear gate in deference to Teddy's hayfever. Just thinking of her sister sent a little frisson of trepidation through Bob. Would Teddy like Raj? Anyone could see he was wonderful, but with Teddy it was still a long shot.

Raj bent to manoeuvre the blossom branches into the spot, and Bob saw tiny white blossoms tumble onto his head. She loved Raj's glossy jet-black hair, it made the dark brunette of her bob seem indecisive, somehow. He straightened, and she noticed a single blossom perched in the middle of the small bald patch on his crown. She wanted to reach out and gently brush it off, but that would just accentuate the fact that she loomed over him like a leviathan. Raj thoughtfully acted as if he didn't notice her superior height, but Bob, a reluctant slave to gender stereotypes, was still fighting self-consciousness.

Raj glanced at his watch. 'Er, what time are you expecting everyone?'

The poor man looked apprehensive, and Bob felt for him. He was about to meet her dad, her seven rowdy brothers and hyper-protective Teddy en masse. Was it too much? Maybe she shouldn't have asked him to come.

'Are you nervous?'

'I wouldn't say nervous exactly, more like completely petrified.'

Bob laughed, but she wondered if she was being fair. 'Would you rather wait and meet them in smaller increments?'

'No, of course not.' Raj smiled up at her. 'I'm looking forward to it!'

Bob felt tears spring to her eyes. Which happened a lot, for all sorts of reasons. She still marvelled at the turn her life was taking. Not only did she now have this amazing man by her side, but Blooming Beautiful was expanding into the vacant store next door and branching out to incorporate her new sustainable floristry workshops.

The store next door, Sew Darn Crafty, had been a mecca for knitters, seamstresses, craft enthusiasts and weavers, and for twenty years its owner, Cicely Bunting, was at the heart of Melbourne's crafting community. But after a family tragedy Cicely had recently closed her doors, and Bob had taken the plunge and rented the store. It was the fulfilment of a personal dream that had crystalised when she'd co-founded Melbourne's Sustainable Floristry Alliance eight years ago.

Sew Darn Crafty was a much bigger store, and Blooming Beautiful was about to quadruple in size. Bob was feeling elated and daunted in equal parts. Financially it would be a stretch, but, thankfully, her first Reducing Your Environmental Footprint workshop had already sold out. And in the meantime, there was work to be done.

Her builder brother, Lee, had already knocked an archway between Blooming Beautiful and Sew Darn Crafty, leaving piles of bricks and shards of plaster behind. On the family WhatsApp group, Bob had requested help this afternoon with cleaning up the rubble, stripping back the wallpaper and carpet in Sew Darn Crafty, sanding back the windowsills and deconstructing Cicely's old counter. Lee and her other six brothers – Kerry, Kym, Robin, Leslie, Mel and Pip – had volunteered, along with their various spouses and kids – and of course, Teddy. Bob was touched by her family's generosity, but she was bracing for mayhem. Teddy often said, aptly, that the collective noun for their clan should be a chaos of Bristols.

'They'll be here any minute,' she told Raj. 'I'm sure they'll love you.'

She almost added, *like I do,* which took her by surprise. But why should it, really, considering how close they'd become?

For five years she'd known Raj as a regular Blooming Beautiful customer who bought flowers for his late wife Holly's grave – until two weeks ago, when he'd floored her by buying flowers for her instead. The next thing Bob knew she was sitting across from Raj at Vue de Monde, and he was warm, engaged and interested. She found herself confiding in him about how she'd become a surrogate mum to her eight siblings at seventeen, and how she'd endured three miscarriages and six failed IVF cycles, and how her marriage had ended in divorce.

To her ears it sounded like a litany of disasters; she'd been mortified about it all spilling out. But Raj's genuine interest and lack of judgement had reassured her. Still, she'd stopped short of confiding that she'd recently fallen victim to an online romance scam that had almost got her killed. That would be a bridge too far, and surely even Raj would think her an idiot. Her cheeks still burned with humiliation at being duped by a catfisher who'd claimed to be a soldier on a top-secret mission in Afghanistan. She'd fallen right into their trap, and it was only Teddy's investigations that had unearthed the truth and literally saved her life. So she supposed she couldn't really blame Teddy for being protective. It was just a shame that Teddy's protectiveness often took the form of vigilantism.

Over that first dinner, Raj had told Bob about the day he'd lost his wife to breast cancer, and she'd surprised herself by spontaneously reaching for his hand. They'd talked about his job as a forensic accountant and his two adult kids, Niall, a maths teacher in Sydney, and Chloe, a first-year physiotherapist in Bendigo. And Raj had revealed a surprising hobby – he'd recently played Willy Loman in Maribyrnong Amateur Theatre Company's production of *Death of a Salesman*. Bob was captivated. The dinner had proven a delightful meeting of hearts and minds, and before they knew it waiters were pointedly putting chairs up on the tables around them, and they were politely ejected from the restaurant.

And yet they still had so much to talk about, so their conversation had spilled over into the next night and the night after that and the night after that. Bob had tried to tell herself to take it more slowly. Her siblings had always accused her of being too trusting, which grated with her, but the fact was, they'd been right in the past. Was she putting too much faith in Raj? But it felt so good, and it wouldn't be fair on Raj if she let her past experiences taint their relationship. Because what was the point of life if you didn't lead with an open heart?

Raj seemed to sense the blossoms in his hair. He reached up to brush them off. 'I feel like a bridesmaid.'

Bob laughed, because all his little jokes were funny to her, even when they weren't.

'Will I start ripping up the carpet?' he asked.

Bob felt a familiar tweak of guilt about the waste involved in ripping up carpet that Cicely had only laid last year, but carpet and flowers didn't mix, and the floorboards in Sew Darn Crafty would come up a treat with a coat of non-toxic stain.

'Actually, Lee's bringing box cutters,' she told Raj, 'so let's leave the carpet for him. Why don't we make a start on the rubble under the archway?'

'Consider it done.'

Raj squeezed between her and the hydrangeas, and as his shoulder brushed against her elbow, she felt an electric charge. Raj seemed to feel it too – he stubbed his toe on a bucket of flannel flowers.

'Ooh. Are you okay?'

'Yeah, yeah, I'm fine, just a bit of a numpty.'

They laughed together, and Raj spontaneously stood on his toes to steal a kiss. The world paused on its axis for a moment, and everything felt soft and sweet. They pulled apart, and it was hard to know who was more flustered.

'Right! Let me at that shovel,' Raj said.

'I'll help.'

Bob shadowed Raj back into the store and was surprised to

find Cicely Bunting at the front door. She rushed over to open it for her.

'Cicely! What a lovely surprise.'

'Hi, Bob!'

They exchanged a hug. Bob always found Cicely nice to embrace, she was warm and voluptuous, and she gave off the scent of home-made lavender soap. Today she was wearing an impeccably hand-sewn gardening smock over jeans, and her prematurely silver-grey curls were gathered in friendly clusters around her rosy cheeks. When they pulled apart, Bob introduced Raj. She could hear the pride in her voice, and she wondered if Cicely heard it too. Raj and Cicely exchanged friendly greetings, and then Raj excused himself and grabbed a shovel. Bob took the chance to check in with Cicely.

'How are you doing?' she asked.

'Oh, you know,' Cicely said, before quickly fashioning a smile. 'I'm fine. I'm good.'

Bob wished that were true, but she knew Cicely was still trying to navigate her way through a series of shattering blows. She and her husband, Duncan, had always seemed to have the world at their feet, but a few years ago Duncan's gym, Body Potential, had gone bust, and Cicely had been forced to sell her house to settle his debts. The new owners had allowed them to stay on as tenants, but then two years later Duncan disappeared while surfing off Cheviot Beach, a treacherous section of the Victorian coastline that was famous for Prime Minister Harold Holt's disappearance in 1967.

Unlike Harold Holt, who'd spawned a hundred conspiracy theories, Duncan's disappearance had quickly faded from the public consciousness. That was around twelve months ago, and recently, Cicely had confided to Bob that she couldn't afford to keep paying rent on both her lost house and her beloved shop. Something had to give, and sadly that something was Sew Darn Crafty.

Bob's heart went out to Cicely, as it always did, and she felt acutely aware of the obtrusive new archway. She wished she'd known Cicely was coming so she could have expedited the rubble removal. Cicely's shop had always been immaculate – did this look like a desecration of Sew Darn Crafty to her?

But Bob had barely formed the thought when Cicely said, 'I like the archway. What a smart idea.'

Bob felt a rush of relief. 'Thanks. But it'll look a lot better once the masses have descended and tidied up. That's not to negate your efforts, Raj.'

'Too late, I feel negated.' Raj chuckled as he tossed some plaster shards into a wheelbarrow.

'Actually,' Cicely said, 'I've got something for you, Bob. Can you help me bring it in from the car?'

'For me? What is it?'

'Come and see.'

Bob followed Cicely out to her station wagon, still poignantly adorned with Sew Darn Crafty signage. Cicely lifted the rear door to reveal a rolled-up rug in hues of orange and black.

'Ta-da!' she said with a smile. 'I thought this might break up the floor space for you. And I know you're fond of mid-century modern.'

Bob was flabbergasted. 'Oh my heavens ... For *me*? Did you weave this yourself?'

'Of course. They're natural, undyed yarns. I hope you like it.'

'I love it! Thank you! I don't know what to say.'

'Can you get into the back seat and push it from the other end?'

Bob and Cicely manoeuvred the rug out of the car and carried it into the store, where Raj cleared away rubble so they could unroll it. It was woven in a bold pattern of intersecting ovals, and Bob couldn't have imagined anything more perfect for the space as she'd envisaged it. She felt bereft of words. Of all the ways Cicely could have responded to losing her shop, she'd chosen to spend countless hours crafting a gift for the person who was benefiting from her loss.

'Oh, Cicely,' she finally managed, her eyes welling again. 'Thank you so much. But all that work! You should keep it for yourself.'

'No, I wove it for *you*.'

So, the least I can do is stop protesting and graciously accept, Bob thought.

'Well, thank you again.' She pulled Cicely into a hug. 'It's beautiful.'

'I'm glad you like it, although I made a mess of this edge over here.'

The edge in question looked flawless to Bob, but she was accustomed to Cicely's perfectionism. She'd once seen Cicely unravel two immaculately knitted socks because she'd dropped a couple of stitches in one. And she'd taken her beautiful signature quilt, a representation of a ballerina inspired by an Edgar Degas painting, off the wall at Sew Darn Crafty because of one tiny biro mark. It wasn't surprising she was now fretting over her rug's non-existent imperfections.

'It looks perfect to me,' Bob said.

'To me too,' Raj concurred. He was leaning on his shovel with an awestruck expression. 'I can't believe you made this yourself.'

'She's ridiculously talented,' Bob said. 'Quick, let's roll it up before everyone gets here.'

'About that,' Cicely said as they rolled. 'I want to help with the working bee.'

Bob waved her offer away with a laugh.

'All this and manual labour as well? I don't think so! You've already gone above and beyond.'

'But it'll keep me busy,' Cicely said with sudden emotion. 'It'll stop me from sitting around the house and wondering what's happened to Dunc.'

Bob scolded herself for her thoughtlessness. Of course Cicely would want to keep busy – but she wished her friend would stop torturing herself about her husband's fate. Poor Duncan's demise had been confirmed when his shredded leg rope washed up in the shallows. Sadly, he was gone for good, but Cicely was still having trouble accepting that. Bob knew it was Cicely's right to grieve in her own way, but she worried as Duncan's first anniversary approached, that her friend's reluctance to accept the truth was tipping into unhealthy denial.

She squeezed Cicely's hand. 'Of course, I get that. Let's put you to work then, eh?'

Just then the door flew open and Bob's burly brother Lee and his handsome Italian partner Marco burst into the shop. Lee clapped his enormous hands together.

'Right, let's get this party started!'

Bob's eyes flew to Raj, who'd taken on the visage of a deer in headlights. She hoped Lee wouldn't judge Raj for being too short or too shy, or make negative assumptions about him because Bob was 'too gullible' to pick a nice guy. Her brothers were so protective of her. Not half as protective as Teddy, of course, but Teddy set an impossible bar. Bob opened her mouth to introduce Raj, but Lee was already towering over him.

'Mate, you must be Raj. I'm Lee Bristol!'

Raj smiled shyly and offered his hand, but Lee bypassed it and pulled him into a bear hug. Bob watched, and her heart unfurled like one of her flowers.

Chapter Five

Ted

As Ted pulled up across the road from Blooming Beautiful, she could already hear her family's racket polluting the classy air of Carlton North. She turned to Miss Marple in the back seat.

'Another chaos of Bristols. Are you sure you don't want to come in?'

Miss Marple looked at her as if to say, *Not a chance, it's like the Hunger Games in there.*

Ted laughed. After a recent family function, when her niece Kelsey and a posse of cousins had dressed Miss Marple in doll's pyjamas and made her jump through a hula hoop, Miss Marple had put her paw down and refused to engage with the Bristols en masse. Ted couldn't blame her. Read the room, kids! Miss Marple wanted autonomy over her body. Ted had tried explaining that Miss Marple was shy and asked the kids to pat her one-by-one, but they'd ignored her request. And when Ted had broached Miss Marple's right to privacy with her brothers and sisters-in-law, they'd just looked at her and said, 'She's a dog, Ted.' Whatever *that* was supposed to mean.

Ted's phone chirped. She glanced down to see a message from Jarrod Beasley.

Hey lovely, you're on my mind today. x

What the hell? She was surprised Jarrod hadn't taken the hint when she'd made such a hasty departure last night. And why hadn't he asked how Miss Marple was? As far as Jarrod knew, Miss Marple's leg was injured. Ted took that as a personal affront, even though she knew it was asking too much of Jarrod, whose memory only extended to himself. She made a mental note to text him and explain that she wasn't interested, and she tossed the phone back into her pocket. She pulled a biodegradable bag from her glove box, removing a dried chicken's foot, then lowered the back windows slightly – luckily it was a cool spring day – and gave Miss Marple the treat.

'I'll be a couple of hours, you stay incognito.'

Fortified by Claratyne, Ted climbed out of her car and crossed the street, passing a sign propped up near a skip: 'Blooming Beautiful is Blossoming Soon!' Ted's heart swelled with pride in her sister. Bob had always been super talented, but now thanks to her growing TikTok following, she was finally getting the attention she deserved. And with these larger premises and her new sustainable floristry workshops, her locally sourced and native floral designs would soon go nuclear.

#bobbristol #bestfloristintheworld

As she got closer Ted could see that Bob had emptied the shop of flowers. She was touched, but she wasn't surprised. It was vintage Bob. On a day that should be all about her, she was busy thinking of everyone else. Ted stepped inside and promptly disappeared in a sea of torsos. As the runt of the litter, she was used to that – Bristol gatherings resembled a festival in the Land of the Giants. She waved to her favourite sisters-in-law, Faizah and Lou, through the crowd as she craned her neck in search of Bob. Then she almost collided with her dad, Cal.

'Teddy!'

'Dad!'

They biffed each other, as Bristols do, and had a little chat about nothing. Ted thought about how grateful she was that things were finally good between them, but then Cal was commandeered by her most annoying sister-in-law, Sandy. Sandy was training to be a counsellor, which was weird because she found her own voice more interesting than anyone else's.

A hairy arm grabbed Ted from behind and wrapped itself around her neck.

'Get off me, dickhead,' Ted said.

It was her oldest brother, Kerry, who was nothing if not predictable. Ted kicked him in the kneecap and he crumpled sideways, setting her free. Ted's brothers Robin, Kym and Leslie, who were shovelling up a small mountain of bricks nearby, laughed their heads off at Kerry's expense.

'Is Chuck here?' Ted asked him.

'Netball ...'

Dammit. Kerry's fifteen-year-old daughter, Chuck, was Ted's invaluable IT expert. She'd been hoping to confer with her niece about a few items on EBI's agenda. It would have to wait until after school tomorrow.

'Teddy! In here!'

Ted somehow discerned Bob's voice in the din. She pivoted and spotted her sister with Cicely Bunting on the other side of the new archway into the old Sew Darn Crafty premises. Ted barged her way through the throng, swapping punches with her brothers Lee, Pip and Mel, and pausing briefly to accept a hug from Lee's partner Marco, her biggest fan.

Marco called through the crowd, 'Make way for your *piccole sorella*, who solves murders!' But no-one was listening. Typical!

'Teddy! There you are,' Bob said. 'Thanks for coming.'

She leaned down to peck Ted's cheek, and Ted's heart did that funny flippy thing it reserved for her only sister. Bob was dressed in old paint-stained overalls and there was plaster dust in her sleek dark bob, but she looked amazing as always. She could wear a hessian sack and make it look stylish – in fact, Ted had a vague memory that once she'd done just that. At forty-nine, Bob was thirteen years older and thirteen centimetres taller than Ted, and, in Ted's opinion, at least thirteen times as gentle and kind.

'Hi, Ted,' Cicely Bunting said. 'I was hoping you'd be here. I'm thrilled to see you!'

'Hi, Cicely! Er, you too.'

Cicely seemed oddly intense, and Ted wondered why she was so stoked to see her when they barely knew each other. Bob had insisted a few times that Ted go to Sew Darn Crafty to replace a button from some blouse or other, when Ted had barely noticed the button missing, but that was as far as it went. Buttons comprised the full extent of their interactions.

'Look at this, Teddy,' Bob said, cutting short Ted's ruminations. She was pointing at a black-and-orange rug that was half unfurled on the floor. 'Isn't it beautiful? Cicely wove it.'

'What? You wove that yourself?' Ted stared at the intricately patterned rug in awe. 'Wow, I'd be lucky to weave a shoelace.'

Bob and Cicely laughed.

'We've been having a spirited discussion,' Bob said, indicating the other side of the shop. 'I was planning to show it off over there, but Cicely wants me to put it here because of the floorboards.'

'What about the floorboards?'

'Exactly.' Bob concurred.

'I had to replace some boards last year,' Cicely explained. 'The stains don't match, and they're not aligned. Can't you see?'

Ted looked at the floorboards, newly exposed with the carpet now removed. If she squinted, she could see where five or six old boards had been replaced, but the new boards were almost identical to the rest. Bob had told her Cicely was a perfectionist, but this took fussy to a whole new level.

'To be honest, I can't notice. And I guess if Bob wants it over there ...'

'No, I'm just teasing,' Bob said. 'I'm happy to lose the argument.'

For a second Ted bristled on Bob's behalf. It was Bob's store now, and interior décor was one of her superpowers. Surely she should be allowed to put the rug wherever *she* thought it looked the best. But then Ted caught something in Bob's expression, and she realised her sister had made the concession because Cicely could do with a victory, no matter how small.

'On second glance, I can see what you mean,' Ted said to Cicely.

But Cicely had moved on from floorboards. 'Bob tells me you solved a murder. Before the police!'

'*Way* before the police,' Bob said.

'Not *way* before,' Ted demurred. 'Well actually, yeah it *was* way before.'

'That's extremely impressive,' Cicely said.

I know, Ted thought. 'Thank you,' she said.

'*I* need a private investigator.'

'You do?'

'Yes, and I want the best. But I suppose you're all booked up now.'

Nope, Ted thought, *but I should be.*

The truth was, when she'd posted about solving the murder and saving an anonymous client (i.e. Bob) from a potentially deadly catfisher on all EBI's socials, she'd been expecting her business to go berserk. But even though her posts had attracted lots of clicks, it had quickly become clear that people weren't prepared to fork out money for investigations unless they were out of other options. Which meant that EBI was still destined to pick up cases the cops couldn't be bothered solving – or cases the client didn't want to take to the cops, like Giselle's. It had been a bit of a kick in the guts for Ted. Not that she'd shared that with anyone, not even Bob.

'I'm busy, but I can always make time for a friend of Bob's,' she said in a professionally friendly manner. 'If it's not too confidential, can I ask what it's about?'

Cicely's face coloured. 'I want you to find Duncan.'

All the decibels in the room were suddenly denuded to nothing. Ted exchanged a stunned glance with Bob. She knew Cicely had been clinging to false hope, but Bob hadn't mentioned that she was delusional.

'I *am* aware of how crazy that sounds,' Cicely said, as if she'd read Ted's mind. 'But I hope you'll do me the courtesy of taking me seriously.'

'Of course I will,' Ted said, because what else could she say? 'How about you come to my office at noon tomorrow?'

'Perfect. Thank you, Ted,' Cicely said. She picked up a wallpaper stripper. 'Well, I suppose this isn't going to strip itself.'

They all got down to business, stripping wallpaper patterned with buttons and scissors off the wall near the new floorboards – Ted had a vague recollection that a quilt with a ballerina on it once hung here.

She felt uneasy about taking Cicely's case. Why had she waited until now to ask for help? But then Ted remembered Bob mentioning that Duncan's first anniversary was coming up. Was

Cicely somehow coping with the painful milestone by telling herself that her husband was still alive when she knew in her heart, like everyone else did, that he wasn't? But if Cicely knew in her heart that Duncan was dead, why would she want Ted to find him? Denial, Ted supposed. But that didn't stop her from feeling uneasy.

As soon as Cicely had left for a Weavers' Guild meeting, Ted said to Bob, 'Is it ethical of me to take on a case when the chances of success are less than zero?'

Bob sighed, but she, surprisingly, seemed open to the idea. 'The more I think about it, this could be exactly what Cicely needs. If you conduct an exhaustive investigation and don't find any trace of Duncan, maybe she'll get closure and finally be able to move on.'

'But you told me she's broke,' Ted pointed out. 'Should she really be spending what little money she's got left on *me*?'

Bob shrugged helplessly. 'Who are we to tell her she can't? Cicely might be a bit wobbly right now, but she's smart enough to make that choice for herself. And I'm sure she'd be prepared to pay *a million dollars* if it would give her some answers.'

'A million, you reckon? Good to know.'

Bob laughed that tinkly laugh of hers. 'Oh, Teddy!'

Ted felt a familiar glow. There was nothing she loved more than making Bob laugh – although she wasn't sure her puny joke warranted quite such prolonged delight.

It took her a few seconds to realise that Bob was now looking over her shoulder. Ted turned and came face-to-face with a compact man with a dark complexion and shiny black hair. The man's brown eyes were set quite far apart, and in an unprecedented event at a Bristol function, they were almost level with Ted's. Ted was thrown. Surely this couldn't be …

'Raj!' Bob said, confirming Ted's suspicions.

So, *this* was Raj Dalal, the Blooming Beautiful regular whom Bob had just started dating? Why had Bob invited Raj to a family working bee already? They'd only been seeing each other for a couple of weeks. Was she giving her heart away too fast, as she'd done so many times in the past? She barely knew the guy! Ted watched as Raj handed Bob a new pair of work gloves.

'Sorry I took so long,' he said. 'Bunnings was packed, and then I had to go back for the sandpaper.'

'Thanks, Raj. This is Teddy,' Bob said, her face the colour of her hottest pink gerberas. 'Teddy, this is Raj.'

She looked so happy that it made Ted petrified for her all over again. But she couldn't, and wouldn't, let that show. She'd promised Bob that she'd stop being so uber-protective. And who was she to say that Raj would turn out to be another bastard who'd scrunch up Bob's heart like a piece of scrap paper and throw it away?

Raj smiled bashfully. 'Hi Teddy. I've heard a lot about you.'

'All of it bad, I hope?'

Raj and Bob laughed as if Ted had cracked the wittiest joke in the world.

Raj started helping them strip the wallpaper and Ted tried to make small talk, but inside, she was busy catastrophising. Raj seemed like he was genuinely into Bob, but people could seem all kinds of things. Was it wise for Bob to invite him into the bosom of her family so soon? Wouldn't that make things worse if the worst happened? Which it usually did. What if Bob's life ended up in danger again?

'Raj has been amazing,' Bob told her as he enthusiastically peeled back a strip of wallpaper. 'He's been working his heart out all day.' Their eyes locked.

Raj smiled. 'You're too kind, babe.'

Babe? Wasn't it a bit early for *babe*?

Kym and Leslie materialised and invited Raj to join them out in the courtyard 'for a bevvy'. Bob seemed transfixed as she watched him walk away, and it was only when he'd disappeared out the door that she turned her attention back to Ted. Her pretty oval face was glowing under its light smattering of freckles.

'So, what do you think? I'm right, aren't I? He's wonderful.'

Ted bit back a million words of warning and said instead, 'Yeah, he seems awesome.'

You couldn't hear a plane land in the din, and yet Ted heard Bob exhale.

'Really? That means everything, Teddy. You really like him?'

'Yeah. He seems great.'

Bob threw her arms around Ted and Ted playfully pushed her away.

'Get off me.'

It was one of their sisterly rituals. They both laughed, and Ted saw Bob's eyes moisten.

'Seriously, Teddy. It feels so right. I really think it's different this time.'

It had better be, Ted thought.

She framed a supportive smile. 'That's brilliant, Bob! I'm happy for you.'

Bob dabbed at the tears of joy that had started to trickle down her face. 'But aren't you going to lecture me about falling in love too fast? Or at least warn me not to be gullible?'

'No,' Ted said. 'How many times do I have to tell you? I trust your judgement.'

Chapter Six

Ted wanted to trust Bob's judgement, but let's be real. How could she, when Bob's romantic judgement had almost resulted in her murder? The fact was, Bob needed protection from the lowlifes who preyed on her good nature, and she needed protection from *herself*.

Ted took out her phone and pulled up her address book, scanning the list of surveillance agents she'd met through the Surveillance Agents Australia Facebook page. She hesitated. Should she do this?

She glanced across the road to Blooming Beautiful, now empty except for Bob and Raj, who were bringing the flowers back in after Ted and her hayfever had vacated. They were laughing at something as Raj replaced a tub of hydrangeas. Ted had been telling the truth when she told Bob that Raj seemed nice, and she'd discreetly canvassed her family and they all thought he was nice too. But so what? The Bristols weren't exactly known for their emotional intelligence, and a lot of the world's vilest people made it their business to *seem* nice.

She knew it was exceedingly unlikely that Raj was one of the world's vilest people, but he wouldn't need to be to break Bob's heart. And how many times could her heart be broken before she became unable to put it back together? It made sense to put Raj under surveillance, but it still made Ted feel queasy with guilt.

She turned to Miss Marple in the back seat for counsel, but Miss Marple was preoccupied by a passing poodle.

Ted knew she could have suggested to Bob that she put Raj under surveillance to check his bona fides, but Bob would have been horrified at the very idea. Ted could hear her now, insisting that in spite of her painful history she refused to be driven by suspicion. But someone had to be driven by suspicion, so why not Ted? The thing was, Bob thought the ledger between them was even now. But the ledger would never be even, because Bob had taken Ted into her arms when she was a terrified, traumatised four-year-old and she'd offered Ted (and everyone else) all of herself ever since.

She was too nice, that was Bob's problem. It was as if she had a neon sign on top of her head: 'Heart Available for Breaking'. Would Raj just be the latest user to read that sign loud and clear? Ted hoped not. More than anything, she wanted Raj to be as sweet as he seemed. But her job had taught her that things were rarely what they seemed. And if that included Raj, Bob needed to know ASAP, before she suffered another crushing blow.

Her phone buzzed with a call. She checked the screen. It was rookie surveillance agent Cody Venables, of all people. Was he reading her mind? It was a fun thought, but it was far more likely Cody was just making his latest random call. Cody was in his early twenties, and deaf in one ear. He'd been rejected by the Victoria Police, so he'd set himself up as a surveillance agent, and he was as keen as mustard. He was constantly DMing Ted on her socials and calling her to offer his services (which she'd never taken up), and to ask for her PI tips. Ted pressed Accept.

'Hey, Cody.'

'Ted, hey! How are you? It's Cody. Oh yeah, you said that. How ya doing? Just wondering if you've got any work for me?'

Ted hesitated. Cody was a bull at a gate, and she was dubious about whether he had the subtlety and nuance required to tail Raj. But how would he ever develop subtlety and nuance if nobody gave him a chance? And where would *she* be, if people like her favourite surveillance agent, Wurundjeri woman Aunty June O'Shea, hadn't taken a chance on *her*? Didn't everyone deserve a leg-up?

'Actually,' she said, 'I do.'

'You *do*? Fuck! I mean, great, yeah, I'm up for it! What is it? When?'

'I want you to put someone under surveillance,' Ted said. 'Starting today.'

There was an infinitesimal silence before Cody spoke again.

'Cool, sweet. Yeah, I can do that. Just let me give my brother a call. He's getting married tonight, and I'm supposed to be his best man—'

'Wait, what? That's okay, there's no need to miss your brother's wedding—'

'It's okay, he won't mind—'

Ted seriously doubted that.

'No, go to the wedding. You can start tomorrow.'

'I could start at midnight.'

'No, tomorrow's fine.'

'Sweet! Cool. Tomorrow morning.'

'Awesome,' Ted said. 'Now listen, I need you to be judicious about what you're observing and not always take things at face value, okay?'

'Absolutely.'

'A good surveillance agent is alert to nuance.'

'Nuance, got it.'

'You need to take a step back and look at things from every angle before you jump to conclusions. Can you do that for me?'

'Too easy! Who do you want me to follow?'

Across the road in Blooming Beautiful, Raj was now standing up on tiptoes to give Bob a kiss.

Ted felt her fear for her sister ratchet up a notch. 'I want you to follow a guy called Raj Dalal.'

Chapter Seven

A wattle danced in a shower of yellow spots outside Ted's office window, as she considered Cicely from behind her desk. It was only fair to put it all out there, but Ted tried to do it with delicacy.

'Just so we're clear,' she said gently, 'you do understand it's extremely unlikely that I'll find Duncan alive?'

Cicely reacted as though Ted had punched a kitten. 'But it's not *impossible*, is it? Why are you sounding so defeatist before you even start?'

It was a valid question. Why *was* she sounding so defeatist? Cicely was in distress, and she trusted Ted to find some answers. Sure, the mission was nigh-on impossible, but she wasn't just any investigator – she was Ted Bristol, gun PI, and she already had a murder under her belt.

'I'm sorry, I didn't mean to sound defeatist,' she said.

Cicely seemed placated. She shifted on the navy Ikea sofa that Ted provided for clients, and a beam of sunshine shone through the window and bounced off her framed Certificate III in Investigative Services and her Class 1 Security Providers Licence that were hanging on the wall behind her. Ted noticed that her Certificate III was slightly crooked, and she made a mental note to align it as soon as Cicely left.

'Your office is immaculate,' Cicely had commented when she first arrived, and Ted had felt gratified.

Edwina Bristol Investigations was housed in a converted milk bar in inner-city Abbotsford, and she kept everything about it just so – from her sleek electric desk to the coolly professional colour palate of her navy-blue couch and matching rug, and the box of tissues placed discreetly at a diagonal on the otherwise empty coffee table. Her impeccable office was the polar opposite of her messy apartment, and Ted knew that spoke volumes, if only she could be bothered to listen.

'I know I'm being pushy,' Cicely said, disturbing Ted's musings. 'But I just … I miss Dunc so much.'

Ted nodded sympathetically. 'Of course.'

She had vague memories of Duncan Bunting: tall, blond, in love with himself. He'd been a minor celebrity when he'd starred in cheesy ads for his gym, Body Potential, but when the gym went under his celebrity had evaporated with it.

'I promise, if he's anywhere to be found, I'll find him,' she said.

'I think we should start with the Bass Strait Islands.'

'Er, why?'

'I googled them,' Cicely said. 'There are over fifty, and only a few are inhabited. Dunc's board never washed back to shore. He could have drifted down into the Bass Strait on his board and ended up stranded on any one of those islands. He could be stuck there, waiting for someone to find him.'

So now Duncan was Tom Hanks minus Wilson? It sounded crazy, but Ted knew the outlandish theory just spoke of her client's desperation. She felt for Cicely in all of her stress, and she was reminded of Giselle Tereiti's fraught reaction this morning, when she'd learned that her second potential stalker, Tommy

Braithwaite, had uninjured hands and an air-tight alibi for the break-in on Saturday night.

'What?' Giselle's voice had gone up several octaves when Ted had called her after her fruitless visit to Mother Earth, the organic grocery store where Tommy worked. 'It's not Tommy either?'

'No, I'm afraid not'

'But who else could it be?' Giselle had fretted. If only Ted knew. When Jarrod had proved a dead end, she'd asked Meta to provide a list of Giselle's seven thousand former Instagram followers. She'd comb through the list rigorously, if necessary, but she doubted Giselle had the budget for such an exhaustive search. And personal suggestions were always preferable. 'I need you to rack your brain about everyone you know. Colleagues, casual acquaintances, *anyone*. It could be the person you least expect. Okay?'

'Okay …'

And now in the office a couple of hours later, it occurred to Ted that she was looking for two men at the opposite end of the spectrum; one reviled and the other, in Duncan's case, revered. She reminded herself that she'd just promised to keep her mind open. Were the Bass Strait Islands *totally* implausible? What about the ferries? Wouldn't Duncan have been seen? And Bass Strait was treacherous for big ships, let alone a solitary guy on a surfboard.

'What if the police missed something?' Cicely pressed. 'What if he's washed up on an island with no way of contacting me?'

Desperation was leaking from Cicely's every pore, and Ted had to admit that the Bass Strait Islands idea was starting to get her juices flowing. She had a mental image of herself on every news site in the country being winched into a helicopter above wind-tossed seas, her arms wrapped tightly around a tanned, wizened Duncan, sporting a beard down to his kneecaps. She'd be the PI who'd achieved the impossible! Her business would go bananas.

'Ted? Are you listening?'

Ted re-entered the earth's atmosphere. 'Er, absolutely. But let's start at the beginning. What can you tell me about the day Duncan went missing?'

Cicely told Ted that Duncan had taken up surfing about six months before that fateful day. It was a sunny, spring Wednesday, and low tide was predicted for midday, so on the spur of the moment, he'd decided to drive to the Mornington Peninsula and go surfing at Cheviot Beach. Ted tensed at the mention of the Mornington Peninsula, but she'd been expecting that. Her eyes flew to a framed photo on her desk, showing herself as a tiny four-year-old on Torquay Beach with seventeen-year-old Bob and their mum, Bridget. The photo was captioned in Bridget's hand: *The girls all together*. Ted felt a spasm of that old pain, but she pushed on.

'Cheviot Beach seems an odd choice,' she said cautiously. 'Why would Duncan go there when he wasn't an experienced surfer?'

'He spent all his childhood holidays boogie-boarding on the peninsula with his parents. He knew it like the back of his hand, so he felt confident, and he said that Cheviot always had a good break. I was doubtful, to be honest, but surfing gave him such joy. And I thought he had natural talent, but maybe I was biased.' She gave a sad little smile and reached into her handwoven shoulder bag. 'I've brought these, like you asked.' She pulled out Duncan's frayed leg rope and Apple Watch.

'Thank you.' Ted turned the items over in her hands, careful to treat them with the respect Cicely had a right to expect.

Duncan's beach towel and car keys had been found on the beach, but the frayed rope and Apple Watch had washed up separately in the shallows over the next few days. The leg rope was shredded from what looked like the handiwork of a shark. Ted felt a visceral shudder on Duncan's behalf, and then a sudden catch at her heart that had nothing to do with Duncan.

'The police think a shark did that,' Cicely said, 'but being thrown against jagged rocks repeatedly would have the same effect, don't you think?'

Ted didn't want to lie, so she let the poignant question slide. She turned her attention to the Apple Watch. The band was missing its buckle. Duncan's name and address were written on a tiny piece of paper affixed to the back of the watch face with waterproof glue.

Ted handed the leg rope back to Cicely, but she kept the watch. 'Can I keep this for now? Hopefully my IT expert can retrieve the data. I can't promise that will give us any answers—'

'But will it tell you which way he was drifting?' Cicely cut across intensely. 'I was thinking, if we know what direction Dunc was drifting in, it might pin down what island he ended up on.' She qualified, probably more for Ted's benefit than hers, 'I mean, *if* he's on an island.'

'Let's see what we find before we start speculating,' Ted said.

Cicely nodded, but her impatience was so tangible that Ted could have spread it on toast.

'His iCloud password is MySissy#79,' she proffered before Ted could ask. 'Dunc calls me Sissy, and I was born in 1979.'

She jotted it down.

'Got it, thanks.' She stole a glance at her watch. She had a meeting in ten minutes with Brad Jorgenson, an under-8s cricket coach who suspected that one of the players' dads was sabotaging him by hiding the kids' helmets. Primary-school cricket sounded brutal. 'I'm afraid I'll have to wrap this up, I have another meeting.'

Cicely nodded and climbed to her feet. Ted's elbow nudged an embroidered bag on her desk that was bulging with Cicely's offerings: four ginger and carrot muffins, a tin of peanut butter dog biscuits, a jar of raspberry jam, an embroidered cushion and a frozen marinade paste of coriander roots that she had no idea what to do with.

'Thanks again for all the lovely goodies.'

'Thank *you* for taking my case.'

Ted walked Cicely to the door. As they stepped outside EBI, they were assailed by the ever-present thrum of traffic from reviled thoroughfare Punt Road just a block away. A gigantic ute with tiny P plates sped past them down the narrow street, and from across the road Ted heard excited barking at Wags Away Canine Day Care, where Miss Marple was currently ruling the roost.

'Morning!'

The friendly greeting came from Ted's next-door neighbour, Chantal Considine, who was wrangling a recycling bin in front of her timber cottage, an anomaly in the semi-industrial street. Ted did the latest in a series of double takes; she was still getting used to the new Chantal. Her neighbour was dressed in a tailored charcoal skirt suit, and her fluffy blonde waves were entrapped in a sleek ponytail. It was a world away from Chantal's former vibe as a bohemian spiritual medium. Ted waved back.

'Morning, Chantal!'

'Isn't it a glorious day?'

Chantal abandoned the bin and wandered over for a chat. It turned out that she'd bought decoupage kits and crochet hooks from Sew Darn Crafty when her daughters were little. She explained to Cicely that she'd been a grief counsellor in Swan Hill fifteen years ago, and she was currently retraining in the principles of Acceptance and Commitment Therapy for Grief and Loss. Ted couldn't help wondering what Cicely would think if she knew that just two weeks ago, Chantal was wearing velvet flares with a rainbow-hued poncho and receiving warnings of danger from Ted's late mum.

Chantal's messages from 'the other side' had ultimately led to Ted saving Bob's life, and yet somehow Chantal had convinced herself they were just stress-induced fantasies brought on by her marriage break-up. She'd closed up shop as a medium and was reinventing herself as a neutral clinician. Ted was trying to support Chantal's pivot, but secretly she found it a shame that her neighbour was turning her back on her gift. Ted could see the irony. Just a few weeks ago she'd despised Chantal and dismissed her as a charlatan. But now, it seemed she was more invested in Chantal's psychic gifts than Chantal was.

'I'd better get on,' Chantal said. 'Nice to meet you, Cicely.'

'You too.'

Chantal's smile stretched all the way up to her big blue eyes, and Ted felt glad that even though she'd ditched the hippie outfits, her earthy warmth had remained intact.

'She seems lovely,' Cicely said as Chantal disappeared into her house.

'Yes, she is,' Ted agreed.

She wondered if Cicely could benefit from Chantal's grief counselling services. She'd have to accept that Duncan was dead, first.

An enormous SUV pulled up across the road, and Ted recognised Brad Jorgenson, the under-8s cricket coach.

'Your next client?' Cicely said. 'I'll be off. But can you tell me what your first step will be?'

One I'd rather not take, Ted thought. Aloud she said, 'I'll start with a visit to Portsea.'

'That makes sense …' Cicely's voice trailed off, and then she said, 'I haven't been to the peninsula since that awful day.'

I can top that, Ted thought dully.

'I haven't been there for over thirty years.'

Chapter Eight

Portsea was at the far end of the Mornington Peninsula, and at just 108 kilometres from the city, it was a playground for Melbourne's rich. But since Melbourne's rich liked to play discreetly, there was no sign of garish designer shops or other such trappings, and the cliff-top mansions were hidden behind high, immaculately pruned hedges. Ted could feel her tummy churning as she passed the beautiful old Portsea pub. Behind her the ocean sparkled at the end of the pier. But the tranquil surroundings didn't soothe her, she'd been avoiding this part of the world for a reason. Her phone rang. She checked the dash – it was Bob. She pressed Accept and tried to sound chirpy.

'Bob, hey!'

'You sound terrible,' Bob said. 'I'm worried about you. I just saw Cicely, and she said you're in Portsea.'

'Yeah.'

'Oh, Teddy, I'm so sorry. I feel terrible. I should have thought it through when I suggested you take the case. I was so focused on Cicely that I forgot … I can't believe I forgot! I think you should turn around.'

'It's too late for that—'

'Well, wait for me. I'll come and join you—'

'Don't be crazy, your flowers need you. And I've got an interview in fifteen minutes. And I'm fine, I'm good. I'm trying to face my demons, remember?'

'But do you have to face them all at once?'

Ted laughed, but she really wanted to cry. It was so like Bob to worry about her. She had trouble accepting that their roles had swapped, and it was now Ted's turn to protect *her*. But Ted supposed that thirty-three years of being a surrogate mum was a hard habit to break.

'You don't have to worry—'

She heard a bell tinkle. It took a second to realise it was the bell above Blooming Beautiful's door.

'Raj!' Ted heard Bob say delightedly, her mouth now away from the receiver. 'What a lovely surprise.'

'Morning. I've brought you a latte.' Ted detected the words in the background.

'Thank you! That's so sweet.' Bob came back on the line. 'Teddy, I have to go. But will you promise me if it gets too much, you'll turn around and come back?'

'I promise.'

'Okay, love you. Bye!'

Bob hung up, and now it was Ted's turn to worry. Why was Raj turning up at Blooming Beautiful with coffee? Was it because he was a genuinely thoughtful person, or was this the first stage in some kind of manipulative game that would be Bob's undoing? Ted couldn't bear the thought. She was glad she'd put Raj under surveillance, even if uber-keen young surveillance agent Cody Venables was driving her nuts.

Over the past two days, he'd sent her thirty-seven texts about Raj.

9.08, *target watered plants on the front verandah.*

9.48, *target went to cafe around the corner for latte, no suspicious interactions.*

11.36, *target came out to check his letterbox.*

11.37, *target went to his car boot and got out some posters about Death of a Salesman and put them in his recycling bin.*

And on and on.

Ted didn't want to dampen Cody's enthusiasm, but this was sending her spare, so yesterday she'd texted him back.

Hey Cody, awesome attention to detail, but no need to tell me everything. Just let me know if anything strikes you as significant. Ted.

Cheviot Beach was only two kilometres south of Portsea, and within five minutes Ted was pulling into the carpark. She was here to meet Don Swift, a witness who'd chatted with Duncan on the beach that day. In an amazing coincidence, Don was a retired detective who'd also been called to Cheviot Beach as a young constable when the Australian prime minister, Harold Holt, disappeared while swimming in 1967. Ted had tracked him down via Facebook and, so far, Don didn't seem to have any issues with private investigators.

As she climbed out of the car with Miss Marple, Ted could feel her anxiety escalate. It was a cloudy day and the grey sky seemed to loom menacingly low over the rugged beach, which was framed by rocks and famed for its dangerous surf conditions. As they descended the stairs to the sand, Miss Marple's fluffy grey ears blew back in the wind. The foaming surf was churning in several spots and Ted recognised treacherous rips. Every part of her wanted to turn and bolt back to the safety of the city, like she'd promised Bob she would. She was glad when she spotted Don Swift, negating that option.

Don was about eighty and as brown as a berry from sunbathing every day, even when there wasn't any sun to bathe in. There were white patches under his rheumy blue eyes, due to sunglasses, Ted surmised. He was wearing red budgie smugglers, and his wizened man boobs were so saggy that you could have hidden a credit card under either one of them. But it quickly became apparent that his brain was still in perfect working order.

'The theories about Chinese subs were a bit of fun,' Don said when they'd dispensed with the introductions, 'but Holt went swimming in treacherous conditions. And all to show off in front of some bird, I heard.' He seemed more engaged by Harold Holt's fate than Duncan Bunting's. 'He was washed out to sea or taken by a shark, probably both.'

For a frozen moment all Ted could see was a shark's gaping maw, but she dragged herself back on track.

'And you think it was the same for Duncan Bunting?'

Don nodded. 'What else?'

'What did you two talk about?'

Don shrugged. 'You know, g'day, great break in the surf, that kind of thing.'

'And how would you describe his demeanour?'

'Good. Upbeat. Friendly bloke. There would have been about, I don't know, fifteen people on the beach that day, walking their dogs or whatnot. I saw him talking to all of them at one time or another. The bloke obviously loved a chat.'

Ted considered this for a moment.

'I got a photo of him,' Don announced unexpectedly. 'You want to see it?'

'Absolutely.'

Don reached down to a towel at his feet and picked up an iPhone 6 and a pair of glasses. He slipped on the glasses. 'I'm a bit of an amateur photographer. It was a good day for photos that day because of the surf. My shots start here.'

He handed Ted the phone, and she flicked through dozens of photos of the surf and the beach and people swimming, until she finally came to a photo of a dog frolicking in the shallows. Duncan Bunting was in the corner of the frame, looking out to sea. Ted enlarged the photo with her fingers and zoomed in on Duncan. He was standing at the edge of the waves, wearing a wetsuit with a swirly blue-and-purple pattern that was pulled down to his waist. His shoulders were ripped from all his gym work, and there was a large birthmark shaped like the South Island of New Zealand under his left shoulder.

Ted sent the photo to herself and returned the phone to Don. She decided to throw something out there to gauge Don's reaction.

'Duncan did have financial problems …'

'Yeah, so the coppers told me, but they're sure it was an accident,' Don said dismissively. 'You think he wanted to disappear? That he's done a runner on his missus?'

'I guess I'm just being devil's advocate. Why would a surfer of limited experience choose Cheviot Beach, especially at a time of year when it's unpatrolled?'

Don shrugged sanguinely. 'Not to speak ill of the dead, but the bloke was obviously a dimwit.'

Ted refrained from comment. After thanking Don for his time, she and Miss Marple climbed the stairs and took a walk along the cliff face, far above the wild sea. Ted was still intrigued about Duncan making such a point of talking to everyone on the beach. Was he just a natural extrovert, or had he wanted witnesses? But witnesses to what? And even if she knew the answer to that question, it wouldn't change the result. Duncan Bunting was long gone, presumably taken by a shark, and proving his death conclusively seemed an even more remote possibility now. But she couldn't fall at the first hurdle. She wanted to find some answers for Cicely and frankly, she also wanted to prove to the world that EBI could achieve the impossible.

Ted was glad she'd asked Chuck to come over tonight to try to access the data on Duncan's Apple Watch. But she was finding it hard to hold Duncan Bunting in her brain, because he was being crowded out by unwanted memories and a sick feeling that she eventually recognised as fear. By the time she was back in the car, she could no longer deny what she had to do.

She turned to Miss Marple in the rear seat. 'We need to take a detour.'

Ted's nerves felt like razor wire as she took the turn-off east to Bushrangers Bay. She seriously thought she might throw up as she pulled into the beach's carpark.

Being a working day and wild weather, Bushrangers Bay was deserted. It was low tide, and small waves were dancing gently against the rocks. The cool weather was so at odds with that sweltering day thirty-three years ago ... As Ted started walking towards the edge of the rocks, she pictured her four-year-old self and her funny, messy mummy, Bridget, playing in the rock pools. Bridget in her big floppy straw hat, Ted in her bright-yellow bathers, both blissfully unaware that within an hour, the world would end.

As Ted and Miss Marple approached the water's edge, a small wave rippled over the rocks. But Ted was consumed by memories of much bigger waves – waves threatening to crash over the top of them, and her mummy telling her to grab her stuff quickly, they had to go *now*. But Teddy had refused, chucking a tantrum until her mummy had agreed to walk right out to the edge of the rocks to pick up her favourite matted old toy, Froggy.

Ted reached the spot where Bridget had been washed away by a rogue wave, and it felt sacred. Had her mum been taken by a shark, like Duncan Bunting and Harold Holt? Or had she been hurled against the rocks and lost consciousness, before being dragged out by the merciless sea? Ted had to accept that she'd never know. For over thirty years she'd thought what happened that day was all her fault, and she'd kept it a guilty, agonising secret, because it was *she* who'd robbed her siblings of a mother and her dad of his soulmate. But, somehow, she'd recently found the courage to tell her family. She was so grateful they'd all forgiven her.

Miss Marple's sturdy little body pressed against her leg in comfort as Ted stared out at the ocean, sea spray dampening her cheeks. But then she realised it wasn't sea spray, it was tears. After all those decades of blaming herself for ruining everyone else's life, she was finally crying for that little girl.

Chapter Nine

Ted was still feeling shaken when she pulled into the Macca's carpark off the Eastern Freeway in Scoresby. She was planning to salve her emotional wounds with a Big Mac, fries and a caramel thickshake, because why not? She turned off her engine and tried to muster a smile for Miss Marple.

'I'll get a large fries, so you can have some too.'

Of course McDonald's fries weren't technically good for Miss Marple, but they weren't technically good for humans either. Ted figured a few fries now and then wouldn't kill her dog, just like they hadn't killed *her* yet. If she was Bob or Cicely Bunting, she would have prepared a delicious picnic and taken it to the peninsula with her. But she wasn't. So she hadn't. So what?

She walked into the restaurant, full of tradies eating burgers the size of their heads, and went straight to the ladies. She saw in the mirror that her eyes were red-rimmed and her face was swollen, both dead giveaways that she'd been crying. More emotionally evolved people probably wouldn't care if strangers knew they'd been crying, but it felt untenable to Ted. She splashed water all over her face, but it only seemed to make things worse.

She left the ladies and went to the counter to order, and ninety seconds later her number was called. She grabbed her bag of greasy foodstuffs and her caramel thickshake and headed outside, where she almost collided with Spike Tereiti. *Spike!* Ted's heart performed a star jump. Spike smiled down at her in surprise, and she suspected his heart might have done the same thing.

'Ted!'

'Spike! Hey.'

Spike turned to his companion, a podgy middle-aged guy in an ill-fitting suit. 'I'll catch you up in a second, Enzo.'

Enzo nodded and disappeared through the door. Ted and Spike stepped to the side and paused near the play equipment where little kids were screaming and running around like maniacs.

'What are you doing here?' Spike asked.

Ted held up her Macca's bag.

Spike grinned. 'You know what I mean.'

'I'm on my way back from a job.'

'Same,' Spike said.

And then they fell silent. Ted wondered where her banter had gone. Had she left it in her glove box? But Spike wasn't delivering on the banter front either. She looked up and noticed his eyes had softened, and he was studying her face with concern.

'Are you okay? Have you been crying?'

If he was anyone else Ted would have denied it, but Spike had made himself vulnerable with her, so shouldn't she do the same in return? And the surprising truth was, something about Spike made her actually *want* to share.

'I've just been to the beach where my mum died,' she said. 'I haven't been there since ...'

She couldn't quite finish the sentence, but she didn't need to. She'd told Spike all about the awful day on the night she'd almost taken him home.

'Oh, Ted.' His warm brown eyes were liquid with sympathy. 'That must've been tough.'

Spike opened his arms as if he wanted to hug her, but Ted thought if she allowed that to happen, she might never let him go. And then she remembered Giselle's stalking case, and how as the father of Giselle's kids, Spike had a right to know about it, and how she was denying him that right. It felt like the shameful secret it was. If she let herself draw comfort from Spike, would that make her lie seem even worse when he found out about it? Would he think she'd willingly betrayed him?

She sidestepped the hug. 'I'd better get going.'

She saw disappointment flicker across his features before he nodded understandingly. 'Sure, you go.'

'Cool ... Bye.'

But she seemed somehow stuck to the spot.

And then Spike leaned down and moved his face so close that she could have counted his bristles. He gave her a smile that was so sexy, she almost dropped her thickshake on her foot.

'One day you might let me touch you ... And, trust me, there'll be no going back.'

Ted's legs suddenly had the consistency of golden syrup, but nevertheless, she managed a snort. Spike had tickets on himself!

'You might want to order a slice of humble pie with your quarter pounder.'

Spike threw back his huge head and laughed before turning and sauntering in to Macca's. 'See you at Swordcraft on Saturday.'

Chapter Ten

It was now 7.30 pm, and dusk was illuminating the cityscape through Ted's floor-to-ceiling windows. Across the road, Ikea loomed like a land of promise, as Ted and her niece and IT expert, Chuck, slurped down the last of their Vietnamese take-away. A vermicelli noodle got stuck on Chuck's chin and Ted watched as she wiped it away, creating a streak in her thick make-up.

'This is, like, the first time I've worked from your apartment,' Chuck noted.

'Yeah, I know. Thanks for coming.'

When Chuck's IT services were required, she usually dropped into EBI after school. Kerry, Chuck's father, had only let her come over tonight on the strict condition that she'd have answered all her *Macbeth* comprehension questions by the time he picked her up on his way home from indoor cricket. Ted grabbed their food containers and dumped them on her kitchen bench, then she took a couple of Cokes from the fridge and rejoined Chuck at the card table.

'Thanks, Aunty Ted.' Chuck took a big slurp and opened her laptop.

'It's all about accessing Duncan Bunting's data,' Ted told her. 'Hopefully it'll give us some clues.'

Chuck nodded vigorously, and her long dark hair cascaded down her back in curls. It was the first time Ted had seen her niece's hair going free-range.

'Your hair looks excellent, by the way. I like your curls.'

Chuck pulled the kind of face you'd expect if someone had waved a dead mouse under her nose. 'OMG, are you serious? It's, like, a nightmare! My Prestige Pro Hair Straightener broke, and I had to go to school like this.' She gestured expansively at the horror, and her eyes furrowed in such a frown that her eyelash extensions looked like two black caterpillars about to collide.

Ted pulled Duncan's Apple Watch out of her backpack. 'This was Duncan's. It washed up in the shallows a couple of days after he disappeared.'

Chuck grimaced ghoulishly. 'Do you think he was, like, taken by a shark?'

'Probably.' It didn't take a genius to form that conclusion, although Ted was still trying to examine it from every angle, no matter how unlikely. 'I want you to work your magic and see if you can access any data that might give us a clue.'

'Too easy,' Chuck said. 'What's the password?'

Ted handed her a post-it with the password on it. *MySissy#79.*

'Perfect,' Chuck said. 'I'll research the best data recovery software.'

Ted nodded, but she was still mulling over a couple of anomalies that could mean something or nothing. 'You know what's weird? Duncan went out of his way to say hello to people on the beach that day. It's almost like he wanted to establish witnesses.'

But Chuck seemed preoccupied with the laptop screen. Her acrylic nails were making little clicking sounds as she tapped away at the keyboard.

Ted's phone rang. She checked the screen. Giselle. Ted's gizzards pre-emptively curdled. Oh no, had the stalker struck again? But how could he have when she was watching Giselle's security footage and doing regular drive-bys? Had that snake somehow managed to slip through her net? Ted hurried into the bedroom and found Miss Marple already there, ghosting Chuck. She pressed Accept.

'Giselle! Are you okay?'

'I'm fine, are *you* okay? You sound hysterical.'

Ted was surprised to discover that relief and irritation could co-exist.

'Yeah, I'm good,' she said, hiding the irritation part. 'I'm glad you are too. What can I do for you?'

'I've thought of someone else who could be my stalker.'

Ted grabbed an old-school pen and notepad she kept on her bedside table. 'Awesome. Who?'

'I don't know why I didn't think of him before. Brent Knox.'

'Brent Knox?'

'Yeah. He used to be Ava's teacher, but now he's a traffic management consultant.'

Ted blinked. 'What's a traffic management consultant?'

'He holds the Stop/Slow sign at roadworks,' Giselle said over the line. 'He had an epiphany during Covid, so he changed careers. He said he gets seventy dollars an hour for holding the sign.'

'Seventy bucks an hour?' Ted briefly contemplated a side hustle as a traffic management consultant. 'Okay, and what makes you think it could be this Brent guy?'

'He's super friendly, and he always made my parent/teacher appointments the last one of the night – even when I specially requested an early one. And he always wanted to have dinner after. I made excuses, but he kept asking.'

Ted was incredulous. Why hadn't Giselle mentioned this guy before? 'Well, thanks for telling me. I'll get straight onto it.'

Ted hung up, feeling like the emoji with the exploding head. She hoped to God it would be third time lucky with this Brent Knox guy. Working for Giselle was doing her head in, and, most importantly, catching the stalker would mean she could finally stop lying to Spike. She felt her cheeks pinken as she remembered that moment outside Macca's. Once Spike had recovered from the news that she'd been working for Giselle in secret, the two of them could start something. But *what*, exactly?

'OMG, Aunty Ted!' Chuck suddenly called from the living room. 'Come and see this! Quick!'

Ted was at Chuck's side within a millisecond. 'What?! What is it?'

'I've retrieved some data from the Apple Watch!'

Chuck showed Ted how she'd recovered Duncan's photos and phone-call records, but it soon became clear what really had her frothing.

'This GPS data's, like, epic!' she said. 'Look.' Chuck pointed at a map of the Point Nepean National Park, which was less than a kilometre from Cheviot Beach. 'Duncan Bunting travelled to this exact spot three times in the two weeks before he disappeared.'

'Three times?' Ted squinted at the screen. 'To a remote spot off the walking path?'

'I know.'

Ted exchanged an intrigued look with Miss Marple, whose curiosity had triumphed over her aloofness and drawn her out of the bedroom. Why would Duncan go to the same spot in the middle of nowhere three times, in the two weeks before he disappeared? Ted felt as if someone working her gears had just switched her into overdrive.

'This is awesome, Chuck! Excellent sleuthing, you're a star.'
'Thanks!'
The doorbell rang.
'That'll be your dad.'
Ted went to answer the door. Before she could say a word, Kerry grabbed her in his traditional headlock.

Ted struggled against his sweaty armpits. 'You stink! Get off me!'

'Hey, sweetie,' she heard him say affably to Chuck above her head.

'Hey, Dad,' Chuck replied.

'I said get off me!'

'Let's get you home. Your mum's on the warpath 'cause I let you come to Aunty Ted's on a school night. Well, any night, really.'

In a masterstroke, Ted reached back and elbowed Kerry hard in the gut. Kerry gasped and doubled over, releasing her.

Miss Marple looked up at Ted as if to say, *Well played!* and Ted looked back at her as if to say, *Why, thank you.* Meanwhile, as Kerry gasped for air, Chuck casually tossed her schoolbooks into her bag.

'Have you ...' Kerry rasped to his daughter, 'done your ... Macbeth comprehension questions?'

Chapter Eleven

It was an atypically hot day for early October. Ted could feel the sun leaping out of the cloudless sky and landing squarely on the back of her neck. Thank goodness for sunblock. She was glad she'd soaked a bandana in cold water and wrapped it around Miss Marple's neck. Not that Miss Marple was complaining. She was bush beating through the untamed scrub like a trooper.

Technically, Miss Marple wasn't permitted in a national park, but Ted was breaking the rules in the interest of furthering her investigations. The average dog's sense of smell was over one hundred thousand times more powerful than a human being's, which probably meant that Miss Marple's was at least two hundred thousand times more powerful. Ted was hoping that would prove invaluable, although she hadn't quite worked out how. Luckily, it was still too early for snake season, and Miss Marple was contained on her retractable lead for the safety of any small native fauna.

They'd left the walking track behind at least twenty minutes ago, and they were trying to forge a path through the thick scrubland in a rugged pocket of the Point Nepean National Park, which was Bunurong country. They were heading for the spot where Duncan Bunting's Apple Watch had been pinged three times before his disappearance. Ted checked the coordinates on her GPS app.

'We're nearly there.'

Could Duncan really have come *here* three times? This area seemed impenetrable. There was no evidence of human footprints or brush pushed out of the way. Ted could hear the boom and crash of the ocean getting closer, and she knew from her GPS app that they were nearing one of the national park's wild, pristine beaches. Thank God for the app, or they'd never get back.

Her phone chirped, and she reached into her pocket. Hopefully, this would be a text from the guy she'd spoken to at BHL Traffic Management, who'd promised to make some enquiries and let her know where she could find Brent Knox. But when she pulled out her phone, she saw a photo of Jarrod Beasley wearing nothing but Lululemon yoga pants and striking a pose at sunrise. Beneath the photo he'd written:

Awakening to a new day with Trikonasana and an open soul. Wouldn't you like to open your soul too? x

The guy was a dickhead. Ted realised she'd forgotten to text him and tell him she wasn't interested, but right now, she had more important things to do. She slipped the phone back into her sweaty pocket.

'I'm starting to wonder if Chuck got it wrong,' she said to Miss Marple. She could hear herself panting from the heat and her back was soaking with sweat under her backpack. As she bent to squeeze Miss Marple's bandana and trickle more cooling water onto her dog's neck, her eye caught what looked like a narrow path bashed through the scrub up ahead.

'Oh my God, look. There.'

Ted pushed her way to the rudimentary path, taking care not to let any sticks or foliage flick back into Miss Marple's eyes.

They reached the path and followed it to a clearing. Ted's GPS told her they'd arrived at the spot Duncan had visited before his disappearance, but she couldn't see any signs of human disturbance beyond the barely discernible path. The sound of the waves got even louder, and she walked just beyond the clearing and saw they were atop a small cliff. Vivid blues rose and fell in the ocean below, and white foam crashed against jagged rocks. It was a magnetic sight, but Ted forced herself away and retreated to the clearing.

She removed her backpack and pulled out Miss Marple's fold-up water bowl. She filled it, and then she chugged on her water bottle. As Miss Marple enthusiastically lapped at her water, Ted looked around the clearing again. She frowned. Was she missing something?

'I can't see anything significant, can you?'

Miss Marple looked up at Ted as if to say, *Nope*. Her fluffy white beard was dripping wet. As Ted waited for Miss Marple to finish drinking, she spotted something on the ground that wasn't indigenous to the surroundings. She snatched it up. It was the plastic tag off a loaf of bread! Ted read the expiry date.

'Miss Marple. This bread expired three weeks *after* Duncan disappeared.'

Miss Marple looked almost as pumped as Ted felt. Ted's eyes scanned the clearing. Maybe she hadn't looked hard enough? Miss Marple clearly agreed because she ran ahead, her snout on the ground, tracking a significant scent. Ted walked in a slow line; eyes fixed on the ground like a cop searching for signs of a missing person. She noticed Miss Marple urgently scratching at some scrub ahead, and when she rushed over, she realised that Miss Marple's digging had dislodged several small branches.

Underneath, the ground was disturbed, as though a hole had been dug and filled in.

'Excellent work, Miss Marple!'

Ted dropped to her knees and started digging beside her dog, although she couldn't keep up with Miss Marple's pace – it seemed she was on the scent of something. It was hot work and droplets of sweat dripped from Ted's forehead onto the dirt. She and Miss Marple dug together for a few minutes without success. Ted was just starting to wonder if she was barking up the wrong scrub when a piece of khaki canvas appeared. She pulled hard at it and eventually yanked it out of the ground, sending sandy soil spraying and revealing a large hole.

The canvas turned out to be a one-person tent, loosely buried with other remnants of a camp. They'd hit pay dirt. There were decaying food scraps, and a loaf of rye with apricot bread that matched the tag Ted had found. She also found the remains of a bar of soap, a few empty packets of Back Country Cuisine lamb and vegetables, a mini camping stove that had been used and – the clincher – a wetsuit with blue-and-purple patterning that was identical to the wetsuit Duncan had been wearing on the day he disappeared.

Ted turned to Miss Marple, reeling. 'He's alive! He did a runner.'

Duncan must have picked this spot as a hiding place and visited three times to stock it with provisions before he staged his disappearance. And then he must have paddled here directly from Cheviot Beach and scrambled up the cliffs. It wasn't far and there were spots where the cliffs dipped quite low, so it was possible. But the bread was dated three weeks after he'd disappeared. Had Duncan disguised himself and snuck into Portsea for supplies? Or had someone else brought supplies to him?

As Ted was pondering these questions, something else caught her eye. She picked it up. It was a handwritten note on the opposite side of a greasy piece of paper that looked as if it had been wrapped around take-away fish and chips. A date on the top of the note said 23 October, five weeks after Duncan's disappearance.

My darling Sissy

I don't know if you'll ever see this, but I thought if my camp is found, I owe it to you to tell you the truth. I'm sorry, but I faked my disappearance. I've let you down so many times, and I thought things would be better for you if I disappeared and started a new life somewhere else. But I've been lying low for weeks now, and I miss you so much that I've realised I don't want to start a new life without you. But I can't bear to keep dragging you down either, and I don't trust myself not to come back and ruin things for you yet again. Let's face it, I'm a waste of space. So, my darling, this is a final farewell. I'm going to end it all on the cliffs, so you'll be free to start again and find a guy who truly deserves you. I love you.

Goodbye forever, your Dunc. Xxx

Somewhere far below, the sea pounded cruelly against the rocks.

Chapter Twelve

Bob

Bob had never felt as helpless as she did right now, sitting here in this silent room, while Cicely read her husband's suicide note. She could feel her friend trying to absorb the tragic news, but was such a thing even possible? In truth, wouldn't Cicely spend the rest of her life trying to reconcile herself to this letter's contents? Bob exchanged a sombre glance with Teddy, who was perched stiffly in a nearby chair. Outside, the joyous trill of birds seemed to be mocking Cicely's plight.

They were at Cicely's renovated Edwardian house, across the road from Merri Creek, on the border of North Fitzroy and Northcote. It was only seven kilometres from the CBD, but Cicely's entire outlook was trees and babbling water. She could have been anywhere in the bush, save for the endless stream of cyclists and dog walkers traversing the Merri Creek trail. Inside, the house was cluttered with evidence of Cicely's passions – a sewing machine, a spinning wheel, a quilting table, hand-crocheted rugs, embroidered cushions, and hundreds of cookbooks and jars of home-made everything. Bob had often thought how sad it was that Cicely had been forced to sell and assume the role of tenant, and now she found herself wondering how such a crowded house could suddenly feel so empty.

She gently rubbed Cicely's back in a futile gesture of support. After what felt like aeons, Cicely glanced up at Teddy with glazed eyes.

'Yes ... that's definitely Dunc's writing ...'

'I'm sorry, Cicely,' Teddy said. 'I wish I could have given you better news.'

'I'm so sorry,' Bob echoed. She squeezed her friend and vaguely registered the smell of fresh baking.

Cicely briefly leaned into Bob, but she soon straightened, and even attempted a smile. 'Well, I suppose I have an answer now. Just not the one I wanted.'

Her plaintive words plucked at Bob's heart. Miss Marple issued a long sigh from her spot on the floor near Teddy's feet and, somehow, it sounded like sympathy. Teddy cleared her throat.

'I hate to do this, Cicely, but in the interests of having the full picture, I need to ask you a few questions.'

'Of course ... What do you need to know?'

It was a good question, Bob thought. Hadn't that terrible suicide note told the whole wretched story?

'How were things between you and Duncan before he disappeared?' Teddy asked.

Cicely shrugged sadly. 'We had our moments, like all couples do ... I knew he felt terrible about losing the house and my savings when the gym went bust, but I kept telling him it didn't matter, all that mattered was that we were together. We were a team, or I thought we were. I thought we could get through it together.' She was trying to sound matter-of-fact but the crack in her voice betrayed her.

'So, you didn't notice anything unusual in his demeanour?'

Cicely pulled out an embroidered hanky and blew her nose. 'He was distracted ... To be honest, I was worried he might have got himself in over his head on another "get rich quick" scheme and he was too scared to tell me. I should have asked, but I didn't want him to think I didn't trust him.' Her face suddenly pinkened with anger. 'That ridiculous man! Surely he knew I would've been prepared to live *on the streets*, as long as we were together. How dare he take that choice away from me?' She dissolved into tears.

Bob threw Teddy a look: *No more questions*.

Teddy nodded, and Bob realised her sister had already decided to stop. She felt proud of her sister's compassion.

'I'm such a fool,' Cicely said between her sobs.

'Don't say that, you're not a fool!' But Bob knew her reassurance would mean nothing to Cicely right now. How could you feel anything but a fool when you'd been duped by the one person you'd chosen over all others – even if that person erroneously thought they were doing the right thing? Bob knew quite a bit about being duped herself, although disappearing on a twenty-year marriage and committing suicide was on another level entirely.

Her heart ached for Duncan in his hopelessness, but how could he have done such a thing to Cicely? Was nobody who you thought they were? She felt a little pinch of fear. Could she be wrong about Raj? But the fear dissolved almost as soon as it appeared. Raj was a good man, and although it seemed a reckless thing to say when they'd only been together for a few weeks, she'd never been surer of anything.

'Can I get you something?' she asked Cicely. 'A cup of tea?'

'I'll do it,' Cicely said. She wiped her eyes and stood. 'I made some baklava this morning, we can have that too.'

Bob wanted to tell her to sit back down, that *she'd* make the tea, but she knew Cicely well enough to know that she'd want to keep herself busy.

'I'll help you,' she offered. 'Teddy, do you want tea?'

Teddy nodded sombrely. 'Sure, thanks.'

Bob followed Cicely into her cluttered open-plan kitchen, dominated by a well-loved Aga. Cicely took a dish of baklava out of her fridge.

'Yum,' Bob said.

'It's a Stelios Niarchos recipe, one of my favourites,' Cicely said, and Bob could tell she was glad for the change of subject. 'Have you ladies got Stelios's cookbook, *Partheyum*?'

'Of course,' Bob said.

Stelios Niarchos was one of Melbourne's most beloved celebrity chefs, and as far as Bob knew, everyone had *Partheyum*. Everyone except Teddy, of course. Bob would have bought her a copy if she didn't think Teddy would use it to prop up a table leg.

Cicely filled the kettle and busied herself with making a pot of tea, and producing jars of caramelised onion and beetroot chutney, as well as some propagated succulents for Bob and Teddy to take home. Bob cut up the baklava, which proved as delicious as it looked, and as they all sipped tea Teddy pulled Duncan's shredded leg rope and his Apple Watch out of her backpack and returned them to Cicely.

Cicely turned her husband's watch over in her hands. 'I gave this to Dunc for his fortieth birthday ...'

It was almost more than Bob could bear. Where to from here for Cicely? Bob didn't like to ask, but she was pretty sure her friend was still paying off Duncan's debts. She'd already been forced to relinquish Sew Darn Crafty, and employing Teddy must have been a stretch for her meagre finances. What if things got so bad that she could no longer pay the rent on the house she used to own and she got tossed out? And what if that pushed her over the edge?

Bob racked her brain for a way to help and then, like kismet, her eye was caught by the open door into Cicely's spare room. The room was stacked with handwoven wall-hangings, intricately embroidered tapestries, hand-sewn cushions, crocheted rugs and other examples of Cicely's handicrafts. It occurred to Bob with a little bump of delight that there *was* a way she could help.

'Cicely, if you'd be willing, I'd love to stock some of your handicrafts at the new Blooming Beautiful. I think they'd fly out the door.'

Cicely's swollen eyes lit up with hope. 'Really? You'd do that?'

'Of course!'

'I don't know what to say, Bob. Thank you, you're so kind.'

'Don't be silly, you'd be doing me a favour.'

'Yeah, your stuff will class the place up,' Teddy joked.

Cicely managed a little laugh, and Bob was struck by another thought.

'And I can put your quilt with the ballerina back up on the wall. It's beautiful, Cicely, no-one cares about a little biro mark. I bet you'll be flooded with offers – you could ask a stiff price.'

But Cicely shook her head. 'I gave that quilt to my cousin for Christmas.'

Bob was astounded. 'You gave it away?'

Cicely nodded regretfully. 'I did. But I'd love you to curate some handicrafts for sale. You're such a good friend, Bob – but please don't sell the rug, that was a gift.'

'No-one's getting their mitts on that,' Bob assured her.

She felt energised by her plan, but the hope was already fading from Cicely's face, and all Bob could see in its place was exhaustion.

'I've put some cash aside,' Cicely said to Teddy. 'Can I pay you now?'

Teddy shook her head. 'This one's on the house.'

'No, I insist. I know you mean well, but it wouldn't feel right not to pay. Please. What's your fee?'

Bob didn't have intimate knowledge of Teddy's charges, but she assumed it must be a few hundred dollars.

'Family discount, fifty bucks.'

Bob threw her a grateful smile. Cicely had run out of energy to pursue the argument, so she thanked Teddy and left the room to get the cash. Bob heard a chorus of bicycle bells and looked out the window to see a line of cyclists overtaking a couple of dawdling walkers on the little pedestrian bridge across Merri Creek. Birds started warbling in the trees, as though they were trying to outdo the tinkle of the bikes.

'Poor Cicely,' she said.

'Yeah …' Teddy agreed somberly.

Bob followed her sister's gaze to Miss Marple, who was now stretched out in a shaft of sunlight through the window. The dog sighed gently, half asleep.

'If Miss Marple ever disappeared, I don't know what I'd do.'

Miss Marple stirred at her name, and her eyes and Teddy's fused. Bob felt a familiar tug at her heart. Would Teddy always save her deepest feelings for her dog? As special as Miss Marple was, Bob hoped not. She wanted her sister to experience the same kind of happiness she was feeling with Raj, but she wasn't convinced that Teddy would allow herself to be that vulnerable, even now.

Chapter Thirteen
Ted

As Ted shut the gate behind Miss Marple, she saw Cicely pull her front door closed.

'Something about this doesn't feel right,' she whispered to Bob.

Bob looked startled. 'What do you mean?'

A jogger appeared from the trees on the other side of the pedestrian bridge, and his panting carried across the creek. Ted decided to put some distance between themselves and Cicely's open windows, so she marched to Bob's small Blooming Beautiful van, parked under plane trees at the end of the street. Dumb move. In an instant, she felt that all-too-familiar tickle in her throat.

'Ah-choo! Ah-choo!'

Bloody plane trees. She stepped back, almost collecting Bob, and jars of condiments collided with clinking sounds in the cloth bag Cicely had given them.

'I'm sorry, Teddy,' Bob said. 'I shouldn't have parked here.'

'Don't be stupid, it's not your fault.' Ted blew her nose.

'What did you mean, something doesn't feel right?' Bob asked worriedly.

Ted pocketed her tissue, her brain buzzing. 'Just what I said. Why would Duncan commit suicide five weeks *after* he staged his disappearance? Why didn't he just kill himself on that day on the beach?'

'Because he was going to start a new life to free Cicely, but then he realised he didn't want to live life without her.'

'Okay, then why didn't he just go back to his old life *with* her?'

'You saw the note, Teddy. He was worried he'd drag her down again.'

But more and more, Ted wasn't buying it.

'So, he's a saint, is he? Duncan Bunting is so madly in love with Cicely and so selfless that he'd literally rather kill himself than risk causing her any more problems. Don't you think that's a stretch? I mean, you knew the guy. Did he seem like a saint to you?'

Bob shifted the bag of condiments to the other hand. 'A saint? No. Do you remember his ads for Body Potential?'

Ted rolled her eyes to the skies. 'Yeah, I thought he was up himself.'

'He was,' Bob admitted somewhat reluctantly. She hated to speak ill of anybody, and it was one of the million reasons Ted loved her. 'But that didn't matter to Cicely,' she added. 'She adored him.'

'But did *he* adore *her*?'

Bob looked stumped. It seemed she'd never considered that question. Ted couldn't help smiling. Trust Bob to assume that all married couples loved each other. Sadly, through her surveillance work, Ted knew different.

'I *thought* he loved her,' Bob said. 'He was always buying her expensive gifts to apologise for his bad financial decisions. Cicely used to despair because he couldn't see the irony.' She frowned. 'What are you suggesting, Teddy?'

'Nothing *yet*. But what if the suicide note was fake?'

Bob gasped. 'But why would he write a fake suicide note?'

'What if there're even more debts that Cicely doesn't know about yet? What if Duncan got involved in something illegal?'

'*Illegal?*'

'Yeah. What if someone was after him for money and he had to make a quick getaway, so he wrote the note to throw them off the scent?'

It occurred to Ted that if Duncan *had* faked his suicide, Cicely's gut feeling about her husband still being alive would be proven right. But at what cost? Meanwhile, Bob was looking dubious.

'Self-absorbed is one thing, but Duncan never seemed like a *criminal*.'

Ted could see where Bob was coming from, but she'd learned not to take anyone at face value. Duncan Bunting had established witnesses by chatting to everyone on the beach, so he must have been more cunning than he'd appeared.

'That's exactly how these arseholes get away with it, by keeping that part of themselves hidden.' Ted could feel hubris and indignation mixing into a provocative stew. 'Well, Cicely might be blinded by love, but Duncan didn't figure on me and Miss Marple. And if that bastard's still out there, we're going to find him.'

Miss Marple gave a sharp little bark in agreement.

Ted half expected Bob to give Duncan the benefit of the doubt, but all she said was, 'Good for you, Teddy. If that's the case, he needs to be thrown in jail.'

Ted snorted. 'I wish. But faking your death isn't illegal.'

Bob crinkled her face in disbelief. 'It's *not?*'

'Not unless there's financial fraud involved. But it's starting to look like there might be in this case – I just need to dig up the dirt on Duncan.' A thought struck her. 'Hey, you don't know the name of their accountant, do you? It's a long shot, but they might be able to tell me something about Duncan's finances that Cicely isn't aware of.'

Bob frowned thoughtfully. 'Accountant, no, but Cicely did recommend her financial adviser once. She said he was excellent with small business. His name was … Matthew? Martin? No, Michael. Michael … and I'm almost certain his surname started with a W.'

Ted googled 'Melbourne-based financial advisers'. There were hundreds of them! She scrolled for yonks to get to the Ws.

'Michael Wade?'

Bob shook her head. 'No, I don't think so …'

'Michael Wall?'

'Yes, that was it! Michael Wall.'

Ted glanced at the address. Michael Wall Financial Solutions was in North Melbourne, conveniently close by.

'Keep things under your hat with Cicely, but I'll pay Michael Wall a visit tomorrow. He might not know anything, but …'

'I wonder if he knows about the quilt?' Bob bizarrely interrupted. 'I'm sure he would've advised against *that*.'

'The quilt? What do you mean?'

'That big ballerina quilt that used to hang on the wall in Sew Darn Crafty. Cicely said she gave it to her cousin for Christmas. I'm sure they're close, but giving it away seems crazy. I know for a fact she was offered five thousand dollars for it last year.'

Ted's eyes bulged. 'Five thousand bucks?'

'Yes, and that would pay *a lot* of rent. But poor Cicely hasn't been thinking straight since Duncan disappeared.' She checked herself. 'That's *if* he disappeared.'

Bob leaned against a telegraph pole, and her apricot silk palazzo pants rode up above her spotted socks and green ankle-length gumboots. As usual, she was making the disparate ensemble sing. Ted knew that if she wore the same outfit, it would look like a serious lapse in judgement – not that it would occur to her in the first place.

Ted noticed the sun sliding down the sky and forming a halo behind Bob's sleek bob. She glanced at her watch. It was almost 7 pm.

'Hey, want to go get a pizza? We could spread chutney on it.'

Bob laughed then turned crimson. 'That would've been lovely, but I'm having dinner with Raj. It's our three-week anniversary.'

'Oh, your anniversary? Cool.'

Ted planted a smile on her face, but inside, little gremlins wrung their hands with worry. Who celebrated their *three-week* anniversary? Was this all part of an elaborate plan on Raj's part, to make Bob fall in love with him and then break her heart? She reassured herself that if so, Cody Venables's surveillance would catch Raj out. She made a mental note to text Cody to tell him tonight was significant and to report to her on everything. All this ran around in her head while she stood there looking up at Bob with what she hoped was a supportive smile.

Bob somehow managed to look radiant and apologetic at the same time. 'I'd invite you to join us, but ...'

'I know. It's early days.'

Bob pulled her into an impetuous hug. 'Thanks for trusting my judgement, Teddy.'

If only you knew, Ted thought guiltily. But she observed their sisterly ritual.

'Get off me.'

Bob laughed, but Ted saw tears fill her eyes.

'I want *you* to be this happy too.'

Of course she did, because she was Bob. Ted could feel herself clenching, but she tried to sound breezy.

'Can we not get into my intimacy issues?'

'I'm serious, Teddy. Now you've finally forgiven yourself and made up with Dad, do you think you might be able to let love into your life?'

Ted snorted, because she couldn't think of what else to do. 'How many times do I have to tell you, Miss Marple's the love of my life.'

'Stop deflecting!'

Woah. Ted gave a little start, and Bob softened.

'Wouldn't you like to open your heart to a man?'

Spike's unshaven mug flashed unbidden in front of Ted's eyes, and she realised she was opening her heart to *him*. Sort of. She knew she should tell Bob about Spike, but somehow she couldn't. All she managed was, 'I've got to get going.' And she quickened her step back to her car.

Chapter Fourteen

Michael Wall Financial Solutions was buried deep inside a soulless 1970s building, and the office didn't have a window or skylight in sight. If it wasn't for her damp hair, Ted could have almost forgotten it was raining outside. She wondered if Michael Wall preferred to be detached from the natural world or if this charmless workplace was an economic decision. Probably the latter – he was savings-focused, after all.

'Cicely Bunting hired you to find Duncan?'

Ted nodded.

Michael Wall gave her a look of barely concealed disgust. 'And you took her case? She *can't* afford a wild goose chase.'

Ted didn't blame him for his disdain. For all Michael Wall knew, she'd been shamelessly exploiting Cicely's grief to line her pockets. She considered explaining that it wasn't a wild goose chase, because she'd already found Duncan's secret camp and his probably fake suicide note, but in the interests of getting objective answers, she decided to keep her powder dry.

'I explained to her that there was a one in a million chance of finding Duncan alive, but she was concerned he might be stranded on an island in the Bass Strait.'

Michael Wall reacted with shock. 'She was? That's sad.'

'I know.' Ted allowed a small space for silence. 'I'm wondering what you can tell me about Duncan's finances?'

'It's been a year. I'm not sure how that's relevant.'

'To be honest, neither am I yet. But I'm trying to cover all the bases.'

Michael glanced down at Ted's phone, which was recording their conversation. 'My clients' financial details are confidential.'

'Of course, and you have my word I'll keep it that way.'

Michael sighed. 'Well ... it's no secret that their situation wasn't good.'

'I know, but more specifically?'

After what looked like a brief internal debate, Michael surrendered to her line of questioning. 'Duncan had a habit of making disastrous financial decisions and leaving Cicely to pick up the pieces. The gym was an example. I advised them against it because they didn't have enough capital. But it was Duncan's dream and Cicely wanted to support him. And then he bought the gym equipment from some fly-by-night discount supplier who charged extortionate interest. It put them behind the eight ball from the start, and the gym went bust. Cicely lost the house, and then the shop. But you know that.'

'Yeah.'

Michael leaned back in his chair, looking pensive. He was fortyish, Ted supposed, and kind of hot, with blond hair and large brown eyes. It was a combination most women would appreciate, Ted suspected. And he was more tanned than you'd expect for a guy who spent most of his life behind his desk in this windowless office that resembled a sealed Tupperware container. Not that he held a candle to Spike, of course. Ted imagined the feeling of Spike's lips on hers, but she shook her head to dislodge the thought. Since when did she daydream about kissing during a case? *Get a grip!*

'So, the gym was part of a larger pattern?' she asked.

'Yes, you could say that,' Michael confirmed. 'Duncan would promise to stick to the financial plan we'd made, but then some shyster would appear, and he'd throw all of their money – what little there was left of it – at them, and the whole cycle would repeat itself.'

'That must have been infuriating for you as their financial adviser.'

Michael shrugged resignedly. 'I wasn't their parent. My role was just to offer advice.'

'Sure, but when your advice wasn't taken ...'

'No-one felt worse about that than Duncan. He was always apologising to Cicely. In fact ... it probably sounds like a terrible thing to say, but his disappearance was almost ironic.'

'Ironic? How do you mean?'

Michael hesitated.

'They were here a few days before he disappeared, and Duncan seemed ... despairing.'

Ted frowned. 'How?'

'Cicely wanted me to help them draw up yet another budget, but Duncan was beside himself. He kept saying, "What's the point? I'm a waste of space ... You'd be better off without me."'

Ted felt a chill descend in the temperature-controlled room. 'He actually said, "You'd be better off without me"?'

'Yes.'

'And that was a few days before he disappeared?'

Michael nodded.

The conclusions were drawing themselves, but Ted asked anyway. 'Did you ever get the sense that Duncan felt so guilty, he might even ...?'

'Leave her, or *worse*?' Michael nodded grimly. 'I'm afraid it had occurred to me. But Cicely always seemed able to drag him back from the abyss. She was obviously very much in love with him. Sounds like she still is.'

Ted nodded. 'Yes.'

Michael's observations were sobering, and Ted was starting to wonder if things weren't as complicated as she'd surmised. After all those weeks of hiding out in isolation, had Duncan genuinely got to a point where he couldn't bear to go on without Cicely, but he couldn't bear to inflict himself on her either? Had she got it wrong? Had he really killed himself in a tragically misguided attempt to spare Cicely from his stuff-ups?

It was a distressingly logical explanation, but Ted reminded herself that a good PI never makes assumptions. There was still the possibility that Duncan had faked his suicide to escape a dangerous debtor, or possibly even jail. She needed to interrogate this from every potential angle, and every angle so far led back to money.

She saw Michael glance at a wall clock behind her and jumped in quickly. 'Can I ask you something else? I know Duncan wouldn't have shared this with you, but do you think he could have been involved in anything illegal?'

Michael considered the question.

'I don't think he would have *intended* to. He wasn't a bad person, from what I could see. But he was suggestible and easily influenced. I *can* imagine him getting swept up in something like that.'

Ted nodded. So could she.

Michael Wall pointedly pushed back his chair. 'Anyway, apologies for cutting this short, but I'm expecting a client.'

'Of course,' Ted said. She needed to be somewhere else too. She'd finally tracked down Giselle's latest suspected stalker, Brent Knox, to a traffic management crew on North Road in East Bentleigh. She grabbed her phone and switched off the recording. 'Thanks for your time.'

Michael Wall saw her to the door. 'I'm sorry I couldn't offer a more positive take.'

Ted smiled sombrely. 'You've been very helpful.'

Her brain juggled bleak scenarios as she left the claustrophobic office and caught the lift down three levels to blessed fresh air. What if what really happened to Duncan was a combination of all three theories? What if Duncan *had* got himself in over his head with some dodgy types, but rather than faking the suicide note to shake off his pursuers, as she'd thought, he'd genuinely killed himself? And what if he'd deliberately composed the note to Cicely in a way that made it clear to his pursuers that Cicely knew nothing about whatever was going on? In that case, he was trying to spare her in either scenario. Ted resolved that if Duncan had killed himself because he was already in fear for his life, then the least she could do for Cicely was try to find out who he'd been so afraid of.

When she emerged from the building, the rain had softened into showers. Ted was relieved, because her windscreen wiper blades made a squeaking noise like fingernails on a chalkboard. It drove her nuts, but she hadn't got around to doing anything about it yet. She drove off and negotiated her way through gnarled traffic for the next forty-five minutes, finally arriving at the roadworks on North Road in East Bentleigh.

A guy was shovelling gravel inside a large hole in the road, while four other guys in high-vis vests stood above the hole, watching him. Google image searches for Brent Knox had proven non-conclusive and he wasn't on the socials, so Ted brought up the pics of the hooded stalker on her phone and reminded herself of his 'average height and build'. Unfortunately, all four guys standing around the hole fitted that physical description – but Ted knew it would only take one question to weed her quarry out.

'Let's see what you've got to say for yourself, *mate*,' she muttered.

Ted climbed out of her car and headed down the footpath, weaving past the orange plastic fencing that proliferated at roadworks, and ignoring the 'Pedestrians This Way' sign. A guy so short he could be a jockey was passing with a 'Slow' sign slung over his shoulder. Ted stopped him.

'Er, excuse me?'

'Yeah?' he said.

'I'm looking for Brent Knox.'

The little guy looked surprised. '*I'm* Brent Knox.'

'You're Brent Knox?'

He nodded. 'What can I do for you?'

'Nothing, as it turns out,' Ted said. 'Sorry to waste your time.'

When she pulled away from the kerb five minutes later, Ted called Giselle and 'pleasantly' pointed out that Brent Knox was at least a foot shorter than the guy in the lamb's heart shots.

'Oh yeah ...' Giselle said vaguely over the line. 'Now I come to think of it, he *is* a lot shorter.'

Ted sighed in frustration.

As she approached Glen Huntly Road in Elsternwick, a rainbow arced the Nepean Highway, and somehow that changed everything. A smile lit Ted up inside. If she was superstitious, she would have thought the rainbow was some kind of positive omen. But a positive omen of what?

She glided to a halt at the lights and heard the chirp of an incoming text. She glanced at her phone on the passenger seat and saw a sword emoji from Spike. In an instant her face felt hot enough to fry an egg, and all she could think was, *I can't wait to see you at Swordcraft.*

But then another thought intruded and killed her joy. If she didn't find Giselle's stalker within the next forty-eight hours, and Giselle honoured their deal and told Spike about the whole thing, how would Spike feel about Ted then? Not flirty anymore, that was for sure. But she'd just have to cop it on the chin. She'd much rather incur Spike's wrath than keep lying to him.

Chapter Fifteen

Ted adjusted an icicle earring as she peered up hopefully at a guy in chest armour, with a black raven painted on his face. He had reddish hair and bright-blue eyes, and Ted had often thought that, unlike Spike, he could pass for an actual Viking.

'Duncan Bunting?' he said.

'Yeah.'

The guy frowned thoughtfully, and the tips of the raven's wings briefly disappeared into the freckled folds of his cheeks.

It was 8.27 pm on a crisp night at the Western Oval in Parkville, a leafy pocket on the edge of the city's CBD. Tonight, the willy wagtails were performing their usual trill in the elm trees that lined the nearby cycling path, but they were barely audible beneath the boisterous clamour of elves, goblins, knights and other fantasy types who were arriving for the weekly medieval battle game, Swordcraft.

As a member of the all-female warband the Ice Elves, Ted was wearing her long blue skirt matched with a silver pauldron, plastic elf ears and silver icicle earrings courtesy of Bob. She had her foam sword in her hand, and she was already itching to use it.

The Viking, Mitch Prowse, was one of Spike's best mates and a fellow member of the Sons of Thor warband. He was a jokey type and, fortuitously for Ted, a detective in the financial crimes squad.

'Duncan disappeared when he was surfing at Cheviot Beach about a year ago,' she reminded him, 'and he had financial problems.'

Mitch nodded. 'Gotcha. Duncan Bunting, the Body Potential gym guy.'

'Yeah. I'm just wondering if he had any dealings with scary dudes on the wrong side of the law.'

Mitch shook his head. 'We did a bit of digging into his business affairs. It seemed like he skated close to the wind, but we never discovered any actual fraud.'

It wasn't the solution wrapped in a neat little bow that Ted had hoped for, but no case worth solving was ever simple.

Mitch grinned. 'Of all the places he could have picked, the bloke went surfing at Cheviot Beach! If you ask me, his only crime was stupidity.'

It was almost the same thing Don Swift had said, and it now occurred to Ted that it was what Duncan had *wanted* people to think.

'Why do you ask?' Mitch said. 'Are you *investigating*?'

Here we go, Ted thought. Mitch had learned bad habits from Spike, who treated her like a little girl playing at being a PI. She was itching to say, *Yes, I am* investigating. *And guess what? I've found the place where Duncan hid for five weeks after he faked his death* and *a suicide note that seems staged*. But of course, she didn't say that. Partly because Mitch was a cop, but mainly because she wasn't going to tell a soul until she had Duncan cornered.

So, instead, she said with her signature smart-arse smile, 'No, I'm too busy investigating why you and Spike are so crap at Swordcraft.'

Mitch laughed, but he was already waving at someone over Ted's shoulder. Ted turned. It was Giselle, of all people. She was wafting towards them in one of her signature floaty dresses, pushing a tiny purple scooter with iridescent streamers hanging off the handlebars.

'Aren't you a bit big for that thing?' Mitch said.

Giselle laughed, and Ted realised it was the first time she'd seen her smile. Which was hardly surprising, when you thought about it. The stalker might have been lying low since the break-in at her house a week ago, but Giselle hadn't come up with any new names since Brent Knox, so they were no closer to identifying her tormentor.

'Ha ha,' Giselle said. 'Hi, Mitch.' She gave Mitch a peck on the cheek and turned to Ted. 'Hi, Ted.' Her eyes swept over Ted's Ice Elves outfit and silently said, *What the hell?*

'Hey, Giselle.'

'Oh, you two know each other?' Mitch said.

'Yeah.'

Ted waited for Giselle to explain that she'd employed her services, but Giselle just said, 'We've got a mutual friend.' Then she glided the scooter towards Mitch. 'I've got to run. Ava's missing this, can you give it to Spike?'

'Too easy.' Mitch took the scooter.

'Thanks, Mitch.'

Ted considered the little girlie scooter and wondered why it made her feel weird, and not necessarily in a good way. Was it because she'd never really thought about the implications of Spike coming as a package with three little kids? Butterflies performed back flips in her chest as she thought about Spike arriving at any second. It reminded her that she needed to clarify something ASAP.

Giselle was waving a lily-white hand. 'I've got to run—'

'No, wait. We need to talk.' Without giving Giselle a chance to refuse, Ted turned and led her over to a quiet-ish spot on the fringes of the Swordcraft chaos.

'What is it?' Giselle asked.

'I wanted to check that you've told Spike about your stalker.'

Giselle shook her head. 'No. I haven't.'

Ted mentally threw her hands in the air. 'We had an agreement, remember? You promised that if I hadn't ID'd the stalker within a week, you'd tell Spike about it.'

Giselle shrugged elegantly.

'I'm sorry, Ted, I've changed my mind.'

'But we had a deal—'

'I know, but this is the right decision.'

'I disagree—'

'I'm *not* telling him.'

'But he'll be here any minute,' Ted heard herself exclaim, 'and I don't want to lie to him anymore!'

Giselle did a theatrical double take. Oops.

'I mean, I don't want to lie to *anyone*, not even an acquaintance.'

And then to Ted's surprise, Giselle fixed her with a level gaze. 'I appreciate that, but I have to prioritise my girls' well-being. They're smart kids. If Spike finds out they'll pick up on his stress, and I don't want them impacted by this. All right?'

Ted found herself nodding dumbly.

'And besides, Spike would feel compelled to rescue me. I'm single now, and as scary as it might be, I have to learn to stand on my own two feet.'

Wow. Ted hadn't realised there was so much substance beneath Giselle's floaty exterior.

'I admire your courage,' she said.

Giselle gave her a long-suffering look.

'I wouldn't need to be courageous if you'd just catch my stalker.'

Ted was speechless, but luckily there was no need for talk, because at that moment a friendly-looking brunette rocked up with a teenage boy who was the spitting image of Mitch Prowse.

'Giselle!'

'Fleur! Ollie!'

The women exchanged a warm hug.

'How are you, gorgeous?' the woman said. 'I didn't expect to see *you* here.'

'I just dropped Ava's scooter off for Spike.'

Giselle introduced the boy to Ted as Mitch's son Ollie, and the woman as his ex-wife, Fleur. Ollie was the exact same height and build as his father, a neophyte Viking, and Ted remembered seeing him watching from the sidelines before. They made small talk for a few minutes, although Ollie was clearly at that awkward teenage stage and seemed too shy to meet Giselle's or Ted's eyes. Giselle kissed Fleur and Ollie goodbye, making Ollie's face turn puce, and then she left.

Ted was heading off to join the Ice Elves, but Ollie nudged Fleur, and Fleur said, 'Ted, before you go – can Ollie ask you something?'

'Of course.'

Ted waited, but Ollie just stared at his feet, his face still aflame. Fleur let a couple of seconds pass, and then she nudged him.

'Ollie?'

'Ah, yeah ...' Ollie finally mumbled. 'Dad said you're a private eye.'

'Yep.'

'That's elite.'

'Thanks!'

'It must be so interesting,' Fleur said, her open face devoid of the mockery that Ted was accustomed to from the blokes.

'It is, I love it.' Ted tried not to fidget as she waited for Ollie to get to the point, but like height and a pleasant singing voice, patience wasn't something she'd been gifted with. 'What do you want to ask me?'

'Umm ... I've got a commerce assignment on careers,' he eventually said. 'Could I interview you?'

'Sure,' Ted replied, smiling up at the boy's nose, because his eyes were still on the ground. She tried to stay focused on the conversation, even though she'd just seen Spike's muddy old ute pull up. Spike was here! But she'd have to keep lying to him by omission. It made the whole thing complicated, and she wasn't sure how to feel about it. 'Do you want to do a Zoom, maybe Monday?'

Spike had climbed out of his ute in his full Viking regalia and was heading in their direction.

'Um, we have to do it in person,' Ollie said. 'Could I come to your office after school?'

Ted did a quick mental calculation. 'Sure, that should be fine.'

Ollie finally managed to raise his eyes, but he had to lower them again to meet Ted's. 'Cool.'

'Hey, Ollie!' Mitch called from nearby. 'Come and meet Roscoe.'

Ollie loped off to join Mitch, and Fleur gave Ted a woman-to-woman smile.

'Thanks for that.'

Ted smiled. 'It's no problem.'

'Hey, you two.'

It was Spike's gravelly voice.

Ted and Fleur spun around as one. Spike was standing before them, a commanding figure in the fading light. His horned Viking helmet was barely restraining his unruly dark curls, and his foam sword was slung over his expansive shoulders. Except for the Māori part, he looked like a Norse god about to do battle.

Ted had a snap fantasy of fainting into his manly arms, but, luckily, Fleur greeted him with an easy hug that gave Ted cover to regroup. Then she and Spike exchanged 'casual' greetings. They all chatted, although God knew what they were chatting about, because Ted was finding it hard to listen. All she could do was *feel* Spike's presence as if it was some kind of invisible, electric forcefield.

Eventually, Fleur wandered off to join Mitch, and Spike and Ted were left alone – if you didn't count the dozens of Vikings, knights, goblins and whatnot gearing up for battle all around them. Ted felt an urge to either fling herself into Spike's arms or to tell him about Giselle's stalker. Since neither was an option, she did the only other thing that came naturally.

'Are you ready to be annihilated?'

Spike laughed down at her. 'Careful, that breeze nearly knocked you over.'

Ted snorted. 'Hilarious. You won't be laughing when I pummel you.'

'Can you send me a postcard? I might not notice.'

Their banter was on the same level as usual, but Ted couldn't help sensing that the vibe felt different, kind of weird and stilted.

And Spike seemed as awkward as she was. What was going on? If this was how emotional maturity felt, Ted wasn't sure she wanted it. She was relieved when Mitch appeared with the tiny purple scooter.

Spike took the scooter and proffered it to Ted. 'I assume this is yours?'

'Stop, my sides are splitting. You'd better be careful, or I'll hit you over the head with it.'

'You'd need a stepladder,' Spike said, and he and Mitch laughed together like the dorks they were.

Ted wondered why she felt relieved, and then she realised she was back in her happy place – mutual sledging, with no confronting emotions involved. The marshal called out, 'Five minutes, combatants!' and her Ice Elves leader, Usma, waved her over to join their elaborately costumed warband. 'Hey, Ted! Come and strategise!'

Ted headed over to join the rest of the Ice Elves, and they spent the next five minutes strategising in a rambunctious rabble. As they took their starting positions at the opposite end of the oval from the Sons of Thor, Usma sidled over to Ted with a cheeky grin.

'Is your new boyfriend here to watch you kick arse?'

Huh? Her new boyfriend? Ted was stumped. But then she remembered Usma seeing her with Jarrod Beasley at Trax last week. She laughed. Boy, did Usma have the wrong end of the stick. Ted was about to set her straight, but the marshal blew his whistle.

'Combatants, go!'

Chapter Sixteen

The Ice Elves and the Sons of Thor charged at each other, and ten minutes later Ted and Spike were the only two combatants still vertical. As their fellow warriors lay 'dead' on the battlefield around them, Ted gave free rein to her inner animal. She parried and thrust, slashing, dodging and blocking Spike.

'For the Ice Queen!' she yelled.

'For Odin!' Spike thundered.

In the exuberance of the moment all their awkwardness had evaporated, and it felt good.

'Get her, Spike!' a 'deceased' Mitch yelled from his prostrate position on the ground nearby. The other 'deceased' Sons of Thor roared their encouragement.

'Belt-hon, Ted!' Usma shouted from nearby, which meant 'kill him' in Tolkien's primitive Elfish. The other Ice Elves yelled support from their various spots splayed on the ground.

'Yeah, belt-hon, Ted!'

'I will!' Ted said.

But in that fraction of a second, Spike's foam sword struck her torso beneath her pauldron, leaving her with only one health point remaining.

'You beauty, mate! That's one for Thor!' Mitch whooped.

Ted charged at Spike and, for once, he didn't react fast enough. She had him up against the wall, metaphorically, but Spike recovered and lunged forward in a flash. As she ducked to avoid his foam sword she lost her footing and tripped over Mitch's 'body'. She ended up toppling over and getting all tangled up with Mitch on the ground. The battle was lost. Ted performed a dying cockroach routine and the onlookers laughed rowdily. The marshal blew his whistle, and all the warriors and watchers-on cheered.

'Victory to the defenders! All projectiles to the centre.'

All the combatants stirred and started climbing to their feet. Ted was laughing so much that she had to catch her breath as she untangled her legs from Mitch's armour and pulled her long ice-blue skirt back over her jeans.

Mitch laughed. 'You okay?'

'I'm good!'

If Ted were honest, she'd never been very fond of losing, but Swordcraft was so much fun that it didn't matter, not even losing to Spike. The sheer exhilaration of the camaraderie and the cut and thrust always seemed to wash her cares away. As she retrieved an elf ear from the ground and scrambled to her feet, she came face-to-face with Spike's chest plate. She tilted her head back to meet his laughing brown eyes, and held out her hand to shake.

'Congratulations, dickhead.'

Spike laughed. He shook her hand, and the minute they touched, it was like one of those scenes from a movie where everything else goes blurry and the only person you can see in focus is the other star of the film. *Steady, Ted. Remember the lying by omission.* But Spike was smiling into her eyes, and it felt so nice that she decided to worry about that later.

'How are you going?' he asked gently.

Ted felt that invisible force field again.

'You mean, seriously?'

Spike nodded with a smile that softened his manly face.

'I'm good,' Ted said, trying to keep it vague. 'You know ...'

Their eyes locked like Velcro.

'How are *you*?' she asked.

'I'm okay, but I'll be better when ...'

She heard the unspoken words: *when I can touch you.* He smiled into her eyes. Everything else was still a blur and she vaguely wondered when the rest of the world would come back into focus.

'So, how long do you think it will take you to overcome your commitment problems?'

About as long as it takes to finish Giselle's case, Ted thought. She wished with all her heart she could tell him about it. She just had to hope he'd forgive her when he finally found out.

'I'm not sure,' she said truthfully.

'That's okay,' Spike replied with a hint of vulnerability. 'It doesn't matter how long it takes, as long as I'm still the first guy you'll practise on?'

'You definitely are.'

'Excellent.' Spike's smile morphed back into sexy. 'Trust me, you won't regret it.'

Ted didn't doubt it. Their eyes fused again and she thought, *How can the world just disappear like this?* But maybe she jinxed herself, because suddenly the world intruded in the worst way possible.

'Hey, has she told you about her new boyfriend?'

Ted turned around to see Usma. Oh no, she was talking about Jarrod Beasley again! Ted freaked. Usma's blue Ice Elf wig was hanging at a lopsided angle over her hijab as she grinned between Ted and Spike.

'What boyfriend?' Spike asked.

'There's no boyfriend,' Ted said quickly.

'So you haven't told him?' Usma said. 'I saw her with a guy at Trax, *holding hands*. That's why she wasn't here last week. It was so cute it made me want to puke.'

'That wasn't a date,' Ted told Spike shrilly. She tried to laugh it off, but her laughter sounded strangled and forced. 'I was undercover on a case.'

But Spike's softness had disappeared, and now he was all sharp edges. 'What kind of case?'

Ted silently cursed Giselle and her non-disclosure agreement.

'I'm sorry, I can't say. But I swear it was work.'

Usma laughed. 'Ha, that wasn't work!' She turned to Spike. 'They were making goo-goo eyes all over each other.'

Ted loved Usma, but in that moment, she would have cheerfully killed her.

'It wasn't how it looked, okay?'

She sounded terser than she'd intended. Usma backed off, even though she clearly didn't believe her.

'Hey, it's cool. I'm sorry, maybe I shouldn't have said anything, I know you like to keep your love life private. But I'm happy for you. Just don't let love make you soft on the battlefield, or Spike'll win again.'

Spike smiled, but the smile didn't reach his eyes. 'Nothing wrong with that. Catch you later.' He walked away, his broad back a brick wall.

Ted wanted to run after him and say, *Wait, I was telling the truth! I only want you!* But there were too many people around for that, and Usma was reminding her about a post-Swordcraft birthday get-together for Becky, one of the Ice Elves. Ted tried to rally as she rejoined her warband, but all she could think about was Spike. He was in the distance, but she was still acutely aware of his every move, and she watched miserably as he left with Mitch without a backwards glance.

The thought of Spike believing she'd lied about her feelings for him was almost more than Ted could bear. She left Becky's party early and as soon as she was back in her car she called him, but he didn't pick up. She left a message reiterating that she wasn't on a date with Jarrod, it was just a job. Then she drove home and took Miss Marple for a late-night walk at Williams Reserve. By the time they got back to her apartment, Spike still hadn't returned her call.

The minutes ticked past like a succession of eternities. Ted tried to occupy herself by catching up on some work, but she couldn't sit still. She felt as if little rodents were gnawing away at soft tissue inside her chest, and she couldn't recall ever feeling like that about a man before. Emotional maturity was overrated!

Ted noticed Miss Marple regarding her quizzically from the floor. She'd always been a genius at intuiting Ted's vibe.

'Do you think I should call him again?' Ted asked.

Miss Marple looked up at her as if to say, *I don't know, what do you think?* And Ted looked back at her as if to say, *I don't know what I think, that's why I asked you!* But in the end she couldn't stand it, and she tried Spike's number again at close to midnight. This time he answered, and Ted hoped he couldn't hear her little gasp of relief or joy or whatever it was – she was finding her emotions hard to identify at the moment.

'Hi, it's me,' she said in a reedy, anxious voice that appalled her.

'Yeah, hi,' Spike said coolly.

'Listen, I hope you didn't believe what Usma said before. I was undercover, I swear. I had to get the guy's trust so he'd give me the info I needed. And I've signed an NDA so I can't discuss the job, but otherwise I'd tell you all about it, I promise.' She waited in silence for a response. 'Spike?'

'Yeah, I believe you.'

'You do? Then why didn't you call me back?'

But Spike just sort of grunted. Ted's ire started to rise; it felt like a welcome return to form.

'Spike? Why didn't you call me?'

There was another silence for a second or two.

'I believe you were on a job, but Usma said you were all over the bloke. And if there's one thing I know you're lousy at, it's faking your feelings.'

Ted took a moment to get his gist.

'Wait, what? So you think I was genuinely hot for the guy?'

'Were you?'

'No! I'm just good at my job.'

'Yeah, sure, whatever,' Spike said in a tone that seemed designed to convey his lack of conviction. 'It's none of my business, anyway.'

Ted felt anger flare. 'You know what? You're right, it isn't.'

'Good. Then we're in agreement.'

Ted suddenly wanted to reach through the phone and punch him in the head. 'This is so typical. You'd rather think I'm just a flirty little girl – because even though I've solved a murder, you still can't bring yourself to believe that a woman could be good at this job.'

'That's bullshit,' Spike said angrily.

'No, it's not. You're a patriarchal dickhead,' she said, even though they both knew it wasn't true.

'And you're a pain in the arse.'

Which they both knew *was* true. Ted pressed End and hoped she got in first, but she was pretty sure that Spike hung up at the exact same moment. She threw her iPhone down on the card table with shaking hands, feeling her breath trapped in her chest. She caught Miss Marple's eye, and Miss Marple looked up at her from the floor as if to say, *That didn't go so well, then?*

'He's an arrogant pig,' Ted said.

Her body was roiling with feelings that made her want to run screaming, and she reasoned with herself that it was better this had happened now. She'd been crazy to think that she and Spike might potentially work as a couple. The man was an idiot – and, besides, he had three little kids! Who needed those kinds of complications? She couldn't be taking kids to music lessons and God knows what, she had an important job to do. And she'd never wanted kids anyway. She could now see that even contemplating a relationship with Spike had been nuts on her part. But at least she'd come to her senses before she'd done anything stupid, like put her heart on the line.

Chapter Seventeen

Ted woke to the sound of Miss Marple's bark ringing in her ears.

Woof! Woof!

She propped herself up on her elbow. Sunlight was streaming through her bedroom window, and she could see a couple having breakfast in the uncomfortably close apartment building next door.

Woof! Woof!

Her eyes pivoted to Miss Marple, who was sitting on the floor beside the bed, staring up at her. Ted checked the time: 9.37 am.

9.37 am!

'Sorry, Miss Marple!' she said blearily, throwing off the doona. 'I was awake all night trying not to think about ... stuff. I think I only fell asleep at about six am.'

Miss Marple looked at her as if to say, *Sure, but I can't feed myself.*

'I hear you.' Ted swung her feet to the floor and padded into the kitchen. Miss Marple followed eagerly. Ted yawned as she reached into the fridge and pulled out her dog's lamb and veggie roll. She cut it into pieces and filled her bowl, giving her a supersized portion out of guilt. 'There you go, apologies for the delay.'

Miss Marple started wolfing down her breakfast, and Ted surveyed the contents of her fridge. Apart from Miss Marple's healthy meal options, there were two containers of leftover Thai, an almost empty tub of yoghurt, a couple of Corona beers and several of Cicely's pristine jams and chutneys. They looked embarrassed to be there, and no wonder. It was a pretty pathetic effort on her part, when Ted thought about it. Would it kill her to make the occasional salad? She took a teaspoon out of the cutlery drawer and sampled Cicely's vanilla and pear jam. *Yum*.

Her phone started ringing in the bedroom, and she jumped so high she almost dropped the jar. Was Spike calling to apologise? Her heart performed an impromptu river dance as she raced back to scoop up her phone.

The caller was Cody Venables.

For a second Ted felt disappointed, but then she remembered that Spike was an idiot, and she'd dodged a bullet. But was he really? And had she really? She didn't want to think about that, so she focused on Cody's call. Surely he couldn't have an update on Bob and Raj already? She knew from his surveillance on Wednesday night that Bob and Raj had held hands over the table at Al Dente Enoteca and then headed back to Bob's place where Raj had stayed the night. And first thing on Thursday morning, Raj had gone out to buy Bob a coffee and some croissants and what seemed like a few things she'd forgotten from the supermarket – a jar of peanut butter, a container of dishwasher powder and a packet of toilet rolls.

Ted had been particularly pleased about the dunny paper, for two reasons: (1) if Raj was a player, there was no way he'd bother to go out and buy Bob's toilet rolls, and (2) Bob would only ask him to do that if she felt truly comfortable with him. And, she had to admit, when she'd talked to Bob on Thursday, Bob had sounded happy and unhurried – but not the hyper kind of happy she'd been in the past, as if she'd known she had to make the most of things before they evaporated. It was a welcome new vibe from Bob, and Ted was finding herself inclined to give Raj the benefit of the doubt. Maybe he really *was* as nice as he seemed, and Bob had finally picked someone who deserved her. Not that anyone ever could.

In fact, this call from Cody was timely, because she'd been planning to call off the surveillance today. Partly for financial reasons, but mostly because the longer Cody's surveillance of Raj continued, the bigger the risk that Bob would somehow find out. Ted liked to think she wasn't scared of anything, but the thought of Bob knowing about this made her paralysed with terror. She knew poor Cody would be crushed, he'd thrown his heart and soul into this gig. He'd probably offer to continue for free, but she wasn't in the business of exploiting fledgling surveillance agents. She pressed Accept.

'Cody, hey.'

'Ted, this is epic! Are you sitting down?!'

The kid sounded like he was in overdrive, although Ted didn't know if he had another gear.

'What? What is it?'

'A woman stayed at Raj Dalal's house last night!'

Ted's blood ran from cold to boiling before she had time to blink. 'What?'

'I saw them come home together at like, ten o'clock. They had their arms around each other. And then she stayed over, and they just went out for a run together.'

'*What?!*'

Cody said something about how they'd just come back from the run and walked right past his hiding spot, but Ted could barely hear him over the blood bubbling in her ears. She tried to pull herself back from the brink. *Don't jump to conclusions.* There could be a perfectly reasonable explanation.

'Hang on, wait. She's probably his daughter.'

Cody made a scoffing sound. 'Close family. She slept in *his* bedroom.'

Little missiles of fury took off in Ted's head. 'How do you know?'

'His bedroom fronts onto the street. He closes his blinds every night and opens them every morning. But this morning *she* opened the blinds, wearing a skimpy nightie thing. That's what they call it, isn't it? A nightie?'

Ted tried to quell her natural instincts to go berserk. *You're a PI,* she told herself, *interrogate this from every angle.* Maybe the woman who'd stayed with Raj last night was actually Bob. Maybe, somehow between now and Thursday night, Cody had forgotten what Bob looked like.

'Wait, is the woman tall?' she asked urgently. 'With dark shoulder-length hair?'

'It's not your sister,' Cody said, smashing Ted's theory to pieces. 'This woman's heaps younger. And she's kinda hot.'

'So is Bob,' Ted heard herself snap. 'She's *very* hot.'

'Er, yeah. For sure.'

Ted tried to calm herself.

'Okay ... I admit this sounds incriminating, but it *could* still be Raj's daughter.'

'No way! If she was his daughter, why would she say to him, "You were amazing last night, my darling"?'

Ted almost self-immolated.

'She said, "You were amazing last night my darling"?'

'Yeah! They walked right past me; I heard every word.'

Ted made a snap decision to murder Raj, but she tried to remain professional in the interim.

'Okay ... Did you get photos?'

'No.' Cody sounded sheepish. 'Sorry. I got kind of excited when they came up so close and I dropped my phone. And I haven't seen her since they went inside, but I've got my binoculars trained on the window.'

'So, she's still in the house?'

'Yeah.'

'I'm heading over.'

Ted put Cody on speaker and tossed the phone onto her unmade bed. She grabbed a pair of jeans from the floor and pulled some clean undies out of a drawer.

'Did I do a good job?' Cody asked needily over the line. 'Are you happy, Ted?'

Happy? How could I be happy when Raj is cheating on my sister? Ted wanted to bark at him. But emotional nuance wasn't Cody's strength, to put it kindly, and he obviously hadn't made that connection. Besides, the findings weren't his fault. She remembered how eager she'd been when she'd started out as a PI a couple of years back – *and* how stupid.

'Yeah, awesome work, Cody,' she said, zipping up her jeans. 'I want you to stay put until I arrive. If this girl reappears, take lots of shots. But be discreet. Okay?'

'Too easy.'

Ted hung up and chucked a T-shirt over her head. She raced into the bathroom to brush her teeth. She tried to breathe deeply to calm her anger, but it just made her hyperventilate, and toothpaste flew up her nostrils. In the bathroom mirror, she saw Miss Marple appear in the doorway.

'It's a shame you've just had your breakfast, or I would have fed you Raj Dalal.'

Ted took Miss Marple downstairs to do a quick ablution, and then she took her back upstairs and gave her a kangaroo tendon. Miss Marple gripped the tendon in her fangs and looked at Ted as if to say, *Go get him.*

'I *will*.'

Ted caught the lift down to her car and rocketed out of the underground carpark. As she headed for Raj's place, she ran through her strategy in her mind. Although she wanted Cody to get pics of the other woman, she had no plans to show them to Bob. Instead, she'd use them as leverage with Raj to make him break up with Bob immediately, before Bob's feelings grew any deeper. He could just say that he didn't 'feel a connection', or one of those kinds of clichés. Bob would be hurt, which tore up Ted, but the relationship was so new that hopefully she'd bounce back quickly. And, most importantly, she'd never know she'd been taken advantage of *again*.

Raj lived in North Carlton, just around the corner from Blooming Beautiful. His street was lined with respectfully preserved Victorian homes that projected a general air of, 'Yes, we're wealthy, but we don't feel the need to make a song and dance about it.'

Raj's single-storey terrace was near the corner, and one of the more modest in the street. It had an iron-lace trim on the porch and front gate, and there was a massive jasmine spilling over the side fence. Dammit.

Ted sneezed pre-emptively. 'Ah-choo!'

She parked her car across the road and searched the street for Cody's hiding spot. She couldn't see him, so she gave him a mental tick of approval. She climbed out of the car and marched across the road. She opened Raj's front gate and held her breath as she skirted the jasmine, but to no avail.

'Ah-choo! Ah-choo!'

She blew her nose as she strode onto Raj's porch and rang the doorbell three times in quick succession. After about half a minute, the door opened and Raj appeared. He was wearing jeans, a blue shirt and slides, and there was a tea towel slung over his shoulder. His thick black hair looked untidy. Was it bed hair? Ted's eyes shot to his open bedroom door and she felt a spasm of rage. And then she was blindsided by a sudden urge to burst into tears when she thought of Bob's potential pain and humiliation.

Raj didn't seem to realise he'd been caught out – in fact, he was smiling like this was a pleasant surprise. 'Teddy, hi!'

Ted flinched at the childhood moniker that only Bob and her dad were allowed to use. And why was he being so friendly when there was another woman in his house? He must've thought he could brazen this out.

'Hi, Raj,' she said coldly.

His smile dropped at her arctic tone. Ted heard rushing water nearby and realised it was the shower in his ensuite.

Raj stepped back from the front door. 'Would you like to come in?'

It was a smart move, inviting her in as if he had nothing to hide.

'No, I *wouldn't* like to come in.'

Raj flinched as if she'd slapped him.

'I just came to tell you I'm onto you.'

Raj blinked. 'Pardon?'

Ted invaded his personal space and eyeballed him – being so short, it was an opportunity that didn't come her way often. Nearby, the bathroom pipes shuddered as the shower was turned off. She could smell toothpaste on Raj's breath.

'I want you to break up with my sister *today*.'

Raj looked flummoxed. 'I'm sorry?'

'You heard me. You need to break up with her now, before she gets in any deeper.'

'What …? Why …?'

Did he think she was a complete idiot? Ted snorted. 'Was that the shower I just heard? The shower in your ensuite?'

'Yes. My daughter's in there.'

His *daughter*? As if! Ted scoffed and Raj feigned mystification. Ted remembered Bob saying something about him being involved in amateur theatre, but it didn't seem to be helping his acting skills.

'This might just be fun and games for *you*,' she said, 'but Bob really likes you.'

'And I really like *her*.'

'Yeah, right.'

Raj was now so flustered he finally forgot to be polite. He threw his hands in the air. 'What's your problem? I can't—'

'You can't *what*? You can't be bothered treating Bob with respect? You can't give a stuff about the hell she's been through?'

Raj pretended he was baffled. Ted snorted again. If he wanted to go around cheating on people, these amateur thespian skills weren't going to cut it. He needed to invest in some professional lessons.

'What do you mean? What hell has she been through?'

Ted was about to snort in his face again, but something in his expression made her realise that Bob hadn't told him. Oh, of course she hadn't. It was classic Bob, trying to spare others from her pain – even people like him, who were destined to compound it.

But, still, Raj's ignorance about the catfishing gave her pause. In truth, wasn't it Bob's story to tell? And wouldn't she be justifiably furious if she found out that Ted had told Raj on her behalf? Being in Bob's bad books felt like the depths of misery for Ted, but surely it was more important to protect Bob from Raj and his lies? And that meant making him see why Bob's good nature *must not* be exploited again.

'She got catfished,' she told him.

Raj's eyes widened in shock.

Chapter Eighteen

Bob

Bob froze and peered past the jasmine. What was Teddy doing on Raj's doorstep? She looked furious – what in heaven's name? She seemed to be giving Raj a piece of her mind. Bob felt bilious. This couldn't be good. She moved closer so she could hear.

'You know how trusting she is?' Teddy was saying. 'She's so trusting she believed a catfisher who said they were a soldier on a top-secret mission in Afghanistan. And not only did she get fleeced financially, but she almost got herself murdered.'

'Murdered?'

'Yes, because she *fell for it.*'

Bob's heart sank, and she almost wished she *had* been murdered. She would have told Raj this story in her own time, when they knew each other better and she felt safe enough. Why was Teddy robbing her of that decision? And what would Raj think of her now? A woman so stupid she was fooled by a transparent scam, and so emotionally incompetent that she needed her little sister to run interference.

'She didn't deserve that, and she sure as hell doesn't deserve to be messed around again,' Teddy told Raj combatively. 'She's too nice. She always believes in the best in people, and she's always being taken for a ride. Well, I'm not letting *you* take her for a ride as well.'

The humiliation! Bob wanted to turn and run, but Raj needed rescuing from Teddy's onslaught. She stepped out from behind the jasmine.

'Morning!'

Teddy and Raj turned in surprise. Teddy's face went a deathly white, and Bob felt a bleak sense of satisfaction.

Raj smiled. 'Bob, hi.'

He sounded warm, but he was probably thinking, *I never realised what an idiot you were.* Teddy looked panicky, and Bob could tell she was trying to gauge how much, if anything, Bob had heard.

'Hey, Bob.'

Bob's body felt like an assortment of miscellaneous parts, but she tried to stroll fluidly up the path.

'Raj. Edwina.'

She saw Teddy flinch when she used her full name. She hadn't been planning to do that – 'Edwina' was a weapon she only deployed in the most extreme of circumstances. It made her realise how incensed she was, although she'd have to take that up with Teddy later.

'I couldn't help overhearing,' she said lightly. 'Although, I'm not sure why Edwina felt the need to share.'

Teddy's face contorted with fear, but Bob tried to forget her and focus on Raj.

'I'm so sorry you went through that,' Raj said.

His brown eyes glistened with sympathy, which meant that thanks to Teddy, Raj now also thought she was a gullible fool. Why not? Join the club. There was nothing like pity to kill romantic feelings, so Bob knew that Raj would never look at her in that way again. And right now he wasn't looking at her at all; he was looking at Teddy, and he seemed just as bewildered as Bob about where her hostility was coming from. But there'd be plenty of time to investigate that later. Right now Bob just wanted her out of there.

'I'm sorry, Bob,' Teddy said, 'but I thought he needed to—'

'Well!' Bob cut across her. 'It's been lovely to run into you, Edwina, but why don't I call you this afternoon?'

Her message couldn't be clearer: Get lost. But Teddy didn't budge. She kept darting looks into the house.

'You're not going inside, are you, Bob?'

'What?'

'Don't go in there, okay?'

'What are you talking about?'

'Just don't go inside, *please*?'

Something lilac flickered in Bob's peripheral vision. A pretty young woman in a fluffy lilac dressing gown materialised in Raj's bedroom doorway. She had Raj's shock of thick black hair, but her oval face and refined features echoed photos that Bob had seen of Raj's late wife, Holly. Bob smiled, but before she could say anything, Teddy suddenly snarled at Raj.

'Good one! Are you happy now?'

Bob was mortified. What was Teddy on about? Chloe (she had to be Chloe) reacted with shock. She took a step back and looked to Raj in confusion.

'Dad? What's going on?'

'*Dad?*' Teddy said.

Teddy's beautiful face turned purple, and something dawned on Bob. Had Teddy mistaken Chloe for a girlfriend? Was that why she was being so rude to Raj, because she thought he was cheating on her? But how had Teddy even known that Chloe was visiting?

'Yes, this is my daughter, Chloe,' Raj replied with astonishing politeness. 'Sweetie, this is Bob. And this is her sister Ted ... er, Edwina.'

'Chloe. It's lovely to meet you,' Bob said.

'You too, Bob.' Chloe smiled the same crooked smile as Raj. 'And, um, Edwina.'

She seemed to be taking the strained atmosphere in her stride, but Bob suspected Chloe was already dealing with conflicting feelings – apparently Bob was the first woman Raj had dated since Chloe's mum died. This would be strange for her. But *were* Bob and Raj still dating? Now that he pitied her, surely he'd end things. And why wasn't Teddy leaving? She was planted on the spot, maintaining a conspicuous silence that seemed to demand an explanation.

'I invited Bob over for brunch to meet Chloe,' Raj obliged.

'So, you're Raj's daughter?' Teddy finally said in a tone that reeked of suspicion. 'But you slept in Raj's room last night?'

Bob gasped. Had Teddy really just said that?

'Edwina! That's none of your business.'

'Yes, she slept in my room,' Raj said. 'The bed in the spare room hurts her back.'

'Dad always sleeps in the spare room when I'm here. Although I agree with Bob, I don't see how this is your business.'

Bob hoped for a humble smile from Teddy, but she should have known better.

'Can we stop the BS now? You're not his daughter.'

What in the world?

'Teddy!'

Teddy turned to her with fire in her eyes. 'Bob. I'm sorry to have to tell you this, but you know what she said to Raj when they got back from their run this morning? She said, "You were amazing last night, my darling."'

A bewildered silence ensued. Bob couldn't make head nor tail of what Teddy was saying and, judging by their stunned expressions, Raj and Chloe couldn't either.

'Yes,' Teddy repeated. '"You were amazing last night, my darling." Try explaining *that*.'

Raj and Chloe exchanged mystified looks, and then Chloe said, 'I actually said, "You were amazing last night *at bowling*." Dad got three strikes.'

A look flickered across Teddy's face, and Bob roughly translated it in her sister's parlance as, *Holy shit, I've stuffed up*.

'Oh, I'm sorry, I misunderstood,' she said in a garbled rush. 'Well, sorry to bother you, Raj. Nice to meet you, Chloe. Could I have a quick word, Bob?'

'Yes. I think we should have a *quick word*.'

Bob could hear how glacial she sounded. Something had just occurred to her that made her even angrier, if that were possible. Raj looked uncertainly between her and Teddy.

'Why don't I start the scrambled eggs then? See you in a few minutes, Bob?'

'Sounds good.'

Raj and Chloe retreated into the house, leaving the front door ajar. Bob turned to Teddy. She looked like a little girl who'd been busted stealing from her mother's purse.

'I'm so sorry, Bob. I got the wrong impression—'

Bob gripped her sister's arm and shamelessly used her superior size to march her out to the front gate.

'I'm sorry. I know I shouldn't have jumped to conclusions—'

'How did you know that Chloe slept in Raj's bedroom last night?' Bob hissed. 'And how did you overhear their conversation?' She had ideas about that, but she wanted to hear it from the horse's mouth.

'Ah-choo! Ah-choo!'

Bob wasn't sure if Teddy's sneezes were genuine or an act of avoidance, but she moved away from the jasmine just in case.

'Have you had Raj under surveillance?'

'Er—'

'Don't lie to me.'

Teddy was silent, and Teddy was never silent, so it spoke volumes. Suddenly, the enormity of it hit Bob like a train. Her heart collapsed into a cavity and, for a moment, all she could feel was the pain. But then that fury reared its head again.

'How dare you invade his privacy like that? You're a hypocrite, Teddy. You told me you trusted my judgement about Raj, and I actually thanked you for it. Which makes me a fool, doesn't it? So you were right all along. Congratulations.'

Teddy looked stricken. 'Don't say that—'

But Bob silenced her with a raised hand.

'You're always going on about how you want to protect me from people who might betray me, but do you know what, Teddy? This is the biggest betrayal of all.'

Teddy burst into tears. It would normally have melted Bob's heart, but it seemed in that split second her heart had calcified into a fossil.

'Bob, I'm so sorry! It's not what you think.'

'What is it, then?'

But the sound of rustling foliage intruded, and then Bob heard an incongruous thump. She turned and saw a long-lens camera lying in Raj's garden bed.

Teddy went white. 'Oh shit.'

There was a streak of something black along the fence line behind the jasmine. Bob started marching towards it.

'No, Bob, don't—'

But Bob ignored her. She fought her way through the jasmine to find a young guy dressed in black clambering over the fence.

'Who are *you*?'

The young guy looked panicked.

'He's no-one!' Teddy said right behind her. 'Ah-choo! Ah-choo!'

The guy grabbed the long-lens camera and tried to scramble back up the fence, but Bob reached out and pulled him down. He was tall and robust, but her rage was giving her supernatural strength.

'Have you been watching this house? Who employed you?'

The young guy pointed at Teddy. '*Not* her!'

Bob released him in disgust, and he scrambled over the fence like a ninja. She moved back towards the house, but in a role reversal, Teddy was now grabbing her arm.

'Bob, wait! Ah-choo! I'm sorry, I was worried about you—'

Bob shoved her away. 'I don't even want to look at you.'

She'd never said that to Teddy before, but she'd never felt that way about her before. She turned her back on her sister and marched up the stairs into Raj's house, closing the door behind her.

Chapter Nineteen

Ted

Ted tried to ignore the miserable knot in her gut and focus on the blood-spattered page on her desk.

See what you're doing to me?

With Giselle's list of suggested suspects exhausted, and her large tally of former Insta followers offering up no clues, maybe the key to ID'ing Giselle's stalker could be found in his handwritten notes with the backwards slant and strange looping t's? Ted tried to study the page forensically, but she may as well have been staring into space. The miserable knot was moving up to her brain and squeezing out everything except the memory of what had happened with Bob yesterday. She was suddenly consumed by panic. What was the point of anything if Bob hated her? She wanted to cry, and she found herself longing for Miss Marple, who was at Wags Away for her regular Monday play day.

Focus!

Ted tried to rally her depleted mental resources. She knew a self-styled handwriting expert, a cluey old ex-cop. Maybe she should take the notes to him. But she swiftly dismissed the thought – he'd probably charge her hundreds of bucks to tell her what she already knew, that the stalker had disguised his writing.

But at least the stalker was lying low, so that was something. Unless he was trying to lull Giselle into a false sense of security ... Ted knew he could strike again at any moment and being back at square one worried her. She felt a fresh pall of despair as she realised she'd have to keep lying to Spike. But did that really matter now? She'd nipped things in the bud with him before there was even a bud to nip. Spike might have his appealing moments, but he'd turned out to be a typical arrogant alpha guy, and she'd done the right thing. Sure, she felt a bit upset about it, but that was only because of Bob. Nothing felt right with the world today.

She had no idea if Bob was okay because Bob had let her seventeen calls go to voicemail. And when she'd driven to her Brunswick cottage last night Bob was out, so she'd had to slip an apology note under the door. She'd slunk home like the traitorous sister she was, and she'd barely slept a wink. This morning her car had driven her to Blooming Beautiful instead of EBI, but she'd forced it to make a U-turn. Bob obviously didn't want to see her yet, and wasn't it Bob's right to forgive her in her own time? That's if she forgave her at all.

The thought had been too terrifying to contemplate, so Ted had tried to drown it out with the car radio. But the news was on, providing yet more evidence that the world was caving in. Ted had switched over to Spotify, which was what she should have done in the first place. But despite Taylor Swift's best efforts, thoughts of Bob were still tormenting her thirty minutes later when she and Miss Marple had pulled up outside EBI and climbed from her car.

And if that was bad, the day had got progressively worse.

After she'd dropped Miss Marple at Wags Away, she'd tried to distract herself by returning a call from an anxious client, Mary

Falkiner, who was worried her husband was being unfaithful. Ted had good news for Mary, which was a ray of sunshine in an otherwise irredeemable day.

'Well, Mary, I'm delighted to tell you that he's not cheating on you.'

'He's not?' Mary sounded ecstatic. 'Oh thank God! He's not cheating!'

'No, he's not,' Ted happily reiterated. 'He's just been going to work and Rotary meetings. You've got a good one there in Don.'

There was a small silence before Mary spoke again.

'John.'

'Er, sorry?'

'My husband's name is John, not Don. And I don't think he's ever been to a Rotary meeting.'

Oh no! Ted rifled through her files, her heart shrivelling like a dried apricot.

'Mary, I'm so sorry. I've confused your case.'

Ted had spent half an hour trying to soothe Mary's distress about John's affair with his podiatrist. Two hours later she was still an emotional mess over the mix-up – although probably not as much of a mess as poor, cheated-on Mary. Ted despised cheaters like John Falkiner and his ilk, although she had to admit they kept her in work.

She abandoned the stalker's notes. There was no way she could muster the mental acuity required to decipher any hidden clues today. As she slipped the pages back into the file, it occurred to her that both her major cases hinged on handwritten notes. Was Duncan Bunting's suicide note fraudulent as she'd originally thought? Or had he genuinely taken his life, as Michael Wall seemed to believe?

Her phone chirped, and she almost took flight. Bob?! But, no, it was another text from Jarrod Beasley.

I'd love to hear from you, lovely. Don't be shy. x

Ted was so *not* in the mood for this! She threw her phone down on the desk so hard that it bounced off the edge and fell to the floor, cracking the glass on the screen. Dammit! She was stuffing *everything* up today. She was wondering if she should go home and hurl herself under her doona, where she couldn't do any more harm, when she heard the tinkle of EBI's front door. She looked up to see Chuck entering in her school uniform.

Ted glanced at her watch. 'Chuck, it's 1.37 pm. Shouldn't you be at school?'

Chuck rolled her grey eyes beneath her lash extensions. 'It's double religion. I told them I'm developing Covid-like symptoms.'

Ted grimaced. 'Are you?'

'No! Duh,' Chuck said, as though that were a ridiculous question. She flung herself into the client's chair on the other side of Ted's desk, flicking her dead-straight tresses out of her eyes. Clearly her Prestige Pro Hair Straightener was back in action. 'I just, like, couldn't stop thinking about how you found Duncan Bunting's hiding spot at Point Nepean, and how you reckon his suicide note is fake. That's, like, epic. What's the latest?'

Ted hesitated. Chuck was only fifteen, and she didn't want to tell her that after talking to Michael Wall, she now suspected the suicide note might be genuine. But she wouldn't make any progress on the case until she knew for sure one way or the other – and with her brain otherwise engaged today, she could do with Chuck's youthful smarts.

'The latest is we have to determine whether Duncan was sneaking out of camp to buy supplies after he wrote the note, which would give us conclusive proof that the note *is* fake.'

Chuck nodded. 'A hundred per cent.'

'But it won't be easy,' Ted told her. 'The local councils and shops only keep their CCTV footage for thirty-one days, so CCTV's a dead end.'

Chuck said 'Bummer!' or something to that effect. Her voice had become faint, because Ted was finding herself derailed again by the photo of herself with Bob and their mum on Torquay Beach. She picked up the framed photo and studied Bob's beautiful, open-hearted face. Her sister had saved her when their mum died. All she'd ever given Ted was love, and Ted had repaid her by betraying her. She searched for a word that could do justice to how awful she felt, and she came up with *wretched*.

'Aunty Ted? Hello?'

Ted tried to reassemble her equilibrium.

'Yes, right … So I decided to research special events in the area that would have generated lots of images in the weeks after Duncan disappeared,' she told Chuck. 'It turns out that the Peninsula Festival was held in late October, a few days after Duncan wrote the suicide note. Most of the activities were centred in a park across the road from the Ritchies IGA supermarket in Sorrento. That means if Duncan bought groceries from the IGA at that time, we might just catch him on Google Images – you know, in the background of happy snaps that people uploaded to Facebook, or wherever.'

'Perfect.'

Ted gestured for Chuck to join her behind the desk. She showed her niece a publicity still of Duncan taken outside Body Potential.

'That's Duncan Bunting. See if you can spot him entering or leaving the supermarket after the twenty-third of October. And there were all sorts of events on at the Peninsula Festival – arts and crafts, music, dodgem cars, a dog show, you name it. Make sure you check out everything.'

'Got it.'

'Awesome.'

Ted gave Chuck her chair at the desk and headed to the couch with her laptop. She opened it to update her notes for another client, small-time pasta manufacturer Freddy Chickley. Freddy was insistent that rival pasta manufacturer Luigi Paracini was sabotaging his business, even though Ted couldn't find any evidence of it. Despite her best advice, Freddy wanted her to keep digging, and she'd come to realise he was more invested in the drama than in a result.

She started typing, but she was still torturing herself over Bob, and she didn't make it through the first sentence. How could she live her life without Bob? Her sister was her anchor and her compass. Could one person *be* both an anchor and a compass? If anyone could, it was Bob. The only person who came close was Miss Marple, who wasn't a person.

She snapped her laptop shut. For the sake of her sanity, or what was left of it, she had to go to Blooming Beautiful and apologise to Bob right now.

'I've got to pop in on Aunty Bob,' she told Chuck. 'Can you keep looking and give me a call if you spot Duncan?'

'Okay, Aunty Ted,' Chuck said, not taking her eyes off the iMac screen.

Chapter Twenty

As Ted sped down the street, she could hear Miss Marple laying down the law at Wags Away. She took the corner and turned onto Punt Road, weaving in and out of the heavy traffic at speed and expertly avoiding collisions, as she'd learned in her defensive driving course. Beeping horns suggested that her fellow drivers didn't share her appreciation of her defensive driving skills, but right now getting to Bob was the only thing that mattered.

By the time she pulled up opposite Blooming Beautiful, her heart had taken up residence in her mouth. What if Bob refused to see her? What then? As she peered across the road, it occurred to her that she'd never been scared of Bob before. She wanted to vomit, but even more than that – more than anything – she wanted to set this right.

A customer was emerging with a bunch of natives, leaving Bob alone in the shop. Ted saw Bob grab a broom and disappear through the new archway into the former Sew Darn Crafty. It was now or never! Ted leaped out of her car and crossed the road. She walked into the shop, and the bell tinkled above the door.

A second later Bob appeared with a friendly smile. 'Hi—'

But her smile faltered when she saw Ted, and Ted's heart sank from her mouth to her knees. She could feel her hayfever kicking in, but she somehow managed to swallow a sneeze. She tilted her head back to meet Bob's eyes.

'I'm so sorry, Bob. I know I don't have any right to expect your forgiveness, and maybe I shouldn't even be here. But I'm just ... I'm so, so sorry.'

Bob stared down at her in silence, as Ted tried to ignore the tickle in her throat. Why wasn't Bob speaking? What was she thinking? Was she going to throw her out? The moment seemed to stretch on forever, until Ted's hayfever got the better of her, and she exploded into a sneezing fit.

'Ah-choo! Ah-choo! Ah-choo!'

Bob frowned. 'Hang on a second.' She went to the counter and grabbed her 'Back in Five Minutes' sign, and hung it on the front door. 'Come through here, there's no flowers yet.' She led Ted through the archway into the new section and paused at a large mid-century modern display cabinet she'd found at a garage sale and restored. 'I can't talk for long.'

'I know.' Ted still couldn't read her sister's face, and it made her feel as if she was standing on quicksand. 'How are you going? Are you okay?'

Bob hesitated.

'You told Raj that I got catfished. You humiliated me.'

Ted's whole body burned with shame. 'I know, I'm sorry.'

'That was *my* story to tell. On my terms.'

'I know.'

'And you put Raj under surveillance! You violated his privacy, and you *lied to me*. I never thought you of all people would lie to me, Teddy.'

Teddy? Bob hadn't called her Edwina. Did this mean there could be a chance for them? Ted dared to feel a flicker of hope.

'I'm so sorry,' she said again. 'There's no excuse for what I did.'

Bob leaned against the timber table and sighed. She was wearing a black roll-neck skivvy under a vintage summer dress with ballet flats, and she looked awesome, like always. Ted thought she might be softening, but was that wishful thinking? She waited for her sister to speak.

'You had good intentions,' Bob eventually said. 'You were trying to protect me from being hurt again.'

'But *I* was the one who hurt you this time. And I ... betrayed you.'

'I'm not sure that was fair of me, Teddy. I know you'd never intentionally betray me.'

Ted felt a catch in her throat. Trust Bob to try to see things from her point of view, even when she'd behaved so reprehensibly.

'But I lied to you about trusting your judgement.'

'And you shouldn't have. But hopefully you realise now that Raj *is* worth my trouble?'

Ted couldn't help noticing Bob's use of the present tense.

'So ... you two are okay?'

Bob nodded. 'I felt like a fool at first, but Raj made me feel I didn't need to. And now that he knows everything ... it's actually brought us closer.'

'So, I did you a favour?' Ted quipped, because if there was an envelope, she felt compelled to push it.

Bob smiled. 'Careful.'

'Sorry, I couldn't resist.' Ted felt so relieved she could almost cry. She hadn't wrecked things for Bob and Raj! 'This is awesome ... I'm so happy for you.'

'Me too. So, I guess you're forgiven.'

Ted sent out a prayer of thanks to God, even though she didn't believe in Her. All was right with the world again. Almost. But there was still one thing she needed to do.

'I'll go and see Raj after work and apologise—'

'No, don't do that,' Bob said quickly. 'He's still getting his head around the surveillance. I'll give you his number and you can text him. I think that's best for now. Maybe we can all get together in a few days.'

'Of course. Can you send me the number?'

Bob forwarded Raj's contact details, and Ted wrote Raj a lengthy apology text, running it past Bob for her approval. She hoped she hadn't blown her chances of having a good relationship with Raj. The idea of not getting on with the man who actually deserved her sister felt unbearable all of a sudden.

She pressed Send. 'There, done.'

'Thank you, Teddy.'

'Don't thank *me*. It should be the other way around.' Ted wanted to cry with relief, so she snorted instead. She could feel emotion swelling inside her, so she changed the subject, checking out boxes of rugs, embroidery and stuff that were sitting on Bob's display cabinet.

'Cicely's crafts?'

'Yeah. I haven't decided how I'm going to display it all yet.'

Ted noticed knitting needles and crochet hooks poking out of a box. 'You're selling these too?'

Bob nodded. 'Cicely thinks you should provide the means for the customer to make the thing they're buying.'

'She'll do herself out of business,' Ted joked. 'Oops, not funny – already happened.' She plucked a small tapestry from the top of a box. It was woven in muted shades of blue and grey.

'I like this one.'

'It's beautiful, isn't it?' Bob said. 'Sad story, though. Cicely got the inspiration from Cheviot Beach. Apparently she'd go there and sit looking out to sea in the weeks after Duncan disappeared. She said it's an homage to the last place he was seen.'

A little guy inside Ted's head tapped her brain on the shoulder.

'Wait, Cicely went back to Cheviot Beach *after* Duncan disappeared? She told you that?'

'Yeah.'

'But she told *me* that she's never been to the peninsula since that day.'

'Did she?'

'Yeah. Why would she say that if it wasn't true?'

Bob shrugged in that trusting way of hers. 'I don't know, but I don't think it matters. People tell silly little social lies for all sorts of reasons.'

Ted was about to argue the point when she remembered that it was her lack of trust in people that had caused her to put Raj under surveillance and had almost ended up costing her the most important relationship in her life. Sure, being suspicious was an occupational hazard, but there was more to it than that – she had to stop approaching the world as a combatant. It was beyond time that she took a leaf out of beautiful Bob's book and started placing some trust in people.

'You're right, it doesn't mean anything,' she said. Her phone started vibrating in her hand. She checked the screen. It was Chuck, calling on FaceTime. She pressed Accept. 'Chuck? Have you found something?'

But Chuck was looking past her to wave at Bob.

'Hey, Aunty Bob. What a pretty dress.'

'Thanks, sweetie,' Bob said, leaning forward to squint at Ted's phone. 'Where are you, at Aunty Teddy's office? Shouldn't you be at school?'

'It's double religion,' Chuck said, as if that explained everything. 'You'll never guess what, Aunty Ted, this is *hectic*!'

'What?' Ted said excitedly. 'Have you spotted Duncan?'

'Wait till you see,' Chuck tantalised. 'There was a farmers' market at the festival, and this was taken on October 26, three days *after* the suicide note.' She adjusted her phone so Ted and Bob could see the Google Images of the Peninsula Festival on Ted's monitor, then tapped the screen with her acrylic nails. 'See this coffee van over here? Isn't that your friend, Aunty Bob? Duncan's wife?'

Cicely?

Ted pulled her phone closer so she and Bob could see the spot on the screen where Chuck was pointing. Behind a young couple smiling into the camera, Cicely was waiting in a queue at a coffee van. It wasn't the sharpest of images, but there was no question it was her. She was carrying a hand-sewn embroidered bag that was bulging with produce – the very same bag that she'd given Ted.

'Oh my God, that *is* her.'

'Yes, that's Cicely,' Bob confirmed.

Ted's adrenaline briefly spiked, until she realised this might not mean anything.

'Excellent ID'ing, Chuck, but we already knew that Cicely's been to the peninsula—'

'Wait! It gets better,' Chuck said, her tone dripping with drama. 'Check out this shot from five minutes later.'

Chuck pulled up a different image, showing a little girl on a merry-go-round. Nearby, Cicely was sipping coffee from a keep cup, and a tall blond guy wearing a surfie's wide-brimmed straw hat was standing beside her with his arm around her. Duncan!

Ted heard Bob gasp. Or maybe that was her.

'Oh my God, it's them!' she said. 'Look at Duncan, he's trying to go incognito. Did he seriously think that hat would fool anyone? Are you certain this was after the suicide note?'

Chuck nodded smugly. 'I checked the metadata three times. It was definitely October 26. They're in on it together!'

It was too much to process. Ted's brain was spinning at ten times the speed of a rotisserie chicken. But she managed to rally enough to congratulate Chuck and tell her she'd be back at the office soon. Chuck said goodbye to Bob and disappeared from the screen.

Ted looked at Bob and Bob looked at Ted and neither of them said anything, until Ted said, 'I have nothing to say.' Immediately followed by, 'That lying, conniving fraud! If she thinks she's going to get away with this, she's got another think coming!'

Ted didn't realise she was yelling until she saw Bob wince. She pressed pause on her vitriol for a second and thought about what this meant for her sister. Poor Bob looked so hurt and, in that moment, Ted realised that rage was just like love – it expanded to fit the circumstances. Bob had given that bloody liar Cicely Bunting the precious gift of her friendship, and *this* was how Cicely had repaid her. Bitch! Ted wanted to march straight over to Merri Creek and strangle Cicely with one of her hand-knitted scarves, but she tried to calm down for her sister's sake.

'Sorry for yelling. Are you okay? No, of course you're not.'

Bob mustered a bewildered smile. 'And to think I was going to sell her handicrafts to help her out.'

'Don't call that off yet,' Ted instructed. 'It might come in handy for us.' She wasn't sure exactly how, but she wasn't sure of anything right now. She needed a beer! 'I'll make some tea.'

'I don't understand,' Bob puzzled a few minutes later, her hands cupping her rosehip tea. 'If Duncan wrote a fake suicide note, they obviously want people to think he's dead. So why didn't he just leave a suicide note on the beach the day he disappeared? Wouldn't that have been simpler?'

'A lot simpler,' Ted agreed. 'But maybe they were worried it would blow away? Or a passer-by would find it and raise the alarm?'

'I guess that could be it … then where's Duncan now?'

'Hiding somewhere else, I suppose. He's probably been on the move.'

Bob nodded, but she was still perplexed. 'It doesn't make sense. If Cicely wants everyone to think that Duncan's dead, why would she hire you to find him?'

'Because it's a clever double bluff,' Ted said grimly, as the pieces fell into place. 'She said she wanted me to find Duncan alive, but what she *really* wanted me to find was the suicide note.' When she thought about it, it made perfect, cunning sense. 'Cicely's been playing a long game … She and Duncan wrote that suicide note five weeks after he "disappeared" and, since then, they've sat it out for nearly a year, waiting for things to die down. And now, when they think it's safe, Cicely's given me the Apple Watch, knowing I'd retrieve the GPS data and find the suicide note.'

The audacity was mind-boggling.

Bob shook her head to try and absorb it all. 'But why?'

'It's got to be money,' Ted surmised. 'Life insurance, probably. Don't forget, if someone's missing, you have to wait seven years before they're officially declared dead – unless you have evidence of their death, like a *suicide note*. Do you know if Duncan had a life insurance policy?'

Bob shook her head. 'No idea, but I know Cicely used ANM for her contents insurance at the shop.'

Ted wondered why ANM rang a bell, and then she remembered hearing about them on the news in the car that morning.

'We're in luck, ANM's had a data breach. I'll get Chuck onto the dark web and see if she can dig up anything.'

'Good idea,' Bob said, but her enthusiasm for sleuthing was clearly waning, and she looked broken. 'To think I've been so worried about "poor" Cicely. Guess I *am* gullible after all.'

'No, you're not!' Ted said fiercely. She felt as if she was being choked from the inside, and she realised she was even more incensed with herself than Cicely. The fact was, she'd allowed Cicely Bunting to play her like a violin. Some gun PI! It was the bitterest pill possible, but she knew she'd never solve the case unless she forced herself to swallow it. '*I'm* the alleged professional who fell for her lies hook, line and sinker,' she told Bob. 'I've unwittingly aided and abetted her plans. If anyone's been gullible, it's *me*.'

Chapter Twenty-One

Back at EBI, Ted looked over Chuck's shoulder as her niece searched a site on the dark web where the compromised data from ANM had been downloaded. It looked like gobbledygook to Ted, but luckily Chuck was great at deciphering this stuff. Within minutes, she'd found what they were seeking.

'OMG! Look, Aunty Ted. Two years ago, Cicely and Duncan took out a 1.5 million dollar life insurance policy on Duncan!'

'1.5 million bucks?!'

'Yeah!'

So, there it was: irrefutable proof that Cicely stood to gain a shitload of money; enough to run away and start a new life with Duncan – providing she had evidence of his 'death'. For the hundredth time, Ted cursed herself for falling into Cicely's trap. Her whole body burned with humiliation. Cicely must think she was such a fool. She wondered why her radar was so off lately. She'd wasted valuable resources tailing Raj, a guy who was beyond reproach, while playing right into the hands of Cicely, who was shaping up to be a sociopath. There was no excuse for dropping the ball like this. But she'd have to deal with that later, right now she had a case to solve.

'So, it's what I thought,' she said to her niece. 'It's all a scam so Cicely can claim on Duncan's life insurance, and they can disappear into the sunset with 1.5 million bucks, leaving all their unpaid debtors behind them.'

'That sucks!' Chuck said. 'What are you going to do?'

Ted pulled her phone from her pocket. 'I'm going to make Cicely and Duncan Bunting rue the day they tried to play me and your Aunty Bob for suckers.'

'Cool. But how?'

'I'm going to catch them meeting up before Cicely can get her hands on that money. And then when she tries to apply for a payout, I'll have evidence of insurance fraud.'

'That's elite, Aunty Ted!'

Ted brought up the number of her favourite surveillance agent, Wurundjeri woman and grandma of six, Aunty June O'Shea. Aunty June had mentored Ted when Ted was a novice, and she'd recently saved Ted's life by felling a would-be killer with a copy of Stephanie Alexander's *The Cook's Companion*. Aunty June was pure awesome, and even in the midst of her rage and self-reproach, Ted was grateful for the chance to see her again. She pressed the number and Aunty June answered.

'Ted! G'day, love.'

Her voice sounded like a motherly smile, and Ted stifled a sudden urge to cry.

'Hey, Aunty. How are you?'

'I'm good. What about you?'

'Oh, you know, I'm fine.'

Ted wondered what it was about Aunty June that always made her want to spill her guts, when she was usually so determined to keep her guts secured? Was it June's warmth? Her decency?

Her grandmotherly demeanour? Probably all three. Ted had often thought that June's comfy persona must have been quite a weapon when she was a homicide detective at St Kilda CID. Had she disarmed murderers by patting their hands and urging them to eat their greens?

'I know this is super short notice,' she said, 'but could you do a surveillance job for me, starting now?'

'Of course, love. You know I've always got time for you.'

'Thanks, Aunty. You're a star.'

Ted briefed June about Cicely and Duncan's scam, and June was as astonished as Ted and Bob had been.

'Cripes! My Kyra used to buy wool for me at Sew Darn Crafty. She says Cicely Bunting's lovely.'

'*Everyone* says Cicely's lovely, that's what she's counting on. I need you to keep an eye on her. Hopefully she'll take us to Duncan – I don't know his current location. I'll send you a couple of pics of him. Could you get to Merri Creek this arvo?'

'Merri Creek? No problem, that's just around the corner.'

'Awesome.' Ted gave Aunty June the address.

'Got it, love. I just have to take a cake out of the oven. I'll be on my way in ten minutes.'

Ted pictured Aunty June in her cluttered kitchen, the throbbing heart of her large and loving family, and she felt a familiar wistful pang.

'Thanks heaps, Aunty. I need Cicely covered until she hopefully meets up with Duncan. I'm assuming that'll be any day, but how are you placed?'

'I'm pretty free for the rest of the week, but I can't—'

'I know, you can't do nights, you've got your babysitting and stuff. I'll find someone else to double with you who doesn't mind staying up all night.'

But they both knew that wouldn't be an easy ask. The glamour of staying awake overnight wore off quickly for most surveillance agents.

'I've got an idea,' Aunty June said. 'I know a young fella who's desperate for experience, and it's always good to give someone new a chance.'

'Absolutely. What's his name?'

'Cody Venables.'

Ted bit back an urge to say, *No way!* She reminded herself that everyone deserved a second chance, and Cody's misunderstanding about Raj and Chloe wouldn't have happened if she hadn't primed him to assume that Raj was a snake. Of course Cody had leaped to that conclusion – although being deaf in one ear hadn't helped. That was probably why he'd misheard Raj's daughter Chloe.

'Okay,' she said, crossing her fingers. 'I know Cody. Let's give him a go.'

'Beauty.'

EBI's front door opened, and an awkward-looking teenage boy with reddish hair entered, a crumpled school shirt hanging out of his pants. Of course! Mitch's son, Ollie. Ted had forgotten about the interview for his school project. She smiled, and his face turned redder than his hair. As she wrapped up her call with Aunty June, she was surprised to see Ollie and Chuck greeting each other like old mates.

'What are you doing here?' Chuck asked.

'I'm interviewing Ted for a commerce project. What are *you* doing here?'

'Ted's my aunty.'

'Yeah? That's epic.'

Chuck preened, and Ted blinked. What was she missing?

'Hey, Ollie. How do you guys know each other?'

As Ted joined the conversation Ollie's swagger evaporated. He stood there, apparently tongue-tied, but chatty Chuck had more than enough confidence for both of them.

'Ollie goes to Christ the Redeemer.'

That explained it. Chuck's school, Our Lady of Sorrows, was a sister school to boys' college Christ the Redeemer, and the two student bodies often got together for debating and musicals and other stuff.

'And you're in Year 10, like Chuck?'

'Yeah ...' Ollie mumbled, looking down at his feet.

Ted remembered her girlhood at Our Lady of Sorrows, and debating sessions with boys from Christ the Redeemer that had almost devolved into fisticuffs because of her smart-arse insults. On occasion, she'd been dragged before both her own principal, the super-scary Mrs Hanley, and Christ the Redeemer's principal, Mr O'Rourke. Mrs Hanley had always been appalled by Ted's mouthiness, but Ted sometimes got the feeling that Mr O'Rourke found it funny. All these years later Mrs Hanley was still principal of Our Lady of Sorrows, but apparently Mr O'Rourke had moved to Daylesford to grow heirloom vegetables.

'Awesome,' Ted said. She gestured towards the chair on the other side of the desk, for Ollie to sit in.

Chuck scrambled to her feet. 'Want to take a seat over here?'

'Cool, thanks,' Ollie mumbled, 'but is there anywhere ... er, can I take a piss?'

'Of course, through there.'

Ted directed Ollie to EBI's small but sparkling bathroom facilities. Chuck giggled as the door closed behind him.

'He's hot for you, Aunty Ted. I can tell.'

Ted laughed. 'Seems like he's hot for anyone over twenty. Do you know each other well?'

'Not super well,' Chuck glanced towards the bathroom and lowered her voice. 'I'm glad he knows you're my aunty now, 'cause he's always bragging about his dad being a detective.' Chuck rolled her eyes. 'But police detectives have got nothing on PIs.'

'See, this is why you're my IT expert,' Ted said with a grin, 'because you innately make sense.'

Chuck plonked herself down on the navy-blue two-seater couch in front of the coffee table. Was she planning to stay all night?

'You should probably get going,' Ted said.

'But your interview isn't like, top secret, is it? I'll just sit over here, I'll put in my AirPods.'

'Well, okay, as long as you use the time for homework.'

'Of course. I'll watch *Macbeth*. We're studying the seminal Orson Welles version.'

Chuck reached into her backpack for her AirPods as Ollie returned from the bathroom. He seemed to have recovered some of his composure, although Ted had no idea how much composure he usually possessed. Considering he was a teenage boy, she guessed not much. He loomed over her as he loped to the client's chair and sat. As Ted skirted around the desk, Ollie met her eyes and smiled at her properly for the first time.

'You look nice.'

'Thanks.' She was wearing one of her tailored black pantsuits she'd bought online from Zara, with a crisp white T-shirt, and her 'urchin' cut was looking tidy, but she suspected Ollie would have been equally impressed if she was wearing her surveillance outfit of jeans and faded hoodie. 'So, what would you like to ask me?'

Ollie pulled out a large exercise book and a chewed biro and proceeded to ask Ted a series of rote questions about her life as a PI. Ted tried to make her job sound as badarse as possible, even though at least seventy per cent of her tasks were pretty prosaic. She wondered why she was trying to impress Ollie, and then she realised she was hoping he'd tell Mitch that she was awesome, and Mitch would pass that on to Spike. She had to remind herself that she didn't care what Spike thought of her anymore. Regardless, Ollie was certainly impressed. He scribbled away so crazily that a couple of times he had to rip pages out of his exercise book and start again.

Ted shot a glance over at Chuck. She could see her niece's phone screen. Chuck definitely wasn't watching *Macbeth* – not unless Lady Macbeth had started doing make-up tutorials on TikTok.

A car horn lightly tooted outside.

'That'll be Mum,' Ollie said.

'Cool. Did you get everything you need?'

'Yeah. Thanks, Ted.'

'You're welcome.'

Ollie gathered up his stuff and Ted saw him to the door. His pimply face went fuchsia as their arms almost touched. Ted waved to Fleur, who was in a family-sized SUV.

'I know you haven't been watching *Macbeth*,' she said to Chuck when she returned inside.

'I needed a mental-health break. There are so many demands on students my age. It's important we take time out to replenish our emotional resources.'

As far as Ted could tell, Chuck spent way more time replenishing her emotional resources than she ever did on her schoolwork, but she couldn't help being impressed by her niece's chutzpah.

'Yeah, okay. But you'd better get going now or your dad'll kill me.'

Chuck started packing up her books. Back at her desk, Ted's eyes fell on Ollie's discarded pages of scribble, and suddenly the whole world stood still. She snatched up a crumpled page and studied Ollie's handwriting up close.

'Oh my God ...'

Chuck glanced over as she zipped up her backpack.

'What?'

'Oh my God!'

'What? What is it?'

Chuck ran over as Ted unlocked her desk drawer and pulled out her hard copy of Giselle's file. She removed the bloodstained note that had been left on Giselle's windscreen – *See what you're doing to me?* – and matched it against Ollie's page.

'Look at the writing's backward slant, and those looping t's – they're exactly the same! And they're from the same exercise book – it's an American Letter size, not Australian A4.'

Chuck flipped out. 'OMG! I can't believe it!'

'Ollie's the stalker!'

They gaped at each other. But even though Ted was stunned, the facts somehow added up. Hadn't she witnessed Ollie's penchant for older women firsthand? Giselle was a close family friend, so he'd had plenty of time to develop an unhealthy fixation. And Ollie's physique was an exact match for the guy immortalised in those shots outside the Australian Ballet. But the lamb's heart, and breaking into Giselle's home? Ted wouldn't have picked that kind of malice in the kid, but look how she'd misread Cicely. And stalkers were nothing if not manipulative. She felt sick to her stomach.

'OMG ...' Chuck said again. 'What are you going to do?'

'I can't do anything right now,' Ted said. Her brain felt like a washing machine on the spin cycle. 'I need to talk to his mum in private. I'll have to wait till tomorrow.'

The wait was frustrating, but at least it meant she could spend tonight serving papers on a few targets she hadn't been able to pin down during the day – a muso, a late-night bus driver, a hospital orderly on an overnight shift.

'Are you sure you want to talk to his mum?' Chuck asked. 'Shouldn't you tell Giselle first?'

Technically, Chuck was right. But Giselle was all over the place emotionally, and who knew how she'd react? Ted thought it was probably wise to forewarn Fleur, who seemed stable and sensible. Ollie would need his mum's support when the truth came out. He might be a stalker, but he was still a kid. She explained all of that to Chuck.

'But what about the NDA you signed?'

'I won't mention Giselle's name, so her confidentiality will be intact. But I still think this is serious enough to warrant Ollie's mother knowing.'

'Maybe you should talk to his dad? He's Ollie's hero.'

Ted had already considered that option. She shook her head. 'No, Mitch might fly off the handle, and that wouldn't help. I'll talk to Fleur first, and she can decide when and how to involve Mitch.'

Chuck nodded. They were both silent as they absorbed the momentous events of the past hour. They now knew that Cicely and Duncan Bunting had concocted Duncan's fake suicide in order to defraud their insurer of $1,500,000 – *and* they'd identified Giselle Tereiti's stalker. Afternoons at EBI didn't come much bigger than this. Ted allowed herself a brief fantasy about future Insta posts: *#dontmesswithebi*. Her business would go berserk!

'Our secret, okay?' she said to Chuck.

'Duh.'

Chapter Twenty-Two

Fleur worked as an early-childhood educator at the Excellence Early Learning Centre in Collins Street in the CBD. Ted arrived at the pre-arranged time of 1.30 pm, and a weary but capable-looking woman asked her to wait in the dining room, which consisted of a bunch of tiny round tables surrounded by tiny round stools. There were bright little flowers on all the tables, and the walls were plastered with toddlers' joyous paintings.

It was the kind of vibe that should have made anyone smile, but Ted found herself feeling uneasy. She wondered why little kids always seemed to press some sort of button for her. Was she simply not a maternal person, as she'd always assumed, or was there more to it than that?

She distracted herself with thoughts of the Bunting case. Cody Venables had agreed to cover nights outside Cicely's place, but after twenty hours of surveillance divided between him and Aunty June, they still had nothing on Cicely.

'I'm sorry I can't give you better news, love,' June had said when she'd called to update Ted a couple of hours ago. 'But I won't let her out of my sight today, don't you worry.'

Little kids' laughter brought Ted back to the moment at the Excellence Early Learning Centre. She watched through glass as tiny attendees scrambled over play equipment in an adjoining room like boisterous puppies. It occurred to her that if they were actual puppies she'd be delighted by them, instead of feeling inexplicably threatened. Still, she couldn't deny the joyful vibe, and she felt bad about sullying it with her unsavoury news.

How would Fleur take it? Nobody wanted to hear something like this about their son. Fleur probably thought that Ollie's thing for older women was no more than a harmless crush. How would she react when she found out he was stalking and intimidating someone? And how would Mitch react?

Ted tried to match Fleur's serene demeanour as she appeared from around a corner wearing a paint-stained smock over her uniform of black trousers and teal polo shirt.

'Hi, Ted,' she said warmly.

'Hey, Fleur. Thanks for seeing me.'

'No problem.'

Ted could read curiosity in Fleur's hazel eyes.

'Why don't we take a seat?' Fleur said. She gestured towards the tiny stools at the tiny tables, in full view of the little bundles of fun who were swarming over the play equipment.

'Er, is there somewhere we could talk more privately?'

'Oh? Okay. Of course.'

Fleur led Ted into an office with adult-sized chairs and a messy desk. A large window with open curtains looked out onto the dining area. Fleur closed the door. 'What did you want to talk to me about? I hope Ollie didn't misbehave yesterday?'

'No, it's not that.'

Poor Fleur looked relieved. But there was no point beating around the bush, so Ted pulled a manila folder out of her backpack and produced Ollie's discarded exercise-book pages.

'I wanted to see you about this.'

'What's that? Did he write something?'

Did he ever. Ted spread the pages out on the desk in front of Fleur.

'I'm afraid there's no way to make this easy. You see the backward slant and these loops in Ollie's t's?'

Fleur looked confused. 'What about them?'

'I'm sorry to tell you this, but I have a client who's being stalked, and I've seen that same handwriting on a note she received from her stalker.'

Fleur looked as if she couldn't process what Ted was saying. The sound of little kids' ruckus permeated through the glass as Ted reopened the manila folder. 'Before I show you this, I want to assure you the blood isn't human.'

'*Blood?*' Fleur's pupils were tiny pinpricks of alarm.

Ted pulled out the stalker's note in its plastic bag with the lamb's heart bloodstains, and laid it out next to Ollie's pages. Fleur's face went ashen. She looked between the three pages and read the stalker's note aloud.

'See what you're doing to me?' She stared at Ted blindly. 'But that writing could be anyone's.'

It was the instinctive response of a protective mum, but Ted could tell that Fleur recognised Ollie's writing.

'Both pages are from the same exercise book,' Ted pointed out gently. 'It's an unusual size in Australia, American Letter size.'

Fleur blanched. She obviously recognised the paper.

'And you said the blood's not human?' she asked urgently.

'No, that's from a lamb's heart,' Ted quickly assured her. 'No-one was hurt, well no-one human, anyway. There was an arrow plunged through the heart.'

Fleur looked so shocked that for a moment Ted thought she might collapse. She'd decided not to show Fleur the photo of Ollie placing the note and lamb's heart on the windscreen in case it identified Giselle's car, but that now seemed a smart move for emotional reasons too. Fleur's eyes briefly flew to the window, and Ted sensed she was trying to reassure herself that the little kids hadn't seen or heard their conversation. She went to the window and pulled the curtain across.

'Ollie's a good kid. He hasn't got it in him to do something like this.'

Ted had expected that reaction. What mum wanted to think her kid was a stalker?

'A passer-by saw the stalker put the heart on the windscreen,' she told Fleur gently. 'He was wearing a hoodie so his face was obscured, but his height and build match Ollie's.'

Fleur shook her head. 'No, no, it wasn't him. When *was* this?'

'Saturday night, ten days ago.'

Fleur gasped, and then fell silent.

'What? Please, you need to tell me.'

'I went away with a girlfriend that weekend, and Mitch was busy, so Ollie stayed home. He said he was old enough to take care of himself ...'

The poor woman looked distraught. In her job, Ted was accustomed to being the bearer of bad tidings, but these tidings felt worse than most.

'I'm sorry I've had to tell you this.'

'Ollie ... stalking ... but who?'

Ted shook her head. 'I can't share that information.'

'It's Giselle, isn't it? Oh my God.' Fleur's eyes bored desperately into Ted's. 'He's always had a crush on Giselle.'

Ted wasn't surprised that Fleur had made that leap, but having signed the NDA, she was in no position to confirm it. And besides, she hadn't even told Giselle about Ollie yet.

'I'm sorry. As I said before, my client's identity is confidential.'

'You have to help me tell Mitch,' Fleur suddenly said with urgency. 'Ollie idolises him, he might have a better idea about how to handle this. He's at Police HQ in Spencer Street, it's only five minutes away. Should I call him?'

But it must have been a rhetorical question, because she'd already picked up her phone and punched in her ex-husband's number. Ted listened as Fleur asked Mitch to come and meet her immediately. She hung up and turned back to Ted.

'He's on his way.'

Ted nodded. She would have preferred to keep things between her and Fleur, but she had to defer to Fleur's wisdom as Ollie's mum. They made awkward conversation for ten minutes, and then the door opened and the weary but capable-looking woman reappeared with Mitch.

'Thanks, Judy,' Fleur said.

Judy retreated, closing the door.

Mitch was wearing jeans and a T-shirt, which seemed incongruous at first glance, but Ted knew that sometimes the 'fraudies' went casual when they wanted to be inconspicuous. She was struck again by how much Ollie resembled his dad. Looking at Mitch was like looking at Ollie if someone had pressed a fast-forward button.

'Ted? What are you doing here?' But without waiting for an answer, Mitch turned to Fleur. 'What's up? What do you need to talk about?'

'Take a seat.'

Mitch remained standing. 'What is it?'

Fleur opened her mouth to explain, but Ted didn't hear a word Fleur said, because she'd just noticed that Mitch was wearing Cariuma Gerry Lopez red canvas sneakers with a white lightning stripe.

Her heart almost tripped over itself. Those were the exact same shoes Giselle's stalker had been wearing when he put the lamb's heart on her windscreen! But it could be a fluke, she told herself, there must be thousands of pairs out there. She discreetly searched Mitch's shoes for any distinguishing marks, and she saw a black smudge near the lightning stripe on his left sneaker. She 'accidentally' dropped her phone, and as she leaned down to retrieve it, she covertly snapped a pic of the shoe.

'This is probably a conversation you guys should have on your own,' she improvised. 'Can you point me to the toilets?'

Fleur gave Ted directions and she made her way into a bathroom that was filled with disarmingly tiny toilets. She lowered herself onto a miniscule toilet seat and pulled up the picture of Mitch's sneaker. Then she reached into a backpack pocket and pulled out the bystander's photo that showed the stalker's sneakers in the glow of a street light. She studied both photos intently. There was an identical black smudge near the lightning stripe on the stalker's left sneaker. They were the same pair!

Rattled, Ted threw the photo back into her pack. Had Ollie borrowed his father's shoes? But what teenager borrows his father's shoes? And hadn't Fleur said that Ollie was on his own all that weekend, and he hadn't seen either parent? A darker, more sinister thought intruded. Had Mitch placed the lamb's heart on the windscreen for Ollie? Was stalking Giselle some kind of sick father–son bonding activity?

Ted's phone vibrated in her hand and she jumped so high that the little toilet seat shook. She checked the screen. It was Chuck. She pressed Accept.

'Chuck, hey. You won't believe—'

'Aunty Ted, OMG! You'll never guess what I found out.'

'What?'

'I've done some investigating of my own …'

Chuck was whispering, and Ted realised she must be in class.

'I rang Ollie at lunch and asked him open-ended questions like you taught me. And guess what?'

'What?'

But suddenly the phone went blurry, and then an icy voice came on the line.

'Edwina?'

Oh no! It was the principal, Ted's old nemesis, Hairy Hanley. Muscle memory kicked in, and Ted couldn't resist a smart-arse comment.

'Hi, Mrs Hanley. I'd love to chat, but I'm sure you're aware that phones aren't allowed during lessons.'

Ted could have sworn she felt a blast of arctic wind in the half-second it took her to end the call. But her amusement quickly fizzled. What had Chuck been about to tell her? It had sounded urgent, but Hairy Hanley was bound to confiscate Chuck's phone. Ted checked her watch. It was only forty minutes until school came out. She'd have to head over to Our Lady of Sorrows and ask Chuck in person.

She made her way back to the office, where Mitch was allegedly reeling from the terrible news. Fleur was probably too nice to notice, but Mitch's 'shock' didn't ring true to Ted. What a poor excuse for a father. No wonder Ollie had gone off the rails. Ted wanted to smack him across the chops and yell, *What kind of lowlife* are *you?*

She carefully masked her suspicions as she told Fleur and Mitch that an urgent job had come up. Before they had time to ask questions she was out the door, and within thirty minutes she was pulling up across the road from her former school – or prison, as she liked to think of it – Our Lady of Sorrows in Preston. Teenage girls were streaming out of the gate in gaggles of laughter and gossip. Ted sprinted across the road and scanned the noisy crowd for Chuck, but Chuck materialised before she could spot her.

'Aunty Ted!'

'Chuck, hey.'

'I thought you'd come. Hairy Hanley confiscated my phone.'

'That'd be right.' Ted snorted on autopilot, but other matters were top of mind. 'What did you want to tell me?'

Chuck gave Ted a look that conveyed more drama than a *Bold and the Beautiful* cliffhanger.

'You'll never guess. I rang Ollie and asked him open-ended questions …'

She paused for effect.

'Yeah, you told me that,' Ted said impatiently, keeping an eye out for Hairy Hanley.

'Well he told me his dad's been doing stalking and coercive control training at work – and he's been getting Ollie to write sample "stalker" notes for his projects.'

It took a couple of beats for Ted to wrap her mind around this information. So, it was even worse than she'd thought. Mitch was Giselle's toxic stalker, and he was manipulating his son into unknowingly being involved. Ted felt sick. Giselle thought Mitch was a dear friend, and so did Spike. Despite herself, Ted felt a flash of protectiveness towards Spike. How would he take this betrayal? But, more importantly, what would it do to Giselle and Ollie?

'This *sucks*!'

'I know,' Chuck said. 'How could Ollie's dad do that to him?'

'You didn't tell him the stalking was real?'

Chuck looked affronted. 'Of course not. Do you think I'm, like, an idiot?'

'Sorry ... I'm just in shock. That was awesome work, Chuck, really excellent.'

Chuck's chest swelled beneath her box pleats. 'Thanks. So, what are you going to do now?'

'Well, the first thing I have to do is tell Giselle.'

'And then what?'

But Ted froze as she spotted a skinny figure on the move behind Chuck.

'Hairy Hanley! I've got to go. Thanks again!'

Ted scarpered.

Chapter Twenty-Three

Giselle was radiating peak ballerina as she spun several times on one foot, while a skinny but muscly guy in tights balanced her with a hand on her waist. Giselle finished effortlessly in a deep arabesque, and a long-necked woman in black leotards and a diaphanous skirt, presumably the director, Marilyn Sparrow, who'd given Ted permission to be here, made some suggestions in French. Ted was surprised – the arabesque had looked flawless to her. But what did she know? She was in awe of her client's contortions. How could Giselle last on her toes for so long? Sure, there was stiffened canvas in the ballet slippers, but still.

She looked at her watch. 8.29 pm. Rehearsals were ending any minute now, and she could finally break the bad news about Mitch. She took a step back and tried to lurk inconspicuously in a corner, but she kept catching curious glances from pale, impossibly elegant dancers who were stretching their pale, impossibly elegant legs at barres in front of floor-to-ceiling mirrors.

Ted fixed her gaze on Marilyn Sparrow, willing her to wrap things up. It must have worked because the next thing she knew, Giselle was rushing across the room, her short tutu radiating around her hips like a tulle pineapple ring. Even in her haste, she looked as if she was floating on air. Spots of sweat on her forehead brought to mind dainty dew drops and, in spite of everything, Ted couldn't help wondering if her armpits smelled like rose petals.

'Ted! Why are you here? What's wrong?' Giselle asked anxiously.

'Can we talk in private?'

Giselle nodded and wiped her face with a towel. 'They'll all be gone in a second.'

But Marilyn Sparrow was on approach. Dammit. Ted realised it was the least she could do to introduce herself and thank her for allowing the intrusion. Those niceties occupied the next few minutes, but still Marilyn and the other dancers lingered, stretching and gossiping. Ted wished she could produce a tray of Big Macs – that would be bound to make them scatter. Eventually the last of them straggled gracefully out of the room. Ted closed the door.

'Well?' Giselle asked, her voice now an octave higher. 'Why are you here?'

'I'm really sorry,' Ted said. She'd decided there was no point beating around the bush. 'I'm afraid Mitch is your stalker.'

Giselle went as white as her lycra leotard. She gaped at Ted incredulously.

'Mitch …? Mitch Prowse?'

'Yes. I'm sorry.'

Poor Giselle seemed lost for words. Ted filled her in on the details, including how Mitch had drafted Ollie to write the notes.

'Oh my God …' Giselle eventually said. 'Why didn't this occur to me before? He's always hanging around, being so "helpful". Poor Fleur. And poor Ollie.'

'I know, the guy's scum. He's betrayed his son's trust and your friendship, *and* he's one of Spike's best mates. Or so Spike thinks!'

Giselle threw her a puzzled look.

'I mean, that's how it seems from a distance at Swordcraft,' Ted said quickly. 'They're always hanging out together.'

Giselle nodded, but she was barely listening. 'Mitch … I still can't believe it.'

'I know.' Ted nodded gravely. 'And I don't want to alarm you, but these things can escalate. I don't think you have a choice anymore – you have to tell Spike.'

Amazingly, Giselle shook her head.

'No. I already told you why I don't want to involve him.'

'What, even *now*?'

'*Especially* now. He'd just go berserk and make things worse, and what would that do to my girls? Mitch is like an uncle to them. I don't want them knowing about this, *ever*.'

'But Giselle, I don't have the power to arrest him or take him in for questioning. If you won't tell Spike, at least tell the police.'

'Absolutely not. They'd just let Mitch off because he's a cop. And he'd be furious with me. Who knows what he'd do?'

Ted threw her hands in the air. 'Exactly! That's why you have to report him—'

'No. For all we know, he's capable of violence.'

'I agree. Which is why I'm saying—'

'I want *you* to handle it.'

Ted blinked. Hopefully she'd misheard.

'What?'

'I said I want *you* to go and warn Mitch off. Tell him that I know it's him, and if he ever comes anywhere near me again, I'll tell Spike *everything*.'

That sounded like a terrible and, frankly, terrifying plan to Ted.

'But you'll have to tell Spike anyway. He needs to know what a vile creep he's hanging around with.'

But Giselle was scribbling an address on a *Don Quixote* score with trembling fingers.

'I'm not telling Spike until I know it's over. What if he tried to get full custody of the kids?'

'On what grounds? He's been exposing them to Mitch too.'

'That's all the more reason he'll go berserk. What if he blames me for letting that happen?'

'Why would he? This is about Mitch's egregious behaviour and no-one else's.' Ted tried to ram her point home. 'Seriously, I'm giving you my best advice. *Please* tell the police.'

'No.'

Giselle handed Ted the scribbled address, and Ted could see the fear in her hooded grey eyes was real. Not that she'd been doubting that.

'I'm scared for my kids' safety, Ted. And for mine. Please?' Giselle pleaded. 'I need you to warn him off.'

Great! Ted refrained from pointing out that while Giselle was scared of putting herself and her kids in danger, she had no qualms about doing it to *her*. But then, wasn't it a PI's job to embrace danger on their client's behalf? And if she wanted EBI to pivot into serious crime, she could hardly pike out when peril presented itself. She reminded herself of her gutsy fight for life against the violent embezzler who'd been intent on stabbing her to death. So what if Mitch Prowse was twice her size? She was Ted Bristol, gun PI.

'All right. I'm on it,' she said, and she couldn't help noticing how heroic she sounded.

There was a weird silence for a second, and then Giselle said, 'What? You look like you're expecting applause.'

By 9.40 pm, Ted was turning into a narrow Collingwood street in the shadow of Victoria Park, the faded footy oval that was once home to the AFL's Magpies. Nearby, a train on the Mernda line rattled along an elevated track, but apart from that, all was still and silent. Ted tried to calm her racing heart as she pulled up outside Mitch's rented cottage, behind his enormous SUV. As she turned off the engine, she noticed her palms were sweaty, and she was grateful for Miss Marple's gutsy presence. She turned to her.

'Let's do this.'

Ted climbed out from behind the wheel and opened the back door for Miss Marple. The street was empty, and the moon was hiding behind the clouds. She felt a shiver run up her spine. Miss Marple must have sensed her fear, because she looked up at her as if to say, *You're a kickarse PI, you're all over this.*

'Thanks, Miss Marple,' Ted whispered, but she didn't share her dog's confidence. How would a malevolent stalker like Mitch react to being warned off by a woman the size of a gnat – even if that woman kicked arse at Swordcraft? And who was she kidding, like Swordcraft mattered. She might be handy with a foam sword, but Mitch was a cop, and he had twenty years' experience with an actual gun.

Mitch's rundown-looking rental was the only cottage in the small street that was still in its original state. Next door an enormous renovation was underway, and the house was unoccupied. As she and Miss Marple walked through Mitch's rickety gate, Ted noticed ring cameras installed and felt reassured, until she realised they were turned off. *Dammit.* They stepped up onto the front porch. From inside, she could hear a TV loudly blaring what sounded like an AFL replay. Ted hoped Mitch's team was winning, so he'd be in a good mood. She strode to the door. She was all over this. She'd maintain a steely calm and tell Mitch in no uncertain terms that if he dared to frighten Giselle for one moment longer, all hell would rain down on him.

She glanced down at Miss Marple for reassurance, but Miss Marple seemed lost in something else. Every fibre of her little body was suddenly stiff, and her snout was twitching urgently. Had she caught the scent of something? A possum?

Ted lifted her hand to knock on the door, but as her knuckles made contact, the door opened, startling her. She examined it and saw the locks were pushed back. Why would Mitch leave his front door open?

Miss Marple's snout was now working overtime, and she was straining at her lead, seemingly desperate to get inside. She started emitting a low growl, which made the hairs on Ted's neck stand on end. Ted held the door still with one hand and knocked again.

'Mitch?' she called.

There was no answer. But he must be here, the TV was on – even louder than she'd first realised. She pushed the door open a little wider and Miss Marple tried to push her way inside, straining even harder at her lead. Ted reined her in.

'Mitch?' she called loudly. 'It's Ted Bristol, from Swordcraft!'

Still nothing.

'Mitch?'

It seemed he couldn't hear her over the footy commentators, who were having kittens about someone kicking a goal. Ted looked down at Miss Marple, but she didn't look back. Instead the little dog yanked hard on her lead. Ted felt an urge to turn and run. But she was so close to confronting Mitch. Was she really going to chicken out now, only to have to return and gird her loins all over again? And who knew what Mitch might do in between? For everyone's sake, including hers, she needed to get this over with.

'Mitch! I'm coming in.'

Ted pushed the door open and Miss Marple practically dragged her down a narrow hall. Large boots and shoes were stacked against one wall, and Mitch's discarded work jacket was slung over the back of an old chair. Ted stopped with a start as she saw his police-issue capsicum spray, handcuffs and extra ammo mag discarded on the chair. She gingerly reached out and lifted the corner of his jacket. His gun was underneath. Why had Mitch left the front door open with his gun in the hall? She was tempted to grab it so he couldn't get his hands on it, but something told her to leave it alone.

'Mitch?'

On the TV, the male sports commentators were banging on about the guy who'd kicked the goal 'feeling the emotions' of the moment. Ted was almost at the end of the hall, and now Miss Marple had started barking urgently.

'Miss Marple, sssh!' Ted hissed.

But there was no reaction from inside. Why hadn't Mitch heard them yet? She took a big gulp of air for courage and followed Miss Marple into the living room.

'Mi—'

The word stuck in Ted's throat, and she grabbed at the nearest thing – a cabinet maybe, who knew – to stop her legs from collapsing beneath her. On the floor in front of the 60-inch TV, Mitch was lying dead in a pool of blood.

Chapter Twenty-Four

Ted's heart was still trying to escape through her ribs, and her stomach was roiling with bile. She needed a glass of water. She stood.

'Sit,' the senior constable said, pointing to the wobbly dining chair that Ted had been occupying. 'We need you to stay put until homicide gets here.'

What was the cop's name again? Senior Constable Dickson? Dibbins? Dinkins? Ted could barely remember the two cops arriving, let alone the niceties of their names. As she sat back down, she felt as if she was observing herself through some kind of haze.

'I was just going to get a glass of water.'

'We can't risk you disturbing the crime scene.'

Ted bit back an indignant response. As if she'd ever disturb a crime scene, especially when she was planning to solve the crime before the cops. Not that she had any intention of sharing that particular information.

She still felt ill when she thought about what she and Miss Marple had stumbled across, although thinking about it wasn't required, because Mitch was still lying in the pool of blood in her peripheral vision. It was obviously the blood

Miss Marple had smelled all the way from the front verandah – she'd been picking up on the stench of death.

They'd found Mitch in the shabby living room, furnished in clichéd bachelor style with just an old couch, a coffee table and the huge TV. He was curled up dead on the threadbare carpet, next to a large pizza box containing a half-eaten Hawaiian pizza. Fresh bruising around Mitch's left eye and broken skin on his knuckles seemed to suggest a fist fight, but it was clear he'd died from a frenzied stabbing. From what Ted could see there were at least eight stab wounds, as well as defensive wounds on Mitch's forearms from attempting to fend off his killer. There was even blood spatter on the cracked walls.

For a second Ted had come perilously close to fainting – but once she'd recovered from her initial shock, she'd quickly taken some sterile gloves and surgical booties from her pocket and slipped them on. Luckily she always carried PPE with her, although she'd never had occasion to use it before.

She'd studied the pizza up close, careful not to touch it. The cheese hadn't yet congealed, which meant that Mitch had probably been murdered within the last ninety minutes. Then she'd searched the room for the murder weapon, but found nothing. Where was the knife? She'd taken out her phone, and while snapping photos of the murder scene she'd noticed that Mitch's wi-fi was turned off. That didn't necessarily mean anything, although it explained why his security cameras weren't operating. She'd searched the rest of the house for the knife, but come up empty. Then they'd gone outside, and Miss Marple had sniffed around the garden for clues while Ted went through the bins at the side of the house, safe in the knowledge that Mitch's security cameras were turned off. She wouldn't have moved the knife, of course, but she would have liked to at least have found it and taken a pic. But, disappointingly, she and Miss Marple's searches proved fruitless. So, she'd deposited Miss Marple back in the car and come inside to call the police.

And while she'd been waiting for the cops, the enormity of the situation had hit her. Mitch was a father. A reprehensible father for sure, but she felt heartsick for poor Ollie, who obviously idolised him. Mitch might have been a manipulative stalker, but he didn't deserve an ending like this. Nobody did. Ted wondered if his murder had something to do with the stalking? But how could it? No-one knew that Mitch was a stalker except for herself, Chuck and Giselle.

'We'll get you some water,' Senior Constable Whomever said more brusquely than Ted thought was necessary. She was slender and pretty, and Ted supposed she felt the need to compensate with a tough demeanour.

I feel you, sister, Ted thought, but all she said was, 'Thanks.' She'd given Senior Constable Whomever and her burly young colleague her name but not her occupation, because she knew how cops felt about PIs, and she preferred to keep her powder dry. She'd told them she knew Mitch from Swordcraft and she'd dropped in for a chat, which was technically true. But she supposed that when the homicide guys arrived, she'd have to tell them she was working on a case or she could be withholding vital information. She felt a little quickening in her heart as she wondered if Spike would be one of the homicide cops called to the scene. How horrific for him. No-one should have to see one of their best mates brutally murdered like this.

The junior cop handed Ted some water. She was still sipping on it when they heard male voices outside, neither of which belonged to Spike. Senior Constable Whomever and her fresh-faced colleague jumped to attention.

'Sounds like homicide's here,' the constable said in a voice that Ted could have sworn was deeper than the one she'd been using three minutes ago. She turned back to Ted. 'Don't move.'

Ted help up her hands in compliance. The front door opened and a heavy footfall came down the hall. A podgy middle-aged detective in an ill-fitting suit appeared, and Ted recognised him as the guy who'd been with Spike at McDonald's. But he flew from her mind in a millisecond, because a trim fiftyish guy with a 1970s porn-star moustache had just appeared behind him, wearing a natty blue suit and shiny brown shoes. Ted recognised the second guy as Chief Inspector Craig Maven, the homicide squad boss who'd refused to give EBI due credit for solving a high-profile murder.

She felt her hackles rise and stand end-to-end. Craig Maven was her nemesis. She'd given Spike vital intel about the murder on the strict condition that the police publicly acknowledged EBI's role in bringing the killer to justice. But despite Spike's best efforts, Maven had refused to share credit with EBI, and when he'd held a televised media conference to announce the murderer's arrest, EBI hadn't garnered so much as a mention. Ted had been incensed. Sure, she'd posted about solving the murder on her socials, but official recognition from the cops would have gone a long way towards helping her pivot into crime-work.

She watched as Maven and the other detective, Enzo Finelli, introduced themselves to the uniformed cops, who looked as surprised to see Maven as Ted was. The big cheese of homicide didn't sully his hands with field work. What was he doing here?

'I'll be leading the investigation,' Maven said in answer to the collective unspoken question. 'This bloke's one of our own.'

The uniforms nodded, slightly awestruck. Senior Constable Whomever stepped back while Maven and Finelli bent to assess Mitch's body. They'd barely registered Ted yet, and she found herself looking forward to the moment when she and Maven came eye-to-eye. But when Senior Constable Whomever said, 'This lady discovered the body,' and they both turned to look at her, only Finelli's face betrayed a flicker of recognition. Ted could tell he was trying to place where he'd seen her before, but infuriatingly, Maven looked completely blank. Ted had assumed he'd google her after learning she'd solved the murder with Spike. It seemed he was even lazier than she'd suspected. He gave her a perfunctory smile.

'And you are?'

'I'm *Ted Bristol*.'

She waited for the penny to drop, but still nothing. Maven dispatched the uniforms to question the neighbours, and once they'd gone, he gave Ted his full attention.

'Can you tell us exactly why you came here and what time you arrived, and take us through what happened, step-by-step, Miss Bristol?'

Ted felt white-hot needles of rage. The arrogant bastard had already forgotten her name, even though she'd solved a murder he'd taken credit for. But she urged herself to put her personal feelings aside. Mitch was dead, stolen from his son in the most savage of ways, and that was the only thing that mattered.

'I'm a private investigator,' she said.

Maven and Finelli looked her up and down with snide smirks.

'*You're* a private investigator?'

Ted nodded. Sure, she might look like a pixie from the bottom of the garden, but at the risk of repeating herself, she kicked arse. She would have loved to tell Maven exactly which private investigator she was, but something told her revealing that might not be to her advantage. She needed to override her natural instinct to get into a barney, and play it safe.

'Yes. I've been working on a case, and I arrived here at 9.40 pm to have a chat with Detective Prowse.'

'A *case,* eh?' Maven asked, barely bothering to hide his amusement. 'What case?'

A case that could be a motive for Mitch's murder, smart-arse. But Ted wasn't inclined to give Maven a leg-up.

'I'm not authorised to disclose that. I'm contractually bound by a non-disclosure agreement with my client.'

For a moment Maven looked as if he was going to tell Ted what she could do with her non-disclosure agreement, but then he said, 'All right, *sweetie*. Then who's your client?'

Ted hesitated. She would have loved to stay schtum, but she knew in all conscience that wasn't an option.

'Your client?' Maven pressed, pen in hand. 'What's his name?'

'Giselle,' Ted said. 'It's a woman. Giselle ... Tereiti.'

She saw Maven and Finelli exchange a look. These were two blokes schooled not to show surprise, but Ted could tell that Maven was thrown.

'Would that be our colleague Spike Tereiti's ex-wife?'

'Er, yes,' Ted said as vaguely as she could. 'I believe so.'

'Hey, that's where I saw you!' Finelli said suddenly. He turned to Maven. 'She was talking to Tereiti at Macca's the other day.'

Maven raised his eyebrows. 'Yeah? Are you two friends?'

'Acquaintances.'

Ted was sure that Maven would finally fit the pieces together, but still her identity seemed to elude him. He returned to the issue at hand, peppering her with questions. Ted explained exactly how she'd arrived and found the door unlocked and entered to discover Mitch's body.

'Did you disturb anything?'

'No, I'm not that stupid.'

The detectives exchanged another look as if to say, *I doubt that*. Ted wanted to punch Maven in his taut, self-satisfied gut, but she caught Mitch's body in her peripheral vision again. She took a deep breath and tried to cooperate.

'Anyway. The cheese on the pizza hadn't coagulated, so I think he was murdered in the last hour or ninety minutes. And as you can see, injuries around his eyes suggest a fist fight before the stabbing—'

Maven silenced her with a dismissive wave.

'Thanks for your expert analysis, but why don't you go and "investigate" something more up your alley, like a missing puppy.'

He exchanged another grin with Finelli. Ted wondered what sound their heads would make if they were cracked together? Maven demanded her contact details. He told her she needed to make herself available for future interviews if required, and then he had Finelli escort her out of the house. Two forensic cops in full PPE had just climbed out of a crime-scene van and were walking up the front path. They stepped past Ted and headed inside. Finelli followed and closed the door behind them, giving Ted one final smirk. As she ducked under blue-and-white crime-scene tape, she was incandescent with rage at being dismissed so contemptuously. Maven and Finelli would regret it when she solved Mitch's murder before they did.

In the moonlight, she saw a cat lope across the road. Miss Marple must have seen it too because Ted could hear barking from her car, and she looked over to see Miss Marple's snout pressed against the window. Ted turned away and scanned the street. Senior Constable Whomever and the other uniform were chatting with a neighbour a few doors down. Ted thought fast. With Mitch's wi-fi turned off and his ring cameras out of operation, the neighbours' evidence would be essential. On impulse, she sprinted through the gate of the house next door. It was a tastefully renovated timber cottage at odds with the garish work-in-progress on the other side of Mitch's place. She glanced at her watch. It was almost 10.30 pm, which was late to turn up on somebody's doorstep, but a murder meant all bets were off. As she rang the bell, she looked over her shoulder furtively. The cops hadn't seen her yet, but she'd have to be quick. She just hoped the next-door neighbour was a busybody who'd seen something and wouldn't mind repeating the information.

The front door opened, revealing a woman who looked to be in her mid-thirties. She was wearing men's pyjama pants and a silk teddy, and vape smoke from an e-cigarette was drifting up in front of her face and obscuring her number 1 buzz cut.

'Yes? Can I help you?'

Ted saw the woman's eyes shoot to the crime-scene van parked outside Mitch's place. Her eyes widened with shock.

'Shit, what's happened?'

It was a lucky break. This meant she hadn't yet spoken to the cops, which gave EBI the inside running.

'I'm sorry to disturb you so late,' Ted said quickly. 'I'm Ted Bristol, from Edwina Bristol Investigations. I'm afraid there's been a murder next door.'

'A murder?'

'Yes, I'm sorry to say.'

The woman looked shaken, but not as surprised as Ted would have expected. She wondered if that meant anything.

'Have you seen or heard anything unusual tonight?'

The woman frowned. 'Who are you again?'

'I'm Edwina Bristol. I'm a private investigator.' Ted whipped a card from her pocket.

The woman scanned it and seemed satisfied. She took a card of her own from a hall table. 'I'm Kip Trammel.' She handed Ted the card: *Kip Trammel, Professor of Queer Studies, Melbourne University, They/Their.*

Ted turned briefly to glance at the cops, who didn't seem to have seen her yet. But she knew that could change at any second.

'Who was murdered?' Kip was asking. 'The detective?'

'I'm afraid so.'

Kip shook their head, but again, they didn't seem overly surprised.

'Well, that's hectic … but I didn't know him well. I can't abide toxic masculinity, so I kept my distance.' Ted saw their eyes widen as they spotted the uniforms emerging from the neighbour's front gate. 'I heard the doorbell a few minutes ago. Was that the cops? I was marking a thesis, so I didn't answer.'

And I love you for that, Ted thought. Aloud she said, 'Yes, that would have been the police. As I was asking, have you seen or heard anything unusual?'

'Actually, yeah. I went out to my letterbox a couple of hours ago, and I saw a guy arrive next door. Another cis alpha-male type. I came back in to work on my marking, but then I heard shouting and I couldn't concentrate. I was almost going to knock on the door and tell them to shut up, but then things went quiet, so I forgot about it.'

They stared at each other as they both absorbed the enormity of the situation. Kip drew on their e-cigarette, clearly shaken.

'Hey!' someone called.

Ted turned. Oh no! Senior Constable Whomever had just seen her at Kip's door, and she and her offsider were heading over. Ted turned back to Kip urgently.

'What did the guy who turned up at Mitch's place look like?'

'He was huge,' Kip said. 'Tall and solid with broad shoulders. He had a lot of curly dark hair. He looked like he could have been an All Black.'

The world stood still.

'An All Black? Do you mean he was a Pacific Islander?' Ted asked weakly.

Kip nodded through vape smoke. 'That's right.'

Ted almost fainted.

Chapter Twenty-Five

Ted's car careened around a corner, tyres squealing. She was glad Miss Marple was strapped in, or she would have been tossed around like a tin can all the way from Collingwood to Moorabbin. Ted was pretty sure they'd copped a parking fine back in East Brighton, but tough. She slammed on her brakes and pulled up outside Spike's house, a few doors down from the corner. It was now past eleven, and the residential street was still and silent, save for the hum of late-night traffic from the nearby Nepean Highway.

'You stay here,' she instructed Miss Marple, and Miss Marple looked at her as if to say, *Hurry!* Ted jumped from the car and raced through Spike's front gate. The second she'd left Kip's doorstep, she'd pulled out her phone and searched Land Titles in the Citec database for Spike's address. She wasn't sure what she'd been expecting, but it wasn't this 1970s suburban brick bungalow with a kids' trampoline in the front yard. A sensor light flicked on and illuminated her path, and she spotted a doll with a tortured hairdo lying abandoned on the porch. There was a tiny comb stuck in its hair, and its spooky eyes seemed to follow her as she stepped up to the door.

She'd seriously thought she might vomit when Kip told her about Mitch's visitor, and hearing what sounded like a fight. Had Spike somehow found out about Mitch stalking Giselle and killed him? But she'd dismissed the idea before she'd reached Kip's front gate. Spike might be a lot of things, but there was no way he was a murderer. She'd raced to her car, 'failing to hear' Senior Constable Whomever, who was calling out for her to stop. Suddenly, more than anything else in the world, she'd needed to get to Spike before the cops did.

But as she rang the doorbell, she realised it could all be a misunderstanding. It wasn't as if Spike was the only Pacific Islander guy in Melbourne. Kip had probably seen someone else. She'd almost convinced herself when a light came on in the hall and the front door opened to reveal Spike, who was sporting a fresh black eye and what looked like a broken nose. Ted's heart sank like a stone.

'Ted?' he said in a surprised sotto voce. He'd obviously been in bed, he was bare-chested above old pyjama pants. He looked as if he wasn't sure whether to be confused or annoyed. 'It's after eleven.'

'I know,' Ted said urgently, 'but—'

'Shh,' Spike cut across. 'The kids are sleeping.'

'Sorry,' Ted whispered. 'Mitch is dead.'

Spike blinked. 'What?'

'I said Mitch is dead.'

'*Dead?*'

'Yeah. Did you do it?'

Spike stared at her uncomprehendingly. Ted tried to ignore his broad, hairy chest that was right at her eyeline.

'Get in here.'

He ushered Ted inside and closed the door. He led her down the hall and as she followed, she noticed a dark mole on his back. She fleetingly wondered if he'd had it checked. He led her into a living room–kitchen area that was littered with little girls' toys and *Frozen* accessories, a few mini-trucks and even a tiny Batman costume. It was the kind of kid-centric scene that would normally have made her tense up, but right now it was impossible to be any tenser. She felt as if a cyclone was ripping up her internal organs and tossing them all around her body.

'What do you mean, Mitch is dead?' Spike hissed. 'What happened?'

'He was stabbed to death.'

'Stabbed? Holy shit!'

'I found his body.'

'*You* did?'

'Yes.'

Spike sank onto a couch, speechless. He looked shocked to the core, but she had to know for sure.

'Did you do it?' she asked again.

'Jesus, Ted. Of course not!'

Ted felt weak with relief, even though, of course, she'd already known that. She brushed a plastic tiara out of the way and sat down on the couch beside him. There was still the matter of his battered face.

'Are you okay?' he asked in a daze. 'That must've been awful for you.'

'I'm fine,' Ted said. 'But what about that broken nose? And Mitch had a cut on his cheek, and a shiner like yours.'

Spike nodded matter-of-factly. 'I was there. We had a fight.'

'That's obvious. Why?'

Anger clouded Spike's brown eyes. 'The prick's been stalking Giselle.'

Ted froze. So, he *did* know?

'Maisy misses Peaches, her cat,' Spike said. 'So, I put a wi-fi camera on top of the living-room cabinet, so she could check in and see her anytime. I told Giselle, but she gets distracted when she's in rehearsals, so she probably forgot it was there.'

Oh my God.

'So, you *saw* Mitch come into the room and leave the note and flowers?'

'Yeah. Not at the time, but I saw it this afternoon. That's why I paid the prick a visit. And I checked his phone and found pics of Giselle, some with the kids. I let him have it, and I told him that if he ever came near my kids again, I'd kill him—'

Ted freaked. 'You told him you'd *kill* him?'

'Yeah, but I wouldn't have done it! And then I left. I tried to call Giselle, but she was in rehearsals, so it went to voicemail. I didn't leave a message. I thought I'd talk to her tomorrow when I'm calmer.'

Ted nodded. They stared at each other in silence for a moment, and then Spike's face creased into a frown.

'Hang on. What were *you* doing at Mitch's place? And how did you know he was stalking Giselle?'

Here we go, Ted thought with a cringe. She metaphorically threw the NDA out the window. It was the least of her worries now.

'She hired me a couple of weeks ago to find her stalker.'

'*What?*'

'I know, I know,' Ted said. She sounded super defensive, even to her ears. 'I wanted to tell you, but she wouldn't let me. She made me sign an NDA.'

If looks could kill, Ted would have been in the same state as Mitch. Spike was clearly livid with her, just as she'd known he'd be. And she couldn't blame him.

'My kids could've been in danger! You should have told her to tell me!'

'I did! *Constantly.*'

The doorbell rang, and they both jumped. Spike's eyes darted towards a door off the hall that was slightly ajar. He leaped to his feet.

'That'll be the cops,' Ted hissed. 'A neighbour saw you and heard the fight.'

He shook his head incredulously. 'When were you planning to mention that?'

The doorbell rang again. Spike sprinted into the hall and quietly closed a door. Ted assumed it must be his daughters' bedroom. She'd almost forgotten there were three sleeping little girls in the house, and the reminder made the stakes feel unbearably high. Spike headed to the front door and she stayed on his heels. She expected him to tell her to back off, but he obviously had other things on his mind.

'It's Maven,' she hissed to his back.

Spike briefly stopped and spun around. 'Maven?'

'Yeah. He's leading the investigation because Mitch is one of you.'

'Christ,' Spike muttered, 'he hates me.' It was only then he seemed to realise she was on his heels. 'What are you doing? Hide, for fuck's sake.'

He shoved Ted into a darkened room, closing the door behind her. She felt around for the light switch and turned it on, and found herself in Spike's bedroom. The bed was roughly made and there were clothes scattered all over the room. Spike's

Viking helmet was hanging off the bedhead. It felt weirdly intimate being in here, but right now she had other things on her mind. She put her ear to the bedroom door and heard Spike greet Maven and Finelli. Their voices were muffled and she couldn't discern what they were saying, and then she heard what sounded like the front door closing. She turned off the light and tentatively opened the bedroom door, sneaking out into the hall. Spike had stepped outside to talk to Maven and Finelli and closed the front door behind him. Ted tiptoed to the door and pressed her ear up against it.

'Mitch, murdered?' Spike was saying out on the porch. 'I can't believe it!'

Ted cringed. It seemed Spike's skill set didn't extend to acting, and his 'surprise' was unconvincing at best. Maven and Finelli were bound to be picking up on that too.

'Where'd you get that shiner?' she heard Maven ask.

'Why don't we cut to the chase?' Spike said. 'We all know why you're here. I *was* at Mitch's place tonight. We had a bit of biffo—'

'What about?'

There was a brief silence. Ted knew that Spike would be loath to share Giselle's personal business, but, frankly, he had no choice.

'The prick's been stalking Giselle.'

'What?!' Finelli said. 'Stalking your missus?'

'My ex – but yeah, he's been terrorising her for a couple of months.'

'That sounds like a motive to me,' Maven said.

'To me too, but I didn't do it. I left at eight thirty. Check the cameras.'

'The cameras were off,' Maven said.

'No, they weren't,' Spike said. 'They were definitely on when I arrived.'

'Yeah, but the wi-fi was turned off at 7.49 pm,' Maven said. 'You're the only person seen arriving, and there's no footage of you leaving.'

'Mitch must have turned it off,' Spike insisted. 'He left the room a couple of times.'

'Or, just to play devil's advocate,' Maven said, 'you killed Mitch in a fit of rage, and then you turned the wi-fi off, so you wouldn't be seen leaving the house covered in blood.'

'That's bullshit!'

'Yeah, I know,' Maven said, but Ted wasn't convinced he meant it. 'But you can see why we need you to come down to the station for a chat.'

There was another brief silence, and then Spike said, 'Sure, just let me get dressed.'

Before Ted could streak back into the bedroom, the front door was abruptly flung open. She felt the thump of her body hitting the hall wall, and then the door was yanked back. Spike, Finelli and Maven all glared down at her.

'What are you doing? Are you all right?' Spike asked irascibly.

'I'm fine,' Ted snapped grumpily, even though – or possibly because – she was the one who'd stuffed up. 'I just wasn't expecting—'

'Shh,' Spike cut across her. He turned to Maven and Finelli and whispered, 'My girls are sleeping. I'll be right back.'

He went into his bedroom and closed the door, abandoning Ted to her fate. Maven was looking seriously pissed off.

'What are *you* doing here?'

Ted tilted her head to eyeball him. 'Like I told you, I'm a private investigator. And I'm conducting an independent investigation into Mitch Prowse's murder.'

Maven's eyes narrowed. 'If you impede a police investigation with your little-girl games—'

'My little-girl games? For your information, mate, *I* solved that North Melbourne murder.'

Maven gawped, and she finally had the satisfaction of seeing him put the pieces together.

'Yeah, that was *me*. And *you* refused to give my business, Edwina Bristol Investigations, due credit.'

She'd been half-hoping he might be chastened, but blokes like Maven didn't do chastened.

'*You're* the one Tereiti was on at me about? Are you two fucking?'

'What? No!'

'Shh!' Spike called from the bedroom.

Maven leaned so close to Ted that she could see a blackhead on the side of his nose.

'You're walking a very dangerous line here, lady. If you've warned a suspect who turns out to have committed murder, I could charge you as an accessory.'

'I dare you,' Ted hissed recklessly.

She heard a little choking sound, and she could have sworn it was Finelli swallowing a laugh. He turned away, red-faced.

'Think you're pretty tough, eh? Well, let me make something crystal clear. You'd better not follow any leads without sharing them with the police.'

'I assume that's a reciprocal arrangement?'

Finelli made another choking sound. Spike emerged from the

bedroom in shorts and a T-shirt. He hadn't made any attempt to comb his unruly curls, Ted noticed, but why start now?

'All right, fellas, let's go to the station and get this sorted,' Spike said in a hushed voice. He sounded less apprehensive than Ted suspected he felt. He turned to her. 'Can you ring Giselle and ask her to come and look after the kids? And will you wait till she gets here?'

'Of course.'

There was an intense moment when their eyes locked, but then Maven put a palm on Spike's back. The gesture was probably designed to appear matey, but Ted sensed hostility.

'Come on then, buddy.'

Maven and Finelli led Spike outside to an unmarked police-issue sedan and drove off into the night. Ted closed the front door and called Giselle. Giselle flipped out, which was fair enough. She promised she'd be there in fifteen minutes, and Ted was left alone to wait in a sea of sparkles and unicorns. She tried to avoid all the kiddie stuff as she tiptoed into the kitchen.

She opened the fridge and took out a beer, and her eye caught a photo on the door, showing Spike with three little girls. Despite herself, Ted was drawn in. She knew the kids' names were Maisy, Ava and Romy, and they were aged ten, eight and four. They were beautiful. Maisy and Ava were tall and olive-skinned, with lustrous curls and dark eyes, and Romy was a mini-version of Giselle, fair and fine-featured. Maisy and Ava were wearing girlie dresses, but Romy was in cut-off denim shorts and a St Kilda Saints jersey. Which knocked the wind out of Ted – she'd had the exact same outfit as a little kid.

Suddenly, she was in fight-or-flight mode. If Spike was charged with murder, these little girls would as good as lose their dad. She knew how it felt to lose a parent – she couldn't let that happen to them. She had to do something! But what? She downed the beer and looked towards the girls' room with trepidation. Thankfully, there were no sounds of stirring.

Over the next several minutes Ted managed to calm herself, but when Giselle arrived shortly afterwards, the ballerina was in a heightened state. Her usually flawless skin had broken out in stress-induced blotches.

'I just wanted to warn Mitch off,' she whispered. 'I didn't want him *dead*.'

Ted was gobsmacked. Surely Giselle wasn't implying—

'I warned you Spike would go berserk, but you didn't listen. And now look what's happened!'

Indignation didn't begin to describe what Ted felt. How could Spike's former wife, the mother of his children, actually suspect him of murder?

'Are you *serious*? How could you think for one second that Spike is capable of murder? He'd never kill anyone in a million years!'

She could hear how protective she sounded, and she felt herself redden. Giselle had obviously noticed too.

'I thought you barely knew Spike?'

Ted tried to group some appropriate words together. 'Er, a bit ... Swordcraft ...'

'And how did you know where he lives? *I* didn't tell you.'

Ted was stumped for an answer, but luckily she was saved by a little girl's voice from the bedroom.

'Mummy? Is that you?'

'You'd better not have taken this job under false pretences,' Giselle hissed. Then she called softly, 'Yes, darling, it's me!'

She headed for the bedroom door, and Ted took the chance to escape.

Out in the car, Miss Marple was waiting for an update. Ted took in her dog's fluffy white face and the inquisitive expression in her big brown eyes, and she felt so grateful she'd gone to the RSPCA on that fateful day. But she cut to the chase as she slipped behind the steering wheel.

'Spike didn't do it.'

Miss Marple looked back at her as if to say, *We never thought he did.*

'I know.'

Ted turned on the engine and pulled away from the kerb. Would Spike call her with an update when he got back from the station? But why should he? It wasn't like they were friends, really. And they certainly weren't anything more. She ignored a small tweak of sadness and turned her mind to Mitch's wi-fi. Why had his wi-fi, and as a result his ring cameras, been turned off after Spike arrived, but before Spike left? The murderer couldn't have turned it off because there was only Spike and Mitch in the house. So, as Spike had pointed out, Mitch must have turned off the wi-fi himself.

But why?

Chapter Twenty-Six

The morning sky was a gloomy grey outside Ted's office window, and it seemed depressingly appropriate. She tried to ignore the sickly sensation in her stomach as she downloaded the murder-scene pics onto her Mac. She could hear Miss Marple's fluttery little snores from under her desk, and she was glad she'd be spared from seeing this twice. Most importantly, Chuck was on a school excursion to a matinee performance of *Macbeth* at the Melbourne Theatre Company, so there was no chance she could turn up unannounced. Ted was going to keep her niece right away from this case. She was only fifteen, and she was friends with Ollie. Who knew what damage it might do if she was exposed to the full horrors of Mitch's murder?

Ollie had been on Ted's mind all night. The poor kid had to be completely destroyed. And would he find out how Mitch had betrayed him? That thought was almost too much to contemplate, and her need to solve the crime on Ollie's account had grown with every passing hour.

She'd woken (not that she'd really been sleeping) to the cheep of a text from Spike at 2 am.

Back home. Maven's just trying to rattle my cage, the prick. Will start secretly working the case myself tomorrow. S

She'd lain awake for the rest of the night, staring blindly at the neon cityscape through her window. Why was Maven trying to rattle Spike's cage? Some kind of grudge? She wouldn't mind betting that Spike's detective skills had shown Maven up in the past, and guys like him did *not* take well to being outclassed. Spike was right, he was a prick. And a dickhead. And a moron. And a misogynist.

She'd tried to call Spike back this morning, but her call had gone straight to voicemail.

She opened the photos on her 27-inch screen. The ugliness of the brutal scene seemed to pollute the air in her immaculate office. She winced as she zoomed in on Mitch's body. Up close, the stab wounds were even more savage than she'd realised. She had no experience with murder scenes, but from what she could see, it looked like Mitch's wounds were a combination of stabbing and sort of ... slashing. She wasn't sure what that meant. Was it something to do with the murderer's knife? A light tinkle intruded, and it was so at odds with the bloody scene on her screen that it took her a second to realise EBI's front door had opened. She quickly clicked out of the photos and poked her head around the screen to see Aunty June O'Shea.

'Aunty! Hi.'

'Morning, love.'

Aunty June was carrying a cooler bag and wearing her usual elastic-waisted jeans and colourful tunic top. She smiled at Miss Marple under the desk, but Miss Marple slept on unawares.

'This is a nice surprise,' Ted said, getting to her feet.

It occurred to her with a little frisson of excitement that as a former homicide detective, June would know how to interpret murder-scene photos far better than she could.

'I've got a spot of news about Cicely Bunting,' June said.

Ted swiftly switched gears. 'About Cicely? Has she met up with Duncan?'

'No, love. Not yet.'

Ted felt a pinch of disappointment. She'd had Cicely under twenty-four-hour surveillance for two days now, but the only activities June and Cody had observed were cooking, sewing, quilting, weaving, knitting, gardening and preserving.

'Sometimes she does all those things at once,' Cody had said, just before he told Ted that he'd taken some free lemons from a bowl at Cicely's gate, and Cicely had come outside and they'd had 'a nice chat'. He was stoked with his undercover work, but Ted was incredulous.

'You *talked* to her? Did you tell her your name?'

'Yeah, I was gaining her trust.'

The kid had no idea.

'It's not your job to gain her trust, it's your job to watch her *inconspicuously, from a distance*. What if she googles you?'

Cody's crest had fallen in front of Ted's eyes. She'd been forced to pull him from the field, but that probably wasn't such a bad thing, since she couldn't afford to keep paying the extra loading for overnight rates. She was still convinced that Cicely and Duncan would meet, she just hoped they'd do it during daylight hours. That way Aunty June would catch them in the act, and Ted could stymy their attempts at insurance fraud.

'She might be starting to action her plan, though,' June was saying. 'First thing this morning, she went to see a probate solicitor in Richmond.'

Ted's synapses exchanged glances.

'A probate solicitor? That's the kind of lawyer you'd need if you were planning on proving your missing husband was dead.'

'Exactly,' June said. 'She was in there for about twenty minutes, and then she came out and went to a scrapbooking workshop. It's on for two hours, so it was safe for me to duck over here.'

Ted picked up a pen. 'Excellent as always, Aunty. What's the firm's name?'

'Robson and Robson, in McCoppin Street.'

Ted jotted it down. Cognisant of June's challenges with technology, she said, 'I'll look up their website and send you pics of the partners, so you'll know them if you see them with Cicely.'

'Rightio,' June said. With the subject having reached its natural conclusion, she pulled a cake tin out of her cooler bag. 'Now, while I'm here ... I baked some muffins last night.'

Ted felt a little flurry in her heart.

'Oh wow! Thanks, Aunty.' She joined June at the coffee table.

Aunty June opened the tin and Ted peered inside to see an array of chocolate chip, blueberry, and orange and poppy seed muffins. 'Three different kinds? You must have been baking up a storm.'

June smiled ruefully. 'To be honest, Cicely's inspired me.'

Ted wasn't surprised. Cicely would inspire anyone except someone like Ted, who was un-inspirable in baking terms.

'I get that. Thank you, they look yum.'

And they did. But in truth, Ted was finding it hard to stay focused on muffins or even Cicely Bunting right now.

'While you're here, can I ask for your help with something?' she asked.

'Of course.'

'Thanks, Aunty.'

Ted pulled up an extra chair at the desk, and they both sat.

'What can I do you for, love?'

Ted briefed June on Mitch's murder, and all the horrific events of the previous night. June looked alarmed, and her face lost its usual affable glow.

'I took photos before I called the cops,' Ted confided. It suddenly occurred to her that as a former homicide detective, June might not approve, so she rushed onwards before her mentor had a chance to comment. 'I know I wasn't supposed to, but I'm glad I did, the cops are barking up the wrong tree. I'd appreciate your expert opinion.'

She clicked back into the murder shots, but they'd barely appeared on the screen before June tilted the monitor away so she couldn't see.

'I'm sorry, Ted, I can't help you. I should get going.'

She was already using Ted's desk as ballast to climb to her feet. Ted was baffled. She stood too.

'I'm sorry, Aunty. I just thought … Are you okay?'

'I'm fine,' June said.

But Ted could tell she wasn't. She clicked out of the murder scene and back into her screensaver, a photo of Miss Marple at the beach.

Aunty June smiled fretfully. 'That's the way. Don't get involved with murder, love, you see the worst humanity has to offer. Why do you think I left homicide? It messes with your emotions in a bad way.'

Ted didn't know what to say. She'd always assumed June left homicide to spend more time with her grandkids, but maybe it wasn't that cut and dried? Had she also suffered from PTSD?

'I'm so sorry. I should have thought …'

'Don't be sorry. But when you're working a murder, you see things you can't un-see, and I don't want *you* living with that too,' June said. 'Promise me you'll stick with jobs that won't keep you awake at night.'

Ted nodded, even though she knew it was a promise she couldn't keep.

Aunty June took her hand. 'I just want what's best for you, love.'

'I know,' Ted said in a voice squeaky with emotion. 'Thank you.'

She impulsively put her arms around June, which was no small victory considering her life-long intimacy thing. She buried her head in Aunty June's ample bosom, and June soothingly stroked her back. Long seconds passed, and Ted realised she'd exceeded a reasonable timeframe for a simple thank-you hug. She pulled away, embarrassed. Aunty June acted like the needy embrace was completely normal, because she was June, and she was awesome. Ted walked her to the door and waved goodbye. Then she headed straight back to her desk. Aunty June's concern was genuinely touching, but she *had* to investigate this murder. And it seemed she'd have to do it alone.

She brought the photos back up and zoomed out so she could examine the living room at large. It was a relief not to be zeroed in on Mitch's bloodied body, although there was blood spatter over almost everything else.

Along with the half-eaten Hawaiian pizza on the floor, there was a can of Red Bull, a half-eaten chocolate bar and a take-away menu for celebrity chef Stelios Niarchos's Carlton restaurant, The Partheyum, on the coffee table. There were also several small rectangular strips of paper. Ted squinted at the scribbled text but she couldn't make it out. She opened GIMP and zoomed in on the strips of paper. They were horse-racing betting stubs issued by a bookmaker called Gail Pettigrove, and they were all handwritten, old-school style. Ted's eyes boggled as she read the amounts Mitch had wagered: $1000, $3000, $2500. Holy moly! Miss Marple stirred under the desk, and Ted looked down at her quizzically.

'How could a guy on a humble detective's salary afford to bet thousands and thousands of bucks?'

Miss Marple looked back at her as if to say, *He* couldn't *afford it.*

'Exactly.'

Ted frowned. Something about Mitch and money was ringing a bell ... And then she remembered Mitch shouting the entire Sons of Thor warband at the pub the other week. Spike had teased him about being flush lately, and he'd told Ted that Mitch usually opened his wallet so rarely that moths flew out. Ted made a mental note to ask Spike if he knew the source of Mitch's extra money, although several explanations had already occurred to her: proceeds from the sale of the family home when he and Fleur divorced, an inheritance, savings or, as unlikely as it seemed, a lottery win – it's not as if he would have advertised that.

She counted the betting stubs. There were seventeen in total, all issued by Gail Pettigrove Bookmaking. The most recent stub was dated just three days ago. If Mitch had won, he would have returned the stubs to Gail Pettigrove, so these were amounts he'd lost. She did a quick mental calculation. Forty grand! Could he really afford to lose that much?

Ted's brain kicked into overdrive. Was Mitch murdered because of an unpaid gambling debt? Maybe he'd had a line of credit with this bookie, but he couldn't pay up, so she'd hired a goon to do him in? Or maybe Gail had done him in herself?

Ted's mobile rang. She checked the screen. Giselle. Her heart leaped into her mouth, leaving a deathly vacancy in her chest. Had Giselle heard something? She pressed Accept.

'Giselle?'

But all Ted could hear was weeping.

'Giselle? What is it? Tell me.' She could hear herself barking at the poor woman.

'Giselle? Talk to me!'

'They found ... Spike's DNA ... at the murder scene ...' Giselle eventually managed between sobs.

Ted nodded darkly to herself. That wasn't good, but it was to be expected.

'That makes sense,' she reminded Giselle. 'Spike got a bloody nose when he had the fight with Mitch. Of course they'd find his DNA. But that doesn't mean—'

'Will you shut up and listen?' Giselle interjected. 'Spike's been charged with Mitch's murder.'

The floor rose up and swallowed Ted whole.

Chapter Twenty-Seven

Gail Pettigrove was older than Ted had expected, but Ted supposed she shouldn't have been surprised. Hadn't the gambling industry been subsumed by online behemoths? It was probably only the most old-school bookies who could still be found at the track, let alone writing their betting stubs by hand.

Ted had tracked Gail down to the Pakenham Racecourse in Melbourne's outer east. It was now 4 pm, and the weather still hadn't made up its mind. It was kind of warm, but sort of cold. The skies were clear except for the clouds, and Ted was still waiting for the rain that her Rain Monkey app had predicted for an hour ago.

Gail was about seventy, Ted surmised. She had a halo of thick blonde shoulder-length hair, a pretty, immaculately made-up face, and her red jersey dress shamelessly hugged the wobbliest parts of her figure. She projected the air of a woman who'd always been sexy and wasn't quite ready to let go of that yet.

Her eyes were scanning Ted up and down. Ted was glad she was wearing her tailored beige Jigsaw pantsuit with her flat streamlined ankle boots, and she had an old-school camera slung over her shoulder – borrowed from her brother Pip. She needed to look like the investigative journalist she'd claimed to be when she'd managed to catch Gail on the phone. Luckily, Gail had bought her spiel about doing a deep-dive profile piece for the *Herald-Sun* on legends of the race track. Ted had already taken lots of shots of Gail with the camera, and asked her questions about her life, her years in horse racing, and her celebrity clients like footballers and breakfast radio hosts. Now it was time to get down to brass tacks.

'If I could bring up something a bit more delicate,' Ted said, 'my sources tell me there were several of your betting stubs found in the home of Mitch Prowse, that detective who was murdered last night.'

Gail nodded with a sigh. 'Yeah, poor Mitch was one of our best clients,' she said in a soft, feminine trill. 'Wasn't he, darl?'

Gail's hulking, sinister-looking husband, Harry, nodded, although he seemed more interested in a group of horses that were doing their training paces around the track. He whooped and hollered as the horses galloped past with pounding hooves. Ted caught a glimpse of sweaty flanks, wild eyes and flared nostrils as they streaked by. She took a step back from the fence and felt glad she'd left Miss Marple snoozing in the grandstand. Gail pointed to a sleek black horse that was leading the pack.

'That's Mr Fantastic,' she said proudly. 'He's ours. We're training later than usual to simulate race day.'

Ted was surprised bookies were allowed to own racehorses, but she didn't feel enough interest to pursue the point. She wasn't a fan of horse racing for lots of reasons and, besides, all she could think about was Spike. His situation was growing direr with every minute. His arrest was still leading the hourly news bulletins. It sounded so bad, a police detective being charged with another detective's murder and taken into custody. It was juicy stuff for the media vultures, and headlines such as 'Killer

Cop!' were plastered all over the internet. Spike was bound to be convicted in the court of public opinion. At least they hadn't named him yet, but Ted didn't know how long his anonymity would last.

She'd tried to call him again but it had gone to voicemail, as she'd known it would. The cops would have confiscated his phone for sure. So then she'd rung the remand centre, but a Corrections woman had told her that she wasn't on the approved list of people allowed to speak to Spike. After a little prodding, the woman revealed that Spike had put her on his list, but Maven had taken her off. That'd be right! She wondered if the next time she spoke to Spike he'd be in jail officially serving a life sentence for Mitch's murder. The thought made her shudder.

'Anyway, back to Mitch,' she said to Gail. 'Did he have a line of credit with you?'

Gail nodded. 'Yeah. We don't give out credit very often, but Mitch was a good bloke, and he always came up with the money, until now.'

Gail and Harry exchanged an inscrutable look, and Ted wondered what lay behind it. She made a note in the notepad she'd brought as a prop.

'How much did he usually bet?'

'Oh, he was a keen punter. Up to about five thousand bucks a pop, wasn't it, darl?'

Harry said something Ted couldn't hear because the horses were galloping past again. Watching Harry watch the horses, she half wondered if he'd done in Mitch himself. But it was highly unlikely, he had to be seventy-five.

'He still owes us ten grand from last week,' Gail said after the horses had passed. 'Don't get me wrong, I feel for the poor bloke's family, but it irks me that we won't see that dough.'

Ted decided to throw the cat among the pigeons.

'How much does it irk you?'

She steeled herself for a walloping from Harry, but the corners of his mouth curled up, and Gail openly laughed.

'Not *that much*, darl! And, anyway, they cleaned things up after Tony Mokbel laundered his money at the track. Now it'd be too risky to even rough up anyone, let alone have them killed. Things aren't like they used to be.'

'You sound wistful about that,' Ted said recklessly.

'I suppose I am,' Gail said candidly. 'Just between us, me and Harry do miss the good old days. I'm not sure we'd ever hire a hitman, but we'd like to still have that option available to us.'

Gail's frankness was disarming, and Ted was starting to doubt her theory about Gail being behind Mitch's murder. It was a body blow. If not Gail Pettigrove, then who?

'Do you know where Mitch got all that money from?'

'It was none of our business, darl.'

'Sure, but you must have wondered. He was only on a detective's salary. Do you know if he had money from selling the family house when he got divorced?'

Gail shook her head. 'They didn't sell it because they didn't want to disrupt the kid. Mitch was always moaning about paying half of the mortgage *plus* the rent on his place in Collingwood.'

Ted nodded. She wasn't surprised. 'Savings?'

Gail laughed. 'Not a chance! The divorce cleaned him out.'

Ted nodded again. She felt like a bit of an idiot for pursuing this line, but she needed to rule out all the legitimate possibilities.

'An inheritance, maybe?'

Gail laughed harder, and now thuggish Harry was laughing too.

'The bloke was from the wrong side of the tracks,' Harry said. 'He'd be lucky if his family left him a pack of ciggies.'

Which confirmed Ted's suspicions. Excluding a lottery win, there was really only one explanation for Mitch having such large sums of money.

Gail raised her immaculately pencilled eyebrows and winked at Ted. 'He was in the financial crimes squad, darl. It doesn't take much imagination to work out where the dough came from.'

Ted nodded. No, it didn't. She tried to maintain her journo persona as she stepped it out in her mind. So, Mitch was not only stalking Giselle, but he was on the take. Had some financial crim been paying off Mitch to avoid prosecution and got sick of it and decided to do him in? Suddenly it seemed like the obvious answer.

She finished her 'interview' with Gail and Harry and headed off, promising them she'd let them know when the special feature was going to appear in the paper. She'd been wasting her time here, when the answer lay in Mitch taking bribes from a crook. But *which* crook? She had no leads. And without any leads, how could she hope to free Spike?

She strode back to her SUV, picking up Miss Marple from the grandstand en route and briefing her on the developments. In the car, she bounced some ideas around while Miss Marple listened intently. Ted mulled aloud over every aspect of the crime scene and the house. All roads seemed to lead to Mitch's wi-fi.

'We already know that Mitch's wi-fi was turned off at the time of the murder,' she mused to Miss Marple. 'What if he knew somebody else was coming? Someone he didn't want any record of?'

Miss Marple's ears went taut with interest.

'And what if that person was the crook who was paying him off?' Ted thought aloud. 'And what if it wasn't their first visit? What if they regularly visited to give Mitch the cash?'

Ted's body felt like an adrenaline factory as her theory reached its climax. 'That might mean the neighbour, Kip Trammel, saw the murderer on a previous visit!'

Miss Marple looked at her as if to say, *You are a gun PI*, and Ted's self-esteem was restored. Miss Marple's respect meant everything.

'Let's go talk to them,' Ted said.

She turned on Google Maps, and fifty-five minutes later, they arrived at Mitch's place. The crime-scene tape outside the house was fluttering forlornly in the breeze, but there was no sign of the cops because the case was closed. Ted snorted. Maven seemed determined to believe Spike was the murderer. He must *really* have a personal axe to grind.

Ted and Miss Marple went to Kip Trammel's house and rang the doorbell. They waited a minute or two, but there was total silence from inside. Damn! Maybe they weren't at home. But eventually the door opened, and Kip stood before Ted in a tracksuit, rubbing their eyes and yawning.

'Hi. Ted Bristol, remember? Sorry, did I wake you up?'

Kip nodded. They yawned so widely that Ted could see their tonsils.

'Yeah, you did. I'm nocturnal, I don't go to bed until 5 am.'

'Sorry,' Ted said again, but she didn't really mean it. Spike's whole life was at stake, so who cared if Kip Trammel missed a couple of hours sleep?

She saw Kip flash a brief glance at Miss Marple. Ted's dog usually attracted rapturous attention, but Kip had looked at Miss Marple in the same way Miss Marple looked at the rest of the world, with disinterest bordering on disdain. And was Ted imagining it, or did Miss Marple look slightly put-out?

'I'm pursuing my investigations into Mitch Prowse's murder,' she told Kip.

'But they've charged someone, haven't they? Wasn't it another cop?'

Ted shook her head. 'I'm of the belief they've got the wrong guy.'

Kip looked surprised. Ted knew she should give Kip some time to absorb this news, but she was too impatient to wait the requisite two seconds.

'I'm wondering if you've seen anyone visit Mitch regularly, or at least the same person turning up more than once?'

Kip shook their head. 'No. I told you, I kept away from the guy. I have no interest in the lives of toxically masculine cops. And if you had queer mates like mine who've been victimised by the police, you wouldn't either.'

Ted nodded respectfully. She could understand where Kip was coming from, but this was a setback. She supposed she could check with the other neighbours, but the house on the other side of Mitch was empty because of the gargantuan renovation, and the couple directly across the road were about a hundred years old, and seemed permanently glued to the TV in their apricot living room.

'They never learn,' Kip said.

For a second, Ted thought Kip was talking about the elderly couple, but then she realised they were talking about the cops.

'They came a couple of hours ago. I asked them why the crime-scene tape's still here, and they said it'll stay in place until the crime-scene cleaners come at 7 am on the day after tomorrow. They wanted me to "keep an eye out" for the murder weapon.' They curled their lip disdainfully. 'Which I assume means they want me to do their job for them.'

Ted felt a little ray of hope. So the cops hadn't found the knife yet; maybe she could still find it first. She darted a glance at Miss Marple, and Miss Marple looked back at her as if to say, *We can do this!*

'What did the cops say, exactly?' Ted asked Kip.

'They said the autopsy had revealed what the murder weapon was, but it was still missing. And they said if they found it and matched the prints to the cop they'd charged, it would make an even stronger case.' They rolled their eyes derisively. 'They even gave me a photo.'

'A photo?' Ted said, her heart suddenly pounding in her ears. 'Can I see it?'

Kip shrugged. 'Sure. It's on my phone.'

Kip stepped back to let Ted into the house. Ted and Miss Marple followed them down a narrow hall, past a large banner with horizontal stripes in yellow, white, purple and black hanging on the wall. Ted recognised it as the non-binary flag. Kip led them to a messy living room, where a desk was piled high with academic texts and papers. They picked up a phone off the desk, and Ted held her breath. Kip flicked through a few photos.

'This is it, they said it's a boning knife.'

'A boning knife?'

Kip nodded.

Ted felt sick. She looked at the picture Kip was holding out on their phone. It was a scary-looking knife about 28 centimetres long, with a white handle and a narrow, curved blade that looked like it matched the stabbing and slashing injuries on Mitch's body.

'The cops said it's a Barbosa boning knife. High carbon, made in Brazil.'

Kip had been playing tough, but Ted could see they were shaken by the horror of this knife being used to slaughter a human being.

'I'm no fan of cops, but I wouldn't wish this on anyone,' they said.

Ted nodded gravely. 'Me neither. Can you send that to me?' She gave Kip her number. Kip forwarded the pic to her, and Ted heard it land on her phone with a chirp. 'Thanks. I'm going to make it my business to find that knife.'

Kip nodded, but they didn't seem to find Ted's quest compelling.

'Why do you think they've got the wrong guy?'

'I know the guy they've charged,' Ted said, 'and you can take it from me, he's no murderer.' She considered Kip for a moment and decided she could trust them. Their relative indifference to Mitch's murder made it highly unlikely they'd repeat anything. 'I think it was someone who was paying Mitch to keep quiet and they got sick of it. Mitch was in the financial crimes squad, and it seems like he was on the take.'

Kip snorted in a manner that reminded Ted of herself.

'That'd be right,' they said.

By the time Ted and Miss Marple left Kip's place and Ted had slipped under the crime-scene tape to conduct another fruitless search for the knife, it was almost 6.30 pm. There wasn't much point going back to EBI so, instead, Ted took Miss Marple for a riverside walk at Yarra Bend. She googled 'Barbosa boning' knife from a picnic bench while Miss Marple sniffed at the base of a River Red Gum. Google didn't offer up any clues about the knife, just that it was sold at catering and kitchen supplies stores, and that it was very effective for butchering animal carcasses. Ted's blood ran cold. *And for butchering Mitch.*

They headed home and up to Ted's apartment. Ted grabbed a beer from the fridge and contemplated the chutneys Cicely Bunting had given her. They now seemed like props used in an elaborate ruse to suck her in, and she wanted to chuck them off her balcony. Should she put them in the bin? But wasting food wasn't on, even in circumstances like these – she'd donate them to Food Bank. She gave Miss Marple her dinner and ordered a burger from Uber Eats. As she ate her burger on her fold-up chair, she updated her apps and then clicked onto Google Analytics to check the traffic on her site. Three hundred and fifty-seven hits today. She wrote a quick Facebook post about cyber-safety and then tried to watch some TV, but she couldn't concentrate so she went to bed.

As she lay staring out at the cityscape, stark against the dark sky, her heart was beating so loudly that it drowned out Miss Marple's fluttery snores. She grabbed her phone and tried to follow a guided meditation that Bob had sent her, but the narrator's voice was so warm and mellow that it grated on her nerves and she was now wide awake. Who was she kidding? All she could think about was Spike sitting alone in a jail cell while the person who'd brutally murdered Mitch with that boning knife was free as a bird out there somewhere. She yawned. She knew in her gut that whoever had been bribing Mitch had also murdered him …

And Spike clearly agreed. He was staring at Ted entreatingly, his huge palms flat against the dirty glass that separated them.

'If you find out who was bribing Mitch, you'll find the real killer.'

'I'll find out.'

Ted noticed holes in Spike's faded orange jumpsuit, and his eyes were two brown saucers of terror beneath the mop of unruly curls stuffed under his horned Viking helmet.

'You have to save me, Ted. Please!'

'I will,' Ted said urgently, her small palms pressed against the dirty glass to meet his. 'I promise.' Their eyes locked, and she felt a flash of fear: *But how would she save him?* 'I just need a bit more time to investigate.'

'But there is no time,' Spike said. 'I'm being executed tomorrow!'

It was as if someone had kicked Ted in the guts and she'd been sent flying across the room.

'Tomorrow?!'

'Yes, tomorrow.' Spike's big eyes were filling with fearful tears. 'They're giving me a lethal injection at 9 am, and then they're hanging me from the electric chair.'

'No!' Ted cried. 'No, they can't!'

Woof woof!

Ted heard a dog behind her. She hadn't realised dogs were allowed to visit prisoners. But dogs were the least of her worries now.

'I'm having my last meal at 8 am,' Spike was saying. 'I've requested a rib-eye steak excised from a cow by a Barbosa boning knife.'

'No!' Ted cried. 'You can't let them put you to death!'

Woof woof!

'I can't stop them!' Spike said. 'My life is in your hands!'

'No-o-o-o-o-o!'

Woof woof!

The dog was getting louder.

Ted woke with a start to find Miss Marple jumping up and down beside the bed. She must have been crying out in distress in her sleep. It had all been a dream, thank God! She leaned down from the bed to pat Miss Marple.

'Thanks Miss Marple,' she said, still shaken. 'I'm okay, I'm okay …'

But Miss Marple didn't look convinced, and why would she? They both knew Ted wouldn't be okay, far from it, until she'd cleared Spike of Mitch's murder.

The distressing dream was already splintering into fragments, but she was left with a feeling of unbearable pain at the thought of Spike being confined behind bars for decades, and not being able to be near him. She stared up at the low beige ceiling. It seemed like there was more going on for her than outrage at an injustice. As if she hadn't known that already.

Chapter Twenty-Eight

Ted leaned on her desk and put her head in her hands, her frustration now flirting with despair. She'd barely slept a wink last night, and today the pressure to solve Mitch's murder had escalated with every minute. She knew she needed to identify the fraudster he'd been blackmailing, or *fraudsters* as the case might be. But it was a big ask. The very fact that Mitch was blackmailing this person or people meant they were flying under the radar and wouldn't be found in any financial crimes squad records. Not that she could ever get hold of those records, anyway. It presented an extraordinarily high degree of difficulty, and Ted couldn't deny that her usual confidence (or cockiness, depending on who you asked) had deserted her.

As a first step, she'd done a deep dive online into media articles and social media posts and the shared online forums that had already started popping up about Mitch's death at Spike's hands. You never knew when a common link might emerge, or a piece of random commentary could prove to be just the clue you needed. But after a few hours going down the rabbit hole, Ted had failed to find any potential clues about who Mitch might have been blackmailing. There was nothing of value there, just a lot of conspiracy theorists pontificating about Spike, and how Victoria Police had gone down the gurgler.

She heard a bark from Wags Away that she vaguely registered as belonging to Miss Marple, but she didn't have the mental space to react. She felt hopeless. What if she *couldn't* find out who'd been bribing Mitch? What if she let Spike down? And, in an even harder blow to the heart, what if his little girls lost their daddy to a life in jail because Ted couldn't solve the crime? She could feel her pulse racing. This wasn't just pressing her buttons, it was hitting them as hard as if it were a game of Whack-A-Mole.

Her phone chirped with a message, and she checked the screen. It was another text from that Jarrod bloody Beasley.

Hey lovely. Your silence tells me you fear your feelings for me.

Ted snorted. Yeah, she feared she might punch him in the nose. Her phone chirped again.

Face your fear with light, I won't bite! x

The guy was unbelievable. She needed to text back and tell him she wasn't into it. She picked up her phone, but it trilled with a call. Ted glanced at her screen. Aunty June O'Shea. She forced her brain back to Cicely Bunting. Had something happened? She hit Accept.

'Aunty, hey. How's everything going?'

'Not bad, love. Nothing to report on Cicely, I'm afraid.'

'Dammit. Well, thanks for keeping me posted anyway—'

'Wait, that's not why I was calling,' June said. 'I wanted to check you're not working that murder.'

'No, no, I'm not,' Ted lied. 'I'm just doing a couple of corporate due-diligence jobs.'

She heard June sigh with relief. 'That's good. Stick with those kinds of cases, eh, love? I've been so worried about you going down the dark murder path. I know how stressful it must have been when you stumbled onto that murder scene, but at least they've caught the bloke now, eh? So you can forget all about it.'

If only, Ted thought. She was so touched by June's concern she almost wanted to blather out everything. Not that she had anything to blather, her investigations had been spectacularly unsuccessful so far. But she comforted herself that they were just beginning. Ted Bristol PI did *not* surrender.

'Yeah, I can forget all about the murder,' she said. She felt lousy for lying to June, and part of her couldn't help wondering what June thought about a fellow homicide cop being charged with another cop's murder? 'But I was surprised the murderer was a homicide cop like Spike Tereiti,' she added as casually as she could manage. 'You met him at my place, remember?'

'Yeah, I remember.' June sighed. 'I'm afraid cops *can* go bad sometimes. This kind of thing makes me sick in the guts, he seemed like a good fella. I suppose that's why he's got a bail hearing.'

Ted's heart skipped a beat.

'A bail hearing?'

'Yeah. I bought a coffee in North Fitzroy and ran into an old colleague. He said Spike Tereiti's lawyers have managed to get him a special bail hearing here at the Supreme Court.'

Ted was astonished. Bail was usually automatically denied in murder cases, so Spike's lawyers must have pulled some serious strings. Which meant there was a strong chance he'd be released on bail and they could solve Mitch's murder together! Her heart was already gambolling in a field of flowers, but she feigned ambivalence for June's sake.

'Oh yeah?' she said. 'When's that on?'

'Two o'clock, apparently.'

'Two o'clock today?'

'Yeah.'

Ted's eyes shot to her watch. It was 1.07 pm, she had time to get there – just! She quickly ended the call and grabbed her keys, but when she raced outside, she almost collided with a doleful Cody Venables. The poor kid looked like a puppy who'd been busted cocking his leg on the carpet.

'Cody?'

'Hi Ted,' he said disconsolately. 'I came to say sorry for stuffing up twice.' I'm spewing about talking to Cicely Bunting.

'It's okay,' Ted reassured him. 'Don't beat yourself up, these things happen.'

'But I'm bummed about letting you down.'

'You don't have to be, really.' Ted tried to gently push past him. 'It's nice of you to drop in, but I'm on my way out—'

'Wait, I want you to have something.' Cody reached into his backpack. 'I went to an investigation conference in Bendigo last month and I got these custom-made, they're sick.'

He pulled out a pair of thick Coke-bottle eyeglasses. Ted tried but failed to see a context.

'They look like glasses, but they're really binoculars!'

Binoculars? Some shonk had seen the poor kid coming. These were just fancy-dress glasses you'd wear to a party, but Ted was too preoccupied with Spike's bail hearing to point that out. Besides, Cody was trying to make amends, she should at least meet him halfway. She smiled gratefully.

'Thanks, Cody, they're awesome.' She tossed them into her backpack and made a mental note to give them to her niece Kelsey for her dress-up box. 'Great to see you, but I've got to go.'

She jumped into her SUV and wove in and out of torturously slow traffic into the CBD, parking in some godforsaken concrete bunker in Lonsdale Street that would probably cost her $50 an hour, but she'd have to worry about that later. She was glad she was wearing one of her pantsuits as she streaked up the street towards the Supreme Court, making it through the metal detector at 1.55 pm.

Ten minutes later, she was sitting in the hushed viewer's gallery above an ornate timber-panelled nineteenth-century courtroom in the Supreme Court of Victoria. Spike's bail proceedings were underway, and the air was heavy with gravitas. Spike was down in the dock and hadn't seen her in the gallery, which ran above and along the side of the courtroom. There were two defence barristers representing Spike, and two acting on behalf of the Crown, and a Supreme Court judge in a wig and red robes who was hearing the application.

The courtroom was packed with media. A cop-upon-cop killing was juicy news, and none of the vultures seemed to suspect or care that the wrong man might have been arrested. Giselle was sitting in the row behind Spike, next to an elegant elderly woman with long grey hair pulled up in a bun and a proud-looking Māori man, who Ted could only assume were Spike's parents. Her heart went out to them. Maven and Finelli were sitting behind the prosecution. Ted could have sworn she could smell Maven's aftershave from up here.

She studied Spike in the dock. It was such a relief to see him and know that he was okay, physically anyway. It was less than forty-eight hours since she'd been at his place on Tuesday night, but it felt like forever since they'd spoken. He was standing erect with a quiet dignity. Ted felt proud of him, even though she supposed she had no claim to. He was holding himself like the innocent man he was.

The barrister for the prosecution, Glenn Bull KC, opposed

bail on the grounds of Spike being a flight risk. Ted almost snorted aloud. But when Glenn Bull told the judge about Mitch stalking Giselle, and how Detective Tereiti had believed his children were in danger, which went to motive, and how his DNA had been found on the deceased, she felt sick. It sounded damning.

But then it was the defence's turn, and her spirits were raised. Spike's barrister, Marianne Cummings KC, argued brilliantly in favour of bail, on the grounds that Spike was innocent. He also had a stable address and strong ties to the area and was of otherwise outstanding character. And his divorced parents were prepared to pool their resources and put up the surety.

To Ted's ears it was a slam dunk, and she found herself zinging with anticipation. *Thank God!* Bail was inevitable, and in twenty minutes she'd be talking to Spike in the flesh, and they could start sorting out this crime together. And then? Well, once they'd nailed Mitch's murderer, who knew? Ted's legs suddenly felt weak even though she was sitting. She held her breath as the judge started delivering her response to the application. To Ted's horror, the judge said the arguments for bail had not convinced her in view of the seriousness of the crime. So, she was denying bail and remanding Senior Detective Tereiti until his committal hearing in the District Court in four months' time.

Four months?! The news hit Ted like a body blow, and there was an audible intake of breath from Giselle and Spike's parents. Ted saw Maven smirk at Finelli. Spike's shoulders briefly slumped before he turned to reassure his parents and stood proudly upright again. Two cops were already taking his arms to lead him out of the courtroom. He'd be gone within seconds and Ted still wouldn't be allowed to talk to him.

She impulsively jumped to her feet.

'For Odin!'

The Viking battle cry that Spike used on the Swordcraft field cut through the hushed air like a torpedo. Spike pivoted, and his eyes flew up in Ted's direction.

'I'll find the real murderer!' she yelled down to him.

'No, don't!' Spike called up to her, ignoring the cops shoving at him. 'I don't want you getting hurt!'

It must have been only a second before the judge was telling Ted to be quiet, and everyone else was in uproar, and Spike was shoved out of the courtroom. But that millisecond seemed to last an hour, and in that hour, there was only Ted and Spike in the world.

Oh my God, she thought, *I'm in love with him!*

The realisation hit her like a train, but there was no time for contemplation because Giselle was staring up at her with a 'What the hell?' expression, Maven was sneering at her contemptuously, and the Supreme Court security guards looked as if they were itching to get their mitts on her. As everyone stood while the judge exited, Ted took the chance to flee. She hurried out of the viewing gallery, into the corridor, and ran down the stairs and out onto William Street.

Trams rattled past, car horns beeped, and barristers and corporate types rushed past her as peak hour rapidly approached. Ted stopped at the bottom of the Supreme Court's stairs, trying to process her realisation. She was in love with Spike! Yikes. What did it mean? It meant a world of pain if she couldn't prove his innocence. And how could she? He'd just been charged with murder and remanded in custody, and she couldn't even speak to him – Maven had made sure of that. The DNA evidence was damning, and Maven seemed fixated on convicting him. And she had no leads – none! As she stood paralysed in a swirling sea of humankind, she could feel herself sinking to rock bottom.

'Ted!'

She turned and saw Aunty June hurrying down the Supreme Court steps, although hurrying was a relative term for Aunty June, because of her dicky knees. Ted blinked as she tried to drag herself back from the abyss. What was Aunty June doing here?

'Aunty?'

'Ted ... Cicely's ... been here ... with her lawyer,' Aunty June puffed. 'I recognised the lawyer ... from the pictures you sent. They just lodged ... some papers for a ... grant of representation.'

Ted could feel her insides screeching as she struggled to switch gears.

'Ted? Are you listening?'

Ted forced herself to regroup. What were the odds of her two major cases converging in the Supreme Court of Victoria on the same afternoon?

'Yes. Yes, sorry, I'm listening. What's a grant of representation?'

'I did some snooping,' Aunty June said. 'Apparently, if you provide the court with an affidavit with evidence that a missing person is dead, and the court accepts that evidence, then they issue you with a grant of representation that allows you to get probate underway *and* claim on the deceased person's life insurance.'

It was exactly what Ted had predicted, but, regardless, little rockets of rage exploded in her chest like fireworks.

'So, Cicely's going through with it,' she said grimly.

'Yeah. And from what I can gather, the court will be kindly disposed to the suicide note.'

'A *fake* suicide note that she set *me* up to find,' Ted fumed. 'Playing me for a fool! I tell you what – we know Duncan's alive, but when I get my hands on Cicely, *she* won't be.'

June reached out and squeezed her arm supportively.

'She must think I'm an *idiot*,' Ted raged on. 'This is so brazen! How does she know I haven't already worked it out and gone to the cops?'

'She strikes me as one of those manipulative types who can read people,' Aunty June said astutely. 'She probably sensed you're no fan of the cops and you're, well, you know, a bit competitive with them.'

Ted resented being so easy to read.

'She thinks she's way smarter than everyone else,' June added.

'She's not smarter than *me*.'

'Of course not,' Aunty June said soothingly. 'So, what are you going to do, love?'

At this point, Ted had no idea.

'I've got a few ideas,' she lied. 'Did you find out how long it takes the court to assess the evidence and issue a grant of representation?'

'It's hard to say, apparently. It can take a few weeks, or sometimes just a few days.'

A few days?! The clock had started ticking a lot faster. It was imperative that Ted find a way to prove insurance fraud before that certificate could be issued. But how? There was no point showing the court the photo of Cicely and Duncan at the merry-go-around – it wasn't conclusive proof because Duncan's face was partly obscured by his straw hat. Which was no doubt exactly what he'd intended. Ted tried to quell a flash of panic.

'I can't let Cicely get her hands on that money.'

'You won't, love,' June said encouragingly. 'If anyone can stop her, it's you.'

Ted wished she could share her confidence.

'I should get going,' Aunty June said. 'I've got to pick up Kyra's oldest from kindy.'

'Of course. Excellent work as always! I'll take it from here, Aunty. Thank you.'

Aunty June gave her a quick hug, and Ted resisted the urge to wrap her legs around her and cling to her like a baby monkey.

'Don't forget to send me an invoice,' she called as Aunty June headed off. 'Get Kyra to help you!'

Aunty June waved, but Ted's eye was caught by a prison van emerging from the rear of the Supreme Court. Was Spike inside? Absurdly, she wanted to run after the van down Lonsdale Street, but she settled for a wave. Was Spike waving back behind those bars? And was it the last time they'd ever wave at each other? Hopelessness descended again. If Spike was convicted in four months' time, would the trauma impact on his little girls forever, creating unhealthy ripples through their lives that might take decades to understand and unravel, like her mother's death had with hers? If she couldn't find out the truth, this wouldn't just be the biggest failure of her career, it would be the biggest failure of her *life*.

Chapter Twenty-Nine

Bob

Bob winced as the ear-splitting clang of a jackhammer started up at the end of the street.

'I just popped over to invite you to Blooming Beautiful's relaunch!' she shouted, but the jackhammer abruptly stopped, and she found herself screaming into the silence.

Chantal laughed. 'That thing drives me crazy. I'm sure it's damaged my eardrums. Did you say your relaunch party?'

'Yes, it's Sunday at 1 pm,' Bob said. 'If you're free?'

'I wouldn't miss it! Thanks, Bob. I'd love to come.'

They shared a smile, and Bob was surprised by a flash of wistfulness. This elegant woman in the restrained navy dress couldn't look more different to the free-wheeling medium who'd sensed the spirits of Bob's miscarried babies, and in some inexplicable way, returned them to her. But since Chantal had chosen to turn her back on that part of herself, all Bob could do was wish her happiness in her new incarnation.

'I'm in between clients,' Chantal said, stepping back from the door. 'Would you like to come in?'

Bob shook her head. 'Thanks, but I have to get back to the shop. And I'm waiting for Teddy.'

As if on cue, Teddy's SUV rounded the corner.

'Speak of the devil. So, I'll see you on Sunday?'

'You will!'

Bob waved goodbye and went to meet Teddy as she pulled up outside EBI and alighted.

'Teddy, hi!'

'Bob ...'

One look at Teddy's wan, preoccupied demeanour told Bob something was terribly wrong.

'Are you okay?'

'Yeah, I'm fine.'

But Bob didn't believe that for a second. Teddy's face was drawn, and her beautiful green eyes looked haunted. She was projecting an incredibly un-Teddy-like air of ... what was that? Hopelessness?

'You're not fine. What's wrong?' she pressed.

'Nothing, I'm good. Why are you here?'

She sounded as if she was asking because she was expected to ask, not because she had any interest in the answer. Bob's reason for dropping in suddenly felt frivolous compared to whatever was bothering Teddy.

'It wasn't important. I was just at Bunnings in Victoria Parade, so I thought I'd drop in and ask if you want to have dinner with me and Raj tomorrow night. It'd be a good opportunity for you two to smooth things over and get to know each other.'

Teddy gave a vague nod that Bob wasn't sure how to translate.

'Teddy?'

And then, out of nowhere, Teddy burst into tears. Bob was so confounded she took a moment to cotton on.

'Teddy? Teddy, darling, what's wrong?' She wrapped her arms around her sister. It always broke her heart to see Teddy in distress, especially when, like now, she had no idea of the cause. 'Don't cry,' she said pointlessly. 'You don't have to come to dinner with us.'

'It's not that,' Teddy said in a small teary voice as she, typically, pulled out of the hug. At least she was behaving like herself in that respect. 'Of course I'll come. But I should never have put Raj under surveillance. It was none of my business.'

'Hey, it's okay ... I know you were only trying to help.'

'But I didn't help, I made things worse.' Teddy sniffled. 'What good am I to anyone if I'm wasting resources on things that don't need solving, and I don't have a clue how to solve the things that *do*?'

Bob was at sea. Was this really her feisty sister talking?

'What's wrong? Talk to me.'

'I'm just stressed about work,' Teddy said unconvincingly.

'It sounds like more than work to me.'

Teddy gave a plaintive little shrug.

'It's a major case. A detective was murdered.'

A penny dropped for Bob.

'Oh, I heard about that. The financial crimes detective? But I thought they'd charged another—'

'They have, but he didn't do it!' Teddy screeched. 'He's not the killer!'

Bob reeled back, rattled. 'How do you know?'

'I just know!' Teddy's passion had the force of a punch. 'And when I think of him rotting in jail for a murder he didn't commit ...' Her voice started breaking. 'He's innocent, Bob. He'd never hurt anyone.'

Bob was astonished and appalled all at once.

'Oh my God ... You *like* this guy.'

Suddenly Teddy seemed lost for words. Bob's hand flew back to her chest.

'I'm so thrilled you've finally opened your heart to someone, but does it have to be someone charged with murder?'

'But I told you, he didn't do it.'

Teddy was fighting back tears again.

'He's a big smart-arse idiot, but he's the best guy I've ever met, and I'd trust all of our lives in his hands.'

Tears sprang into Bob's eyes too. 'Oh, Teddy. Who is he? Do I know him?'

'You know *of* him. It's Spike, from Swordcraft.'

'Spike? Your frenemy?'

'Yeah.'

'Oh ... I thought you just enjoyed insulting each other. I didn't realise ...'

'Neither did I,' Teddy said, her voice wobbling.

Bob looked down at her sister's dear, beautiful face and saw a vulnerability that Teddy would never have allowed herself even as recently as a few weeks ago. She found herself transfixed.

'Stop looking at me like that,' Teddy said.

She stabbed at her eyes, and Bob could tell it was all too much for her.

'Hey, guess what?' Teddy said, abruptly changing the subject. 'Just like I predicted – Cicely's been to the Supreme Court with her lawyer and made a request for Duncan to be declared legally dead.'

It took Bob a beat to catch up, and when she did, she felt betrayed all over again. 'Oh ... I was hoping you might be wrong.'

Teddy threw her hands in the air. 'Stop giving her the benefit of the doubt, the woman's a sociopath!' She was beetroot-red with rage. 'I won't let her get away with it.'

'What are you going to do?'

'I don't have a clue.' But in an instant, her face lit up. 'Oh my God, I've just thought of something!'

'You have? Good for you, Teddy.'

'But I'll need your help.'

'Mine? How?'

'I need to get my hands on Cicely's phone and find evidence she's been talking to Duncan,' Teddy said, firing on all cylinders again. 'I'm thinking you can lure her to Blooming Beautiful to discuss how you're going to display her stuff. I'll wait out in the courtyard, and you can pinch her phone and bring it out to me.'

It sounded like a terrifying plan to Bob.

'You want me to steal Cicely's phone without her noticing?'

'Yeah,' Teddy said as matter-of-factly as if she'd asked Bob to open a jar of Vegemite. 'I'd do it myself, but I can't be in the shop because of my hayfever.'

Bob panicked. This might be all in a day's work for a private investigator, but how could *she*, a mere sustainable florist who couldn't dissemble at the best of times, possibly pull it off? But she couldn't risk sending her little sister into another downward spiral.

'Okay,' she said, aping Teddy's bravado. 'I'll do it.'

Chapter Thirty

Ted

Ted was taken aback to find Raj at Blooming Beautiful the next morning, but apparently Bob had sounded so nervous about Ted's plan the night before, that he'd dropped in to bolster her confidence. Ted was grateful that Raj had her sister's back, and she realised his presence was a positive. It was the first time their paths had crossed IRL since The Debacle, and this meant she wouldn't have to wait until dinner to apologise to him in person.

'I'm so sorry about everything, Raj,' she said. 'Ah-choo! I had no right to put you under surveillance. Ah-choo! Ah-choo!'

Raj smiled graciously. 'Gesundheit. That's okay, I just wish I could have made it more interesting for the poor bloke. I'm surprised he didn't die of boredom.'

Ted and Bob laughed, and then Ted's laugh morphed into a snort, followed by another series of sneezes.

'Ah-choo! Ah-choo! Ah-choo!'

'For heaven's sake, Teddy,' Bob said fondly, 'get out of here!'

They all adjourned to the courtyard, but they hovered near the back door, because Cicely was due at any minute. Ted wished Raj had chosen a better time to turn up. She wasn't sure how, or *if*, he should be incorporated into the operation.

'Well, thank you for being so gracious about everything, Raj,' she said.

Raj's compact face flushed. 'I think it's wonderful that Bob has someone in her life who cares so much. Not that I'm surprised. Who wouldn't care about her?'

'Oh, Raj ... you're so sweet.' Bob slipped her arm around Raj and rested her head on top of his, probably because she couldn't reach all the way down to his shoulder.

Watching on, Ted felt shame ambush her again. Anyone with half a brain could see that Raj was besotted with Bob, so why had *she* chosen not to see it? As a PI she was supposed to be a dispassionate observer, but she'd jumped to negative conclusions about Raj in the same way she'd jumped to negative conclusions about Jarrod Beasley being Giselle's stalker. Sure, Jarrod's positivity was verging on toxic, and his text messages were super annoying, but that didn't make the guy a stalker. And unlike Jarrod, Raj had never seemed anything but nice.

Bob's eyes met hers over Raj's head and she mouthed the words, 'Thank you.' Ted's heart shone like a lava lamp. As long as Bob was happy with her, she could focus on the present moment and put Spike's plight on hold for a minute. And she had to admit she was feeling amped about getting her hands on Cicely's phone. This was like something from a spy movie: a sting, a caper, a covert operation.

'I've been thinking,' Raj said, disturbing her reverie. 'Why don't I help when Cicely comes? I could distract her in the shop while Bob steals her phone.'

'That'd be fantastic,' Bob said eagerly, looking to Ted for approval.

Ted considered Raj. She was impressed by his initiative,

but undercover work was tricky. Would he be up to it? They couldn't afford to arouse Cicely's suspicions.

Raj seemed to sense her hesitation. 'I've acted before. I just played Willy Loman in *Death of a Salesman*. And not to blow my own horn, but the *Maribyrnong* and *Hobsons Bay Star Weekly* said I was excellent.'

'They did,' Bob confirmed. 'He showed me the review.'

Ted admired Raj's desire to help and, more importantly, she realised this covert operation presented the perfect opportunity to prove to Bob that she trusted him.

'All right, we're on! Thanks, guys.'

Raj and Bob exchanged excited smiles, although Bob's was still tempered by fear.

'You'll be fantastic,' Ted told her, inwardly crossing her fingers. 'And don't forget I'll need her passcode. Before you nick her phone, you'll have to get her to google something, so you can watch and see what her passcode is.'

Bob paled with panic. 'Get her passcode? I can't do that.'

'Of course you can.'

'But how?' Bob squeaked.

'You've got this, babe,' Raj said supportively. 'I'll be right here beside you.'

Bob looked at him gratefully, and their eyes fused. Ted could see her sister drawing strength from Raj, and she knew without a shadow of a doubt that this was the Real Thing. Which made Raj the luckiest man in the world, in her opinion, although she had to admit Bob was starting to look pretty lucky too. But her romantic ruminations were cut short when she spotted Cicely approaching the shop.

'Here she is.'

Bob and Raj leaped to attention, and Raj whispered, 'Action!' They hurried back into the shop and Ted hid behind the back door. She peeked around it to watch as Bob and Raj greeted Cicely, and they all wandered through the archway into the former Sew Darn Crafty. Luckily, they were still in Ted's sightline.

Cicely produced some jars of cumquat jam, and Raj engaged her in conversation about the correct soil for growing cumquats. He was very convincing, and Ted felt relieved that he *could* actually act. Cicely chatted away about moist, loamy soil with a pH between 5.5 and 6.5 and, once again, Ted found herself in awe of her gall. It was as if Cicely assumed her many talents would protect her from anyone guessing the truth. And let's face it, they almost had.

Bob sounded stilted at first, but she soon relaxed in Raj's reassuring presence. They all inspected the display cabinet, now arrayed with Cicely's raffia napery, home-made candles and fluffy knitted scarves and such. Cicely said that if Bob wouldn't mind, she thought the Cheviot Beach tapestry would look better hanging where her old counter had been, and she'd prefer that her scarves were displayed in folds rather than rolls, and she wondered if the cabinet should be flush against the opposite wall, on top of the mid-century modern-style rug? She said the sun hit that wall from the most flattering angle in the store, which was why she'd hung her prized quilt there, until she'd had to remove it because of the biro mark.

Ted felt a grudging respect for Cicely's perfectionism. She might be a lousy, duplicitous, traitorous fraudster, but she was passionate about her craft and refused to cut corners. It was the same way Ted tried to operate in her career.

'Of course, whatever you think,' Bob acquiesced with typical generosity. 'But it doesn't bother you that if the cabinet's right on top of your beautiful rug, we'll only see half of it?'

'No, I think that's fine,' Cicely said. 'Otherwise it could be a tripping hazard.'

As Bob, Raj and Cicely moved the rug to the opposite wall and positioned the cabinet on top of it, talk inevitably turned to Duncan. Ted thought Cicely might shut down the subject, but she was obviously so secure in the knowledge that she'd got away with it that she played the stoic victim for Raj. Ted made a mental note to nominate her for an Academy Award when this was all over.

Then, Cicely gave Bob and Raj the first piece of information that Ted didn't already know – unless you counted the correct soil for growing cumquats.

'I'm off to the Barossa Valley tomorrow for a one-day intensive quilting workshop,' she said. 'But don't worry, I'll be back in time for your relaunch party on Sunday, Bob. I wouldn't miss it for the world.'

Ted's antenna twitched. The Barossa! Was that where Duncan was hiding? And was 'intensive quilting workshop' code for 'intensive romantic reunion'?

'That sounds wonderful,' Bob said. 'Quilting's so meditative. I'd love to see the website for the workshop.'

Ted knew this was a ploy to get Cicely's passcode, but she worried that Bob might have overplayed her hand – the quilting workshop probably didn't exist. But Cicely blithely unlocked her phone and showed Bob a Barossa quilting site. Once again, Ted was impressed. The woman thought of everything. But then Cicely slipped her phone back into her bag. Dammit!

In a master stroke, Raj asked Cicely if she'd hold her Cheviot Beach tapestry straight while he fixed it to the wall. With Cicely thus occupied, Bob urgently rifled through Cicely's bag and swiftly retrieved her phone. She raced to the back door, her face crimson with excitement.

'Here! Her password is 3362. I can't believe I've remembered it, thank goodness for Lumosity.'

'3362 – thanks, Bob! You're a star.'

'Be quick!'

Bob disappeared back into the shop. Ted quickly unlocked Cicely's phone and went to her recent calls list. She was disappointed to see a variety of different numbers, and none that recurred more than once every couple of months. But as she clicked out of the list, she saw that Cicely had downloaded the Signal app. Of course! Cicely and Duncan must be communicating via Signal, so their calls couldn't be traced. Ted opened the app and saw a number that had been called repeatedly since 24 October last year, the day after Duncan faked his disappearance, and best of all it had been called just last night! Ted punched in the number. After a couple of seconds, a male voice answered.

'Sissy?'

Sissy! *Ha, the ghost who walks,* Ted thought. She knew she needed to keep Duncan on the line for at least a couple of minutes.

'No, it's Bethany from Signal here. How ya doin'?'

'What? Signal?'

Duncan's voice sounded vaguely familiar, no doubt because she'd heard it a few years ago on his self-aggrandising ads for Body Potential. She heard a clock chime in the background, and the vaguest hint of a cheesy old song. Britney Spears?

'We're just wondering if you're happy with the app,' she said, trying to be as annoying as possible for authenticity purposes.

'We'd love your feedback, and you stand to win a new iPhone. Is there anything you think we can do to improve?'

'But this doesn't make sense,' Duncan said. 'This call came through from, er, a friend's number.'

Got him!

'Did it? Omigod,' Ted said. 'That's one of the gremlins we're trying to improve, we've been getting a lot of reports of that lately. Is there anything else we could improve on?'

'I don't have time for this. Call someone else.'

Duncan hung up in her ear. Ted would have liked the call to last longer, but she wasn't too worried. She was pretty sure she'd recorded enough of his voice to action the next part of her plan.

Chapter Thirty-One

Ted stepped onto the front porch of a 1950s bungalow in a quiet cul-de-sac in the northern suburb of Reservoir. She rang the doorbell and then pulled out a tissue, brushing a cobweb from a small sign that read: 'The Forensic Science Laboratory. We Work Miracles.'

The cobweb was regrettable, but luckily Ted already knew the claim about miracles was true. After a few seconds, the door opened to reveal a bespectacled guy in his mid-thirties, wearing a *Star Wars* T-shirt and a hibiscus-patterned sarong with wooden clogs. Just the person Ted was after, speech scientist John Wong.

'Hey, John,' she said briskly. 'Ted Bristol, remember? Thanks for seeing me at such short notice.'

'Not at all,' John said in a plummy English accent. 'It's delightful to see you again, Ted.'

Ted was astonished. Where had the impeccable Pommy enunciation come from? Last time she'd been here, she'd barely been able to decipher John's distinctly Aussie mumbles. But there was no time to ponder the point, she cut to the chase.

'I need another miracle.'

'Then you're in the right place.'

Ted was counting on it. Recently, John Wong had not only identified Bob's catfisher, but he'd also stripped back the ambient noise from a recorded conversation at a noisy bar, thereby providing crucial evidence in Ted's first murder case.

'Please, do come in,' he said, sounding like a maître d' at the Dorchester.

John led Ted through the suburban house full of nerdy-looking boffins doing mysterious things on intimidating high-tech machines.

She followed him into his office, an unrenovated 1960s suburban kitchen. John invited her to sit at a chipped dining table cluttered with computers and cables. Ted removed a light sabre from a chair and sat. She briefed him on Duncan Bunting's fake suicide and the plan to fraudulently claim on his life insurance. John looked gratifyingly intrigued.

'I've got a recording of Duncan Bunting on a Signal call,' she told him, 'but for evidence purposes, I need you to positively ID his voice. Luckily, my associate, Chuck, has found several YouTube links for Duncan's ads for his gym, Body Potential.'

'Oh, the Body Potential chap?' John said.

'Yeah,' Ted said, 'that's the chap. Can I ask, what's with the Pommy accent?'

'Oxford elocution app. I realised it wasn't appropriate for a speech scientist to be incoherent.'

'Sound decision.'

Ted sent John the Signal recording and Chuck's YouTube links. John slipped headphones on and started tapping away on one of his computers. Ted noticed crumbs on his keyboard. He opened some sophisticated audio software and then Ted's phone recording, and then he brought up one of Duncan's old Body Potential ads and opened that too. Ted fidgeted impatiently as he twiddled knobs and dials with his mouse, listening intently. After what seemed like a century, he looked up and shook his head.

'It's not him.'

Ted's heart landed with a thud in her tummy. 'What? It's *not*?'

'No. That chap you spoke with on Signal is definitely *not* Duncan Bunting.'

Ted was floored. But how could that be? She felt as if her investigation had just been tossed up into the air and had landed in random pieces around her. This didn't make sense! Cicely had been talking to someone on that number since the day after Duncan disappeared. Surely, it had to be him? So, why was somebody else on the number, all of a sudden? Did this mean Duncan wasn't alone? Just who had Cicely been talking to? And, most intriguingly of all, if it wasn't Duncan, why had his voice sounded familiar?

But even as Ted asked herself these questions, she could feel a recent memory break free from its moorings at the bottom of her brain and start bubbling its way up to the surface, until it emerged with an almighty splash. Of course! *That's* where she'd heard the voice!

'Wait!' She grabbed her phone and pulled up a recent recording. 'Can you compare this to the Signal call? Without headphones, so I can hear?'

John removed his headphones and repeated the process. As Ted listened, her heart did a backflip. The two voices sounded identical! But she reminded herself that she wasn't the expert. Finally, John Wong looked up from twiddling his dials.

'Yes, that's the same chap.'

'It is? Are you sure?'

John Wong nodded. 'I'm certain. Who is it?'

Ted's eyes narrowed of their own volition. 'It's Cicely's financial adviser, Michael Wall.'

So, Michael Wall was in on the scam! But why? And what was he doing on Duncan's phone? Were the two of them holed up in the Barossa, waiting for Cicely to come? Ted rang Michael Wall's office and asked to speak to him, but his perky PA told her that he'd 'taken a well-deserved long weekend'.

Busted!

'Cicely's going to the Barossa tomorrow,' she told John, adrenaline pumping. 'She said she's got a quilting workshop, but I reckon she's meeting up with Duncan and this Michael Wall guy.'

'No, she's not,' John Wong said.

Ted frowned. 'What do you mean?'

John pushed his glasses up his nose. 'That guy on your call isn't in the Barossa. The metadata on your call said it was twelve o'clock Eastern Standard Time, and there was a midday chime in the background at his end. South Australia's half an hour behind, so it would only have been 11.30 am there. He's in the same time zone as us.'

Ted was hit by a wave of frustration.

'But that means he could be anywhere on the Eastern seaboard! And that was an untraceable call—'

'Fear not,' John Wong said urbanely. 'I'll replay your call.'

He started replaying Ted's call with Michael, but to what end? Ted's flimsy patience was already exhausted before he'd got two minutes in.

'But how's this going to help?' she asked.

'Can't you hear in the background? That's a back-announce after "Oops, I Did It Again", and an ad for a radio station. The frequency is 100.9.'

Ted was astonished; she hadn't heard any of that beyond a hint of Britney Spears.

'What did you say, 100.9?'

'Yeah.'

Ted grabbed her phone and googled '100.9 Radio'. The answer popped up on her screen: HIT 100.9 in Hobart.

'Michael Wall's in Hobart!' she told John Wong. 'Thanks heaps. Another miracle to add to your list.'

Chapter Thirty-Two

That night, Ted joined Bob and Raj as promised at The Partheyum in Carlton, the original in celebrity chef Stelios Niarchos's chain of cheap and cheerful Greek restaurants. The whitewashed walls were lined with blue-and-white posters of the starkly beautiful Greek Islands, and Greek paraphernalia like cloves of garlic and wine carafes in rope holders hung from the ceiling. The whole effect suggested holidays on sun-soaked Greek isles, but the conversation at Ted's table was strictly business.

'Oh my God,' Bob was saying. 'Cicely's financial adviser is in on the scam?'

Ted nodded with a derisive snort. 'Yeah. Some financial advice – let's split the 1.5 million bucks three ways.'

Raj made a whistling sound through his teeth. 'The plot thickens.'

'But I don't get it,' Bob puzzled. 'Why would a financial adviser risk his career and his credibility to hook up with two liars?'

'Because he doesn't *have* any credibility,' Ted informed her. 'I did some research on Michael Wall this arvo. Turns out he's got three cases lodged against him with the Australian Financial

Complaints Authority, and another former client is suing him for negligence.'

'Goodness.'

'Yeah. And if he loses that case, I'd imagine he'll be needing the five hundred grand.'

A waitress appeared at their table to take their orders, forcing a halt to proceedings. As she departed with their menus, Bob sighed sadly.

'I'm still so disappointed in Cicely. Maybe if she'd just asked for my help …'

Raj squeezed her hand in comfort. 'Oh, babe.'

'Don't waste any sadness on her,' Ted scoffed. 'She was lying about the quilting workshop too. But she lies about everything. She's not really going to the Barossa, she's on a 9 am flight to Hobart. And guess what? So am *I*! And I'm going to bust all three of them.'

Ted had snared a seat four rows behind Cicely on the 9 am Virgin flight to Hobart, VA116, thanks to Chuck convincing a Virgin customer service operator to give her Cicely's flight number. Some well-timed tears on Chuck's part and talk of a surprise family reunion had eventually done the trick. Ted had felt both proud and perturbed by her niece's powers of manipulation.

Back at The Partheyum, Raj was looking at her admiringly.

'I can't believe you've found all this out so fast,' he said.

'Teddy's a brilliant PI,' Bob ventured proudly.

'Just doing my job,' Ted said.

She would have liked to bask in her own awesomeness, but it was hard to feel good about anything when Spike was still in jail for Mitch's murder. She was desperate to get back to the case, and as soon as she got home from dinner, she was planning to do an online search for every Victorian importer and supplier of the Brazilian Barbosa boning knife. And then, somehow, even if she had to visit every store and perform a miracle of persuasion, she was going to find out the name of every person and/or establishment who'd bought one of those knives in the past three years.

At the next table, a party of eight burst into a raucous rendition of 'Happy Birthday'. Stelios Niarchos was standing at the head of the table, conducting the singing, and the birthday girl was shrieking with laughter.

Ted grinned along with everyone else. She didn't get the whole celebrity chef thing, but Stelios was hard not to like. He was one of those larger-than-life types, and he had a cheeky twinkle going on. In person he was almost twice the size and a decade older than the photos on his cookbooks suggested, but wasn't that par for the course with famous types?

Ted spread her napkin out on her lap, and the silk of her dress felt slippery under her fingers. She'd pulled out all the stops on Raj's behalf tonight and ditched her jeans for the black halter-neck she'd worn on her undercover date with Jarrod.

Stelios Niarchos passed their table and greeted them expansively.

'Chaírete! Welcome!'

'Thanks, Stelios!'

They'd never met the guy, but everyone called him by his first name.

'Enjoy!'

Stelios headed back into the kitchen, where eight or nine chefs and kitchen hands were producing meals like a well-oiled machine in full view of the diners, behind a glass window.

'I hope this isn't inappropriate,' Raj said to Ted, 'but I *loved* that sting today.'

Ted could tell he was still frothing about it, and it made her smile.

'It was fun, hey? You were awesome, Raj. You both were.'

'*I* couldn't have done it without Raj's acting skills,' Bob said adoringly.

'And I couldn't have done it without Bob.'

'You make an excellent team,' Ted said, and she realised she believed it.

'But you were our inspiration,' Raj ventured shyly. 'I hope I don't sound like I'm trying to suck up, but I agree with Bob. You're a brilliant PI.'

Ted wondered if she should demur, but that would be disingenuous when they all knew that Raj was right. So, she simply said, 'Thanks, Raj.'

'I guess talent runs in the family,' Raj said, giving Bob another besotted smile.

Bob's face lit up, and Ted thought, *I've never seen her so happy.* She reached for her wine to toast the blissful couple, but her glass didn't make it to her lips, because the restaurant door opened and Mitch Prowse's ex-wife, Fleur, entered with their fifteen-year-old son, Ollie, and a guy who resembled her so much that he had to be a relative.

Ted froze as her two major cases unexpectedly collided for a second time. Bob's and Raj's voices became a blur. She felt a dead weight sitting in her stomach as she saw the grief etched on poor Ollie's young face. Mitch's murder scene flashed before her, and all the travails of the past few days came back sharply into focus.

As the sombre little group made its way to a table, Stelios re-emerged from the kitchen and wrapped Ollie in a bear hug.

Then he shook Fleur's and the guy's hands gravely, offering his sympathies. Ted hadn't realised that Mitch's family knew Stelios personally, although there was no reason she should have. They took their seats. Stelios hovered for a brief chat before heading back to the kitchen.

'That boy over there,' Ted whispered to Bob, 'he's the son of Mitch Prowse, the detective that Spike's been wrongly accused of murdering.'

Bob gasped. 'Oh no! How tragic.' She looked over to Fleur's table, her features soft with compassion. 'The poor kid only looks about Chuck's age.'

'He is,' Ted said. 'They're friends. Ollie goes to Christ the Redeemer.'

Bob's hand flew to her chest, and Raj reached up to put his arm around her shoulders.

Ted pushed back her chair. 'I should go offer my condolences.'

But as she headed across the restaurant, Ted could feel her nerves stretched as tight as piano wire. Would she be intruding? She was frightened of saying the wrong thing, although she knew from her experience with grief that saying nothing was the worst thing of all. The room was ringing with raucous laughter, and she wanted to yell at everyone to show some respect, although it wasn't the other diners' fault that they were oblivious to Ollie and Fleur's plight.

She arrived at their table with an awkward smile. 'Umm, hi. Fleur. Ollie.'

Fleur's face looked pale and drawn, but she managed a wan smile. 'Oh. Ted. Hello. Ollie, it's Ted Bristol.'

Ollie's eyes were downcast. 'Hi …'

'I'm so sorry about your dad,' Ted said to the top of his head.

Ollie mumbled a thank you, but his eyes remained fixed on the floor. Fleur thanked Ted for her thoughts and introduced her brother, Anthony, who seemed to be keeping a protective eye on Ollie. Nobody mentioned Spike, a glaring omission by unspoken understanding.

'Ollie wanted to come here tonight to honour his dad,' Fleur told her.

'Oh? That's a lovely idea.'

Ollie finally lifted his gaze. 'This was Dad's favourite restaurant,' he mumbled. 'Him and Stelios were mates.'

So, that explained the embrace.

'This was a special place for you fellas, wasn't it, bud?' Anthony said.

'Yeah. We come here a lot when I'm staying at Dad's.'

Ted noticed Ollie's use of the present tense, and her heart contracted on the kid's behalf.

'Stelios gives Dad a discount, and we pig out on, like, so much food. And then Stelios always gives Dad a take-away bag with marinated octopus.'

'Octopus?' Fleur looked surprised. 'Your dad's taste buds must have changed. He's always hated octopus.'

Ollie shrugged. 'He likes it now. I mean, *liked* it.'

A pall fell over the table, and Anthony slung an arm across the back of Ollie's chair. Meanwhile Ted's brain was accelerating so fast it had almost left her body behind.

'Did your dad order octopus often?' she asked casually. It sounded like the answer was inconsequential when the opposite was actually true.

'Nah,' Ollie said, avoiding Ted's eyes. 'He never ordered octopus. He didn't have to, 'cause Stelios always gave it to him.'

Ted nodded, trying to keep her face neutral. So, Mitch and Stelios were mates. But what kind of mates? And why would Mitch suddenly start liking octopus if he'd always hated it? And if he *did* like it, why did he never order it? You had to wonder. What if it wasn't marinated octopus in those bags that Stelios regularly handed Mitch? What if it was something else, like money?

'That's very generous of Stelios,' Fleur was saying.

'Yeah,' Ted said, 'isn't it?'

She turned to look through the window into the kitchen, where Stelios Niarchos was now carving up a side of lamb – with a Barbosa boning knife.

Chapter Thirty-Three

Three minutes later, Ted was pacing in tiny circles in a toilet cubicle, her phone to her ear.

'Be there,' she muttered. '*Please* be there.'

The tables had suddenly turned and she was now desperate to talk to Jarrod Beasley. After seeing Stelios with that Barbosa boning knife, she'd remembered Jarrod's story about reporting a celebrity chef to the cops for financial malfeasance. Could that celebrity chef have been Stelios Niarchos?

She jumped as Jarrod picked up.

'Tiny Ted. Finally you call. How are you, lovely?'

Ted wished she'd remembered to text Jarrod and tell him she wasn't interested. She couldn't bring herself to flirt with him again, even to get the intel she needed.

'I'm good. I'm just calling because I thought you should know that someone's been bringing your skills as a life coach into question,' she improvised.

'My skills into question? What do you mean?'

'I mean, somebody's spreading rumours.'

'What kind of rumours?' Jarrod asked indignantly. 'Who?'

Ted winced. This was a leap in the dark.

'I met Stelios Niarchos yesterday—'

Jarrod made a huffing sound. 'Stelios Niarchos?'

'Yeah, at dinner at a friend's place.'

She paused to see if Jarrod would say he'd never met Stelios, but instead he said, 'Was *he* spreading rumours about me? What did he say?'

Ted felt a clutch of excitement. She was on the right path.

'Well, we were just making small talk, you know how it is. And I'm not sure how we got onto the topic, but Stelios said he used to have a corrupt accountant, so he sacked him—'

'Corrupt? What the fuck?'

'And I asked the corrupt accountant's name, and he said it was you.'

'That lying prick!' Jarrod exploded. 'It was the other way around. Niarchos was the corrupt one. He wanted me to launder hundreds of grand! *I* reported *him* to the cops.'

Ted wanted to do a victory dance, but that would be premature. She told herself to keep it cool.

'Oh my God, that was Stelios Niarchos? I remember you telling me about that, but you wouldn't say who the chef was.'

'Yeah, because he's a scary dude, even though everyone thinks he's Mr Nice Guy. That prick! What else did he say?'

'Just that. The conversation moved on to something else. But I know rumours like this could compromise your life-coaching business, so I thought I should let you know.'

'Yeah, thanks,' Jarrod said tersely. 'I'd sue him for defamation if I didn't think I'd end up wearing concrete shoes. That good-bloke persona is an act, trust me.'

Ted's heart was hammering so loudly that she half wondered if Jarrod could hear it. It now seemed almost certain that Stavros was Mitch's murderer, but she needed to make this watertight. And that started with establishing a motive.

'What happened when you called the cops? Was it the local North Carlton station?'

'No, this was serious stuff, what could they do? I rang the financial crimes squad and spoke to a detective.'

Ted's breath held its breath.

'Oh, financial crimes? My brother's got a mate who works there,' she lied. 'Was the detective's name Steve Peters?'

'No, that's not it. It was a few years ago now, but I think it was something with an M. Mike? Max?'

'Mitch?'

'Yeah, that was it. Mitch Howes? No, Mitch Prowse. Yeah, Mitch Prowse.'

Ted wanted to faint.

'And what happened after you spoke to him?'

'Nothing, as far as I know. He never called me in to make an official report.'

'Why not? Didn't you think that was weird?'

'Yeah, but I'd done as much as I could, it was up to him to take it from there. And by then I'd started studying at the Life Coaching College.'

'So, as far as you know, Stelios was never investigated?'

'I don't know. But if he was, they did a shit job. I haven't heard of him being arrested, have you? And it would've been big news.'

'Yeah, it would've.'

Ted's grey matter was grinding fast. Had Mitch gone to Stelios and demanded that Stelios pay him off to avoid prosecution? And was Stelios the source of those large amounts of money that Mitch had been betting with Gail Pettigrove? And had Stelios tired of paying Mitch off and murdered him with the Barbosa boning knife? The pieces were all fitting together. She needed to get off the phone and work out her next move.

'Anyway, I thought you should know. Nice to chat—'

'Wait,' Jarrod said, his tone softening and becoming more intimate. 'There's something *you* should know too.'

'Yeah? What's that?'

'I'm afraid it's not going to work out for us,' he said gently. 'You've wasted too much time fearing your feelings for me, and I've met an actress who's more evolved. But you're a good human – I'm sure you won't be alone forever.'

Ted snorted. The male ego was more indestructible than a cockroach.

'Thanks for telling me. I'll try and move forward with my life regardless.'

She hung up and thought hard about her next step. Within seconds a plan had dropped into stark relief, and she knew exactly what she had to do. She stepped out of the cubicle and was about to exit the toilets when Bob entered and they almost collided.

'Teddy. What happened to you? I was about to send out a search party.'

Ted tried to smile, but she was so wired it probably looked like a grimace. Bob frowned.

'Are you okay? You seem strange. Did something happen with the murdered detective's family?'

Ted hesitated. She knew Bob would be petrified if she shared her plan, so she needed to protect her from the truth at all costs. And that meant keeping her trap shut.

'Stelios Niarchos murdered Mitch!'

Dammit, her trap was wide open.

Bob blinked as she tried to process what Ted shouldn't have said.

'What …? Stelios …?'

She obviously couldn't believe it, and who could?

'I'm afraid so,' Ted said. 'I won't go into how I know. I'm going to head home and get Miss Marple, and we're going to wait for the restaurant to close, and then we're going to steal his knife and lift his fingerprints, so I can prove it.'

Bob looked every bit as petrified as Ted had expected.

'What? You can't do that!'

'I have to.'

'No, you don't. Call the police!'

'No way!' Ted scoffed. 'They're out to frame Spike, even though he's a better homicide detective than any of them will ever be. Or maybe *because* of that.' She could feel emotion rising and threatening to overwhelm her. 'I'm the only one who can clear him. I have to do this!'

She expected Bob to protest again, but Bob was now staring at her in what looked like wonder.

'You'd risk your life for him? Oh my goodness, this is so much more than a crush. You love him.'

'So?'

They both heard Ted's single syllable wobble.

Bob threw her arms around her. 'Oh, Teddy,' she said, her own voice wobbling. 'I'm so happy for you.'

Ted knew she should be happy that Bob was happy for her, but, frankly, part of her felt peeved. Was that it? Had Bob officially abandoned her role as Ted's designated worrier? She pulled out of her sister's embrace.

'Hey, I just told you I'm planning to steal a knife off a murderer, remember? This being in love stuff is all very nice, but aren't you at least going to tell me to be careful?'

Bob laughed sheepishly and wiped her eyes. 'I'm sorry, Teddy. Be careful.'

Chapter Thirty-Four

By midnight, Ted and Miss Marple were lurking behind a large skip in the laneway at the rear of The Partheyum. A crescent moon was casting a faint glow on the cobblestones, and the late night was spookily silent.

Ted had replaced her black silk dress and strappy sandals with surveillance-friendly jeans and runners, a baseball cap and an oversized grey hoodie. Her hands were squeezed into sterile gloves, and she was carrying a backpack containing a plastic sandwich bag from her emergency investigation kit.

She checked her watch. They'd already been waiting for several minutes without incident. She exchanged a glance with Miss Marple – time for a reconnoitre. She put her finger to her lips, and they stepped out from behind the skip. Ted's heart was in her mouth as she tiptoed over to The Partheyum's back gate. She peered through a gap in the latch. Past a mulberry tree in the restaurant's courtyard, she could see the kitchen door propped open. Stelios was alone in there, save for an acne-scarred kitchen hand who was mopping the floor. The open door was a lucky break, and Ted gave Miss Marple a thumbs-up. But her jubilation was short-lived. Sure, she might be able to slip into the kitchen, but how was she going to get her hands on the boning knife without being seen?

She started when she saw Stelios wrest the mop from the young guy's hand. He pointed at a spot on the floor.

'Look, a dirty mark! I should rub your face in it, you pig!'

The kitchen hand cowered, and Ted recoiled. Jarrod hadn't been kidding about Stelios's jovial persona being an act.

'Get out of here before I kill you!' Stelios screamed.

Ted felt a chill of fear, because she was 99.9 per cent certain that Stelios had already killed once. She was glad for the kitchen hand's sake that he didn't share that knowledge.

'I said, get out!' Stelios yelled.

The kitchen hand threw off his apron and scampered out the back door, and Ted and Miss Marple sped back to their spot behind the skip. Ted heard the click of the latch as The Partheyum's rear gate opened, and a few seconds later the kitchen hand loped past, muttering, 'Psycho arsehole!'

Ted waited for the guy to disappear around the corner, and then she re-emerged from behind the skip. He'd left the back gate ajar! It was manna from heaven. She gestured to Miss Marple: *Let's do this*. They sprinted to the gate, and Ted saw that the kitchen door was still open. She could hear Stelios swearing in Greek as he took half a lamb out of a fridge and started prepping cuts of meat for tomorrow's service – with the Barbosa boning knife!

Ted swallowed back the bile of fear. This was a highly dangerous operation, and she was starting to have second thoughts about involving Miss Marple. The idea of Miss Marple coming to harm was more than she could bear. There was a killer in that kitchen who had access to a lot of deadly utensils, including a probable murder weapon. She couldn't subject her dog to that risk.

She whispered, 'You stay out here and keep watch.'

But Miss Marple looked back at her as if to say, *Get real!* And before Ted could object, she was running through the gate and down the back path towards the kitchen. What a badarse! Ted held her breath as Miss Marple ran brazenly into the kitchen, barking like a banshee.

Stelios turned and went ballistic. 'Gamóto! You filthy dog! Get out of my fucking kitchen!'

Stelios grabbed a meat cleaver – oh God, a cleaver – and he started chasing Miss Marple around the kitchen. But Miss Marple was nothing if not wily, and she wove under and around benches and food preparation tables, distracting him. Ted streaked inside. Miss Marple was creating so much ruckus at the other end of the kitchen that Stelios didn't notice her, but she knew that could change at any moment. She raced to the cutting board and grabbed the knife with her gloved hands, slipping it into the sandwich bag. Meanwhile, Stelios seemed to be closing in on Miss Marple.

'I'll cut you into pieces!'

Ted's brain was in overdrive as she tried to work out a way to get Miss Marple safely out of the kitchen. But she must have been too busy thinking because she knocked a heavy pot off a bench and it clattered to the floor with a loud clang! Shit!

Stelios shot around and saw her. His eyes went straight to the knife in the sandwich bag, and his face contorted with rage.

'What the fuck?!'

Miss Marple sank her teeth into his calf.

'Oww! Maláka!'

The meat cleaver clattered to the ground, and Miss Marple looked at Ted as if to say, *Run!!!* But Ted wasn't going anywhere without her. As Stelios reached down to grab the cleaver, Ted leaped forward like a ninja and kicked him in the guts. He doubled over, gasping in pain.

'You ... putána!'

Ted scooped up Miss Marple and raced out of the kitchen, somehow managing to slam the back door shut. She slipped the sandwich bag into her backpack. But Stelios had already rallied. The door flew open and he appeared with the cleaver. Ted ducked behind the mulberry tree with Miss Marple still in her arms. Thank God mulberries didn't make her sneeze. She saw Stelios rampaging past, the blade of his cleaver glistening in the moonlight.

'I'm going to get you, putána!'

Ted felt faint with terror. She had little doubt that he'd use the cleaver if he found them. Only silence stood between them and death. But, horror of horrors, Miss Marple suddenly stiffened in her arms and bared her fangs. Ted followed her gaze to see a possum high in the mulberry tree, sneering down at them. Oh no! Possums were Miss Marple's mortal enemies. If she got into an affray, it would all be over.

Ted whispered desperately, 'Forget the possum.' But she could tell that every fibre of Miss Marple's being was dying to take on the creature.

'Where are you, putána?'

Stelios was marching around, kicking over garbage bins and pots. Through the mulberry tree Ted could see the open gate beckoning like a lifeline, but Stelios was obstructing their path. A loud guttural hiss shattered the silence, and Ted cursed the possum as Stelios froze. Then he started approaching the tree. Ted could barely breathe. She tightened her arms around Miss Marple, but Miss Marple strained against her and leaped to the ground. The miniature schnauzer then skirted the tree trunk and hurled herself into Stelios's path, tripping him over. Stelios fell heavily to the ground.

'Skatá!'

Ted sprang out from behind the tree and high-jumped over his prostrate body.

'You ... bitch!'

Ted and Miss Marple pelted to the back gate as Stelios struggled to stand. Ted shut the gate behind them, and as she shot a quick look back, she saw him wincing and dragging his left foot – it seemed he'd sprained his ankle.

'I'll get you!'

But Ted knew he couldn't get them now. They bolted down the rear laneway and around the corner and leaped into Ted's waiting SUV. Ted locked the doors and turned on the ignition, feeling giddy with elation. She met Miss Marple's eyes in the rear-vision mirror.

'You're a superstar.'

Miss Marple looked back at her as if to say, *So are you*, and as Ted pulled away from the kerb, she realised she'd never felt so alive.

'We're two kickarse females fighting for justice, and woe betide anyone who gets in our way!'

She drove off through the Carlton streets until she'd put enough distance between herself and Stelios, and then she swerved to the kerb and stopped. She took the sandwich bag out of her backpack and checked the knife against the photo the cops had given to Kip Trammel, Mitch's next-door neighbour. It was the exact same model of Barbosa boning knife, although obviously Stelios's knife showed more wear and tear. Ted felt bilious at the thought that Stelios had probably slaughtered Mitch with this very knife. Would he really be so brazen as to use a murder weapon at his restaurant? But when she thought about it, it was evil genius. If he'd thrown the knife away it would almost certainly have been found, and would have eventually led back to him. But who'd ever suspect a murder weapon would actually be in use in a popular restaurant's kitchen?

But she was getting ahead of herself. She couldn't prove it was the murder weapon until she'd lifted Stelios's prints off the handle. She climbed out of her car and opened the boot and pulled out her latent fingerprint kit. Her phone rang, startling her. For a terrifying moment she thought it might be Stelios, but then she remembered that Stelios didn't even know who she was. *Yet.* She checked the screen. It was Bob. Of course. Ted pressed Accept.

'Bob, hey.'

'Teddy? You're okay?'

'Yeah, we're both fine.'

She heard Bob exhale. 'Oh thank God.'

'Yeah. Miss Marple was awesome. I've got the murder weapon—'

'Oh my God, you've got it? Did Stelios see you?'

Ted considered the question for a second. Bob didn't need to know *everything*.

'Nope. We got in and out unnoticed.'

'Thank God.'

'Yeah,' Ted said. 'Thanks for checking on us, but it's so late, you should be in bed. And I need to dust the knife for prints.'

'Okay,' Bob said, her voice still light with relief. 'But be careful.'

'I will.'

Ted pressed End and slipped her phone back into her pocket. As she opened her fingerprint kit, she felt a fresh burst of rage that Stelios was swanning around like some kind of celebrity while poor Spike was wrongly charged with Mitch's murder. She wondered what Spike was doing right now. Was he lying wide awake, staring through prison bars and trying to come to terms with the possibility that he might never be released?

'I'll get you out, Spike,' she whispered into the darkness, and for the first time since his arrest, she thought that might actually be possible.

Chapter Thirty-Five

Ted took out her fibreglass fingerprint brush and dusted the boning knife's handle with latent powder. Then she used fingerprint lifting tape to lift a print from the handle's surface. Stelios's print showed distinctive little scars from knife cuts along the top of his index finger. Yes! Ted quickly grabbed a fingerprint card and stuck the lifting tape to it to preserve the print. It was an excellent result, but there was no time to pat herself on the back, because the print still meant nothing unless it was matched to the murder scene. According to Kip Trammel, the crime-scene cleaners were coming at 7 am – which meant Ted needed to break into Mitch's house and match that fingerprint *tonight*.

She quickly secured the fingerprint card back in her kit. Then she threw the kit and the bagged knife into her backpack, along with some surgical booties and a second pair of sterile gloves. She jumped from the car and opened the rear door.

'Come on,' she called to Miss Marple, who was sniffing a nearby telegraph pole. 'We have to go.'

Miss Marple rocketed into the rear seat, and as Ted closed the door behind her, she felt an irrational fear that Stelios would spring from the darkness and stab her. Spooked, she scrambled back into the car and locked the doors. The city was sleeping as she drove through the empty streets to Mitch's place in Collingwood, turning off her headlights at the corner for maximum discretion. It was 2.20 am when she and Miss Marple pulled up outside. Mitch's dark house was encircled by police tape and all the doors and windows were closed. It looked like a ghoulish fortress. How the hell was she going to get in?

She climbed out of her car with her backpack, and Miss Marple alighted behind her. There was no sign of movement anywhere else in the street, and the deathly silence felt depressingly appropriate. Ted and Miss Marple padded stealthily through the front gate and slipped under the police tape. They crept around the deserted house to the back door. It was locked, just as Ted had expected, but it was still a blow. She lifted the doormat hoping to find a key, but no luck. She looked under a couple of rocks and an ancient garden gnome nearby, but all she unearthed was worms. Dammit. She turned her attention to the windows and tried to lift them with her fingertips, but she couldn't get enough of a grip. She could feel herself starting to panic. She *had to* find a way inside. The crime-scene cleaners would be here in a few hours and Stelios's fingerprints would be washed away.

Miss Marple disappeared into the darkness, and Ted scanned the house in desperation. Should she smash a window and just pray she'd have time to match the prints before the cops arrived? But then she heard a tiny bark in the blackness and realised Miss Marple was whispering to her. She followed the sound and found Miss Marple wagging her tail outside a large doggie door that was obscured behind a bushy potted plant. Salvation!

'Excellent work, Miss Marple,' Ted whispered.

She moved the pot plant and made a final check for a key. No luck. It looked like the doggie door was her only way in.

Miss Marple barrelled through it, and Ted figured she was small enough to wiggle through too. It was the first time in her shortish career as a PI that she'd been grateful for her diminutive size. She felt in her backpack for her sterile booties and gloves – she'd need to put them on as soon as she got into the house. She threw her backpack through the doggie door behind Miss Marple, and then she got down on her knees and started wiggling her body through, but she got stuck halfway.

'Shit!'

Miss Marple reappeared from behind the backpack and looked at Ted as if to say, *You can do this!*

'I know I can,' Ted whispered.

She couldn't stand the thought of letting Miss Marple down. Ted kept wriggling and eventually managed to get her shoulders through, but now she was stuck at her hips. Dammit! Miss Marple took Ted's hoodie sleeve in her teeth (carefully avoiding Ted's flesh) and tried to pull her inside. It was a valiant effort on her miniature schnauzer's part, as always, but at just six kilos, she couldn't take all of Ted's weight.

And then suddenly they were both flooded in light, and Ted heard someone say behind her, 'What are you doing?'

Oh no! Ted grabbed her bag and wriggled all the way back out into the yard. She looked up to see Kip Trammel from next door, shining their iPhone torch on her.

'Oh, Kip, hi,' she said lamely, scrambling to her feet. 'Sorry if I woke you.'

'I was already awake,' Kip said. 'I told you I'm nocturnal, remember? What the hell are you doing?'

'Oh yeah, nocturnal. I forgot.'

She winced in the torchlight, and Kip redirected the beam so it wasn't shining directly into Ted's face. Meanwhile Miss Marple barrelled back out the doggie door, but Kip barely gave her a second glance.

'Why are you here at two thirty in the morning?'

It was a valid question. Ted contemplated lying, but she decided there was little point. From what she knew of Kip, they were pretty unlikely to call the cops, so she told them the truth – that she'd tracked down Mitch's real murderer and the actual knife, and she needed to match the prints on the knife with the prints at the murder scene before the crime-scene cleaners turned up at 7 am, but she couldn't get into the bloody house and it was incredibly f%$#ing frustrating!

Kip let her finish, and then they pointed to the bushy pot plant that had been obscuring the doggie door.

'Have you looked in there?'

Ted nodded. 'There was nothing under it.'

'What about *in* it?'

'What?'

Kip shone their phone torch at the pot plant. It hadn't occurred to Ted to check *inside* the pot. She started rifling through the bushy plant and sure enough, lying in the potting mix like some kind of magic talisman, was a key.

'It's a key!'

'Yeah,' Kip said caustically. 'I can see that.'

'Thanks a million,' Ted said. 'How did you know it was there?'

'I didn't. But it's not like it took much imagination.'

That was a fair call, Ted had to admit.

'Well, thanks again,' she said, striding to the back door with Miss Marple. 'And sorry to disturb you.' She stopped as it occurred to her that Kip might follow. 'Er, it's probably best you don't come in. It's a pretty horrific scene.'

'I've got no intention of going in,' Kip said, and Ted thought she detected a hint of judgement. 'I'm not a ghoul who gets titillated by other people's violent ends.'

So more than a hint of judgement, then.

'Neither am I,' Ted said defensively. 'I'm only here in a professional capacity.'

Kip shrugged as if it was of no import to them either way.

'Sure, whatever. But I'm trying to mark some sex, gender and power essays, so keep the noise down.'

Kip disappeared back into the night. Ted looked down at Miss Marple.

'Cross your paws.'

She held her breath as she slipped the key into the back-door lock. It worked! She opened the door and they both stepped into the darkened laundry. Ted opened her backpack and took out her sterile gloves and booties. As she put them on, she gave Miss Marple an apologetic glance.

'Sorry, but you'll have to stay out in the hall.'

Miss Marple looked at her as if to say, *Duh*.

Ted proceeded to the living room. She steeled herself as she turned on the light and was confronted by the murder scene again. A shudder travelled through her. Mitch's body had been removed, but it was still a shock to bear witness to his blood spattered over the walls, the half-eaten pizza, the betting stubs, the open can of Red Bull – all the signs that Mitch had no idea his life was about to be snuffed out.

Ted felt queasy with the brutality of it, but she forced herself to remain on task. She took out her latent fingerprint kit and started lifting prints from the scene. She found a lot of different prints, presumably from Mitch and people who'd lived here before him, but none of them seemed significant – until she dusted a section of wall streaked with blood, and found multiple prints with distinctive nick scars on the top. She took the fingerprint card out of her kit and matched it with the other prints. They were identical! Stelios Niarchos's fingerprints were all over the murder scene!

'Miss Marple, we've got him!' she called.

Miss Marple appeared in the doorway. She looked at Ted as if to say, *You are a bloody legend,* and Ted could only concur. She'd now solved *two* murders, she obviously had a knack for this. But she told herself to pull her head in. There'd be plenty of time to love herself sick when she'd found justice for Ollie and freed Spike. Right now she needed to share this evidence with the police, whether they wanted to hear it or not. She checked her watch. It was just past 3 am. The cleaners would be here in four hours, and all evidence of Stelios in situ would be scrubbed away. She stripped off her booties and gloves, and she and Miss Marple raced next door – it was lucky Kip was nocturnal. She rang the bell and Kip answered in a haze of vape smoke. Ted coughed. She could see *The Kardashians* were on on a TV in the living room, but she didn't have time to contemplate the incongruity.

'Sorry to disturb you again. I just wondered if the cops had left you an after-hours contact number?'

Kip nodded. They went to a bowl on a hall stand and rifled through it, but not with enough urgency for Ted's liking. *Hurry up!* she thought. *This is life or death.* Eventually Kip retrieved a business card and returned, handing it to Ted.

'Thanks,' Ted said.

'Is that it?' Kip said. 'Can I get on with my life now?'

'Er, yeah. Thanks for everything.'

Kip closed the door behind Ted without so much as a see you later. Ted looked down at the business card, and despite everything, a sneaky smile found its way onto her face. She waved the card at Miss Marple.

'What I have here in my hot little hand, is the number for Chief Inspector Craig Maven. What a shame to wake him at three am.'

Miss Marple gave a wicked metaphorical chuckle.

Maven was glowering when he alighted from his snazzy Audi outside Mitch's place, where Ted and Miss Marple were waiting. Even though he'd been roused from sleep his linen suit was uncreased, and Ted found that a character defect.

'I told you to fucking keep out of this case,' he scowled.

'Yes, and aren't you lucky I ignored that advice?' Ted said, smiling up at him sweetly. 'Otherwise you'd go down in history as the homicide boss who didn't do his due diligence and sent an innocent man – *one of his very own colleagues* – to jail for a murder he didn't commit.'

She could tell he wanted to throttle her.

'You'd better not be wasting my time, little girl.'

Ted couldn't let that pass. 'Why would I waste your time when you've already wasted so much of it yourself? That would just be adding to the problem, right?'

Ted knew she was being a smart-arse, but it felt so good. She checked herself.

'But, seriously,' she said gravely, 'your murderer is Stelios Niarchos.'

Maven gave a little start of shock.

'Yeah, the celebrity chef,' Ted affirmed. 'He's been fiddling the books for years, and Mitch found out. My belief is Mitch was blackmailing him, and I can only assume that Niarchos got sick of handing over the dough.'

She could see that Maven's wheels still weren't quite spinning, so she briefed him on Jarrod's evidence about reporting Stelios's financial crimes to Mitch, and the large amounts on Mitch's betting slips – which surely Maven had also noticed, but had decided to dismiss because he was obsessed with Spike's DNA. And then, in the coup de grace, she pulled Stelios's bagged knife from her backpack. Maven's eyes nearly popped out of his head.

'An uncanny resemblance to the murder weapon, hey? You'll find the distinctive prints on this knife are matched all over the murder scene. But you'll need to investigate faster than usual, because the cleaners will be here in a few hours.'

That last smart-arse part just slipped out.

If it was possible to be eaten up by resentment, Maven's eyeballs would be the only part of him left. They both knew he detested Ted for proving him wrong, but they also knew he had nowhere to go. As he reached out to snatch the bag with the knife, he seemed to finally get his shit together, and his usual sneer reappeared.

'I suppose you think we're going to put your pathetic little investigation agency in our media releases. Well, think again.'

Ted was stunned. Not because Maven was refusing to credit EBI with solving the crime, but because she'd been so intent on proving Spike's innocence that negotiating credit for EBI hadn't even occurred to her. Wow.

'I don't give a stuff whether you credit me or not,' she said, and she was surprised to realise that was true. 'I just want you to release Spike Tereiti.'

Chapter Thirty-Six

At 8.20 am Ted was sitting at a crowded departure gate in Terminal 3 at Melbourne Airport. Outside the windows, rain as soft as a whisper danced in the breeze above the tarmac. Ted usually enjoyed watching the comings and goings of airport ground staff, but this morning she was way too wired. She was subsisting on two and a half hours sleep, and three and a half cups of coffee, and all she could think about was Spike.

She must have checked her phone a million times already for breaking news that he'd been cleared, but so far, nothing. She'd even tried calling him, but her call had gone straight through to message bank, which meant that Spike's phone hadn't been returned to him. Did that mean he didn't know the good news yet? Was he lining up for a ladle of gruel, unaware he was about to be sprung from the slammer? Ted pictured Spike's face when he found out she'd saved his future. She imagined ways he might choose to thank her. Bring it on!

She was dying to announce to the world that she'd proven Spike Tereiti's innocence and snared the real murderer of Detective Mitch Prowse, but she had Ollie and the rest of Mitch's family to consider, and she couldn't let her hubris take precedence over their feelings.

#secondmurdersolved #dontmesswithEBI

She needed to wait a respectful interval before getting on her socials. And, besides, she didn't dare breathe a word until Spike had been officially freed. She knew they'd have to hold a special hearing to release him, which wouldn't be scheduled until Monday. And she had no intention of jinxing things by pissing off Maven, even though that was turning out to be her favourite hobby.

She stole a glance across the packed departure gate at Cicely Bunting, who was knitting an intricately patterned sock. She was chatting with the woman beside her, who seemed to be complimenting her handiwork. Cicely had so many talents, Ted mused, it was a shame they extended to fraud and false pretences. Cicely happened to glance in her direction, but Ted felt unfazed thanks to her disguise.

She was wearing a long blonde wig and sandals with a lilac paisley maxi-dress and a purple cardigan. The ultra-feminine outfit was anathema to Ted's usual taste, but Chuck had been frothing at the prospect, so Ted had let her design the ensemble. It was the least she could do for the kid, who always went above and beyond. Chuck had chosen the outfit from the disguise box Ted had put together when she first opened EBI a few years ago. And her niece had insisted on adding Cody Venables's ridiculous Coke-bottle eyeglass 'binoculars', in spite of Ted's scoffs.

'I've got the real thing, Chuck. You know, actual binoculars that actually work.'

'But have you tried these?' Chuck asked.

Not technically, but Ted didn't need to – poor old Cody wasn't known for his smart choices. Nonetheless, she'd humoured Chuck by tossing the novelty item into her bag, and then she'd let Chuck slather makeup all over her. She'd even allowed her niece to apply false lashes, and a couple of hours later, she still felt as if she had two dust brushes attached to her eyelids.

A baby started crying nearby, and Ted thought, *Please God, don't let that kid be sitting next to me on the plane.* A couple of overly groomed flight attendants emerged from the air bridge and positioned themselves at the desk, and some guys in suits started queueing for priority boarding. Ted's eye was caught by a ruby-red spoodle on a nearby passenger's screensaver, and she felt a pang of longing for Miss Marple. Still, she was glad she'd decided against bringing her. There was a risk Cicely might recognise her miniature schnauzer and, besides, Ted wasn't prepared to lock her in a crate and stuff her in a cargo hold for three hours.

It had been awesome to see Miss Marple enjoying simple canine pleasures on this morning's walk at the crack of dawn, especially after she'd heroically saved Ted's life for the second time. Ted had felt a sudden pinch of guilt for asking so much of her beloved dog. Was she being unfair? In a reflective moment, she'd looked at Miss Marple as if to say, *Would you rather live a carefree doggy life than fight crime at EBI?* And Miss Marple had looked back at her as if to say, *Are you kidding, I'd be bored witless.*

But still, she knew she'd made the right decision by leaving her miniature schnauzer with Chantal. For some reason Miss Marple adored Chantal, and in a rare exception, she always lavished Ted's neighbour with affection.

Ted's phone rang and she jumped. Spike?! She whipped it out of her pocket, but the caller was Giselle. Ted felt a lurch of disappointment, but at least she could now tell Giselle that Spike was innocent – as the mother of Spike's kids, she deserved to know that despite the secrecy. The subject matter felt too personal to discuss in this cheek-by-jowl space, so Ted strode out of the departure gate and into the wide thoroughfare, pushing past the masses, who were shuffling into a messy line for general boarding. She pressed Accept.

'Giselle, hey—'

'Hi Ted,' Giselle said breathlessly. 'I'm calling with some good news.'

'What?'

'Spike's mum just called me. He's been cleared!'

Ted almost collapsed with relief, and she realised how worried she'd been that Maven would somehow block the truth for the sake of protecting his ginormous ego.

'Oh my God, that's awesome!'

'I know!' Giselle said. 'They've found the real murderer, but they're not saying who it is yet. I'm so happy for my girls. And for Spike, of course. And ... for *you*.'

Ted blinked. Come again?

'For *me*?'

'Yes, for you. I'm still mad you tried to make out you barely knew him, but ... When I saw you both in the courtroom yesterday, I realised how much you mean to each other ... so I thought you'd want to know.'

For a second, Ted couldn't access any vocabulary. Giselle was being as gracious as one of her pirouettes. Ted felt a lump form in her throat and she coughed to clear it.

'Thank you, Giselle. And I *am* sorry for misleading you.'

'Well ... let's just leave that behind us. Spike's the father of my children, and if you're the woman he wants, then you and I need to get along.'

Ted nodded, even though she knew that was an ineffective way to communicate over the phone. Was she really the woman Spike wanted? Or did he just want a fling? And did *she* just want a fling? Wouldn't that be preferable? After all, Spike was the father of three little kids, and for a woman with a bereaved childhood and intimacy issues, that was almost scarier than a murder charge. What if she and the girls bonded, but then she got hit by a truck? Or had a heart attack? Or fell off something? Romy was only four. Ted would be responsible for inflicting the same kind of grief and unhappiness that *she'd* experienced at that vulnerable age. Ted could feel herself starting to spiral, but Giselle brought her back to earth with a verbal slap.

'You've got to hand it to Maven. Even though he and Spike don't get on, he's righted this wrong very quickly.'

Ted snorted indignantly. Trust Maven to take the credit.

'*He* didn't right the wrong. *I* did.'

'You?'

'Yeah. Maven's clouded by his personal hatred of Spike, *and* he's lazy. It's a terrible combo. I did all the investigating and found the proof, and then I gave him the evidence. If it was left up to Maven, Spike would never get out.'

'Really? Then you must know who *did* kill Mitch.'

Ted hesitated. She would have loved to tell Giselle about Stelios, but she couldn't risk blabbing.

'I'm sorry, I can't say right now. But Spike's been cleared, that's the bottom line.' Suddenly none of this chit-chat mattered, because there was only one thing Ted really cared about. 'Did Spike's mum say when they've scheduled his release hearing? Monday morning?'

'No, today.'

'*Today?*'

'Yeah.'

'But it's Saturday!' Ted shrieked. She only just managed to stop herself adding, 'And I'm going to Hobart!'

'I know it's Saturday,' Giselle said in a tone that suggested Ted was a child. 'But they work on weekends when it's important. They're holding a special hearing at the Magistrate's Court at 4 pm.'

'4 pm?'

'Yeah. Enzo said they need time to organise transport to get Spike back from Hopkins Correctional Centre in Ararat.'

Ararat? That was a three-hour drive from Melbourne, but at least Ted knew where Spike was now.

'Have you spoken to him?' she asked Giselle.

'No, just to his mum. And judging by the way he was looking at you yesterday, you'll hear from him way before I do.'

Ted was overcome by a jumble of emotions that she couldn't sort through efficiently. She tried to sweep them all aside and match Giselle's generosity.

'You know what, Giselle? Consider your invoice wiped clean.' As she mentally waved goodbye to payment for all those endless hours of blood, sweat and tears, Ted took a moment to be impressed by her own magnanimity. 'There'll be no charge for my services.'

'Just as well.'

'Er, sorry?'

'I said just as well. You wasted a lot of time on wild goose chases with Jarrod and Tommy.'

Ted was incredulous. *She'd* wasted time? It seemed Giselle was still inhabiting her alternative planet. But that didn't matter, because all Ted wanted to do right now was get off the phone. She ended the call, torturously torn. Spike's hearing was at 4 pm, and FOMO wouldn't begin to describe her feelings if she missed it. But as much as she wanted to turn and run from the departure gate, she forced herself to stay put. She was on the verge of busting the Buntings and Michael Wall's $1,500,000 fraud – was she really going to drop the ball at this vital point for personal reasons? *As if!* She knew Spike would understand. She'd call him now and explain why she couldn't be at the hearing.

Ted googled the Hopkins Correctional Centre and punched in the jail's number. An incongruously chirpy male receptionist answered. Ted asked to speak to inmate Spike Tereiti.

'Who may I say is calling?'

'Ted Bristol.'

Ted pictured Spike's smile when he heard she was on the line.

'Oh. Did you say *Ted Bristol*?'

'Yes, that was my name last time I looked.' Ted knew the smart-arse comment was unwarranted, but all this anticipation was getting to her.

'I'm sorry,' chirpy guy said, 'but you're not on the list of approved contacts.'

'Yeah, I know I wasn't before. But now Spike's been cleared surely he can talk to whoever he wants.'

'Technically that's true. But we had a call from Chief Inspector Maven from homicide this morning. He mentioned your name specifically and said you're still not approved for contact.'

Ted's blood boiled.

'So, I'm afraid you'll have to wait until Detective Tereiti is released. Have a good day!' He hung up in Ted's ear.

Ted hurled her hands in the air and almost sent a passing passenger's Boost juice flying.

Meanwhile at the departure gate, one of the overly groomed flight attendants switched on the microphone. 'Good morning, ladies and gentlemen. Flight VA116 to Hobart is now ready for priority boarding.'

Chapter Thirty-Seven

As Ted followed Cicely to the Avis car rental counter in the Hobart International Airport terminal, she congratulated herself for booking a car online with Thrifty, just in case. Luckily the Thrifty counter was right next to Avis, so she could keep a covert eye on Cicely while they both signed about six hundred forms before being granted their keys.

She'd been hoping that Duncan and Michael would meet the plane, so she could snap some pics of the allegedly deceased Duncan, and then jump on the first flight back to Melbourne in time for Spike's special hearing. But, of course, things never unfolded that seamlessly. A good PI had to be nimble. You needed to constantly navigate disappointment, think on your feet at every second, and be prepared to chuck an instant U-turn in your investigation. It was exhausting, but it was also exhilarating.

Cicely stepped away from the Avis counter at almost the same moment as a frazzled Thrifty employee dropped Ted's keys into her palm. Ted thanked him and discreetly followed as Cicely wheeled her overnight bag out of the terminal and into the delightfully temperate Tassie day. Ted breathed in the crisp air. The skies were clear, and the breeze was soft, and it was as if this place had never heard of humidity. No wonder mainlanders flocked down here for a less sweaty life.

Ted hung back as Cicely marched into the rental car carpark and unlocked a red Subaru XV. Ted sent out a silent prayer of thanks to Avis for the bright colour – it would make her easier to follow. But Cicely was already climbing into the SUV. Ted quickly pressed her unlock button, and a pleasingly nondescript white Camry started flashing its lights. Ted sprinted to the car and hurled her large tote into the passenger seat. She jumped into the Camry and put her foot down, managing to catch Cicely as she exited the carpark.

Cicely followed the Tasman Highway from the airport to the city, and within fifteen minutes they were crossing the Tasman Bridge over the River Derwent, with Hobart elegantly arrayed on gentle hills before them, and majestic Mount Wellington straight ahead, its summit lost in the clouds.

On the other side of the river, Cicely took a left turn off the bridge. Ted assumed she'd drive into Hobart's CBD, but instead Cicely turned onto the Southern Outlet/A6, and they skirted the city and drove south-west through forests, lush green countryside, and villages with cute names like Snug and Oyster Cove.

About fifty minutes after leaving Hobart they arrived in Kettering, a fishing village nestled at the bottom of forested hills. Cicely turned left at a large sign that read 'Bruny Island Ferry'. Ted turned left behind her and saw the ferry up ahead, lowering its ramp for a line of cars.

So, Cicely was going to Bruny Island. Cool. Ted didn't know a lot about Bruny Island, just that it was isolated and by all accounts beautiful, and it had become a bit of a foodie destination – she was pretty sure she'd heard something about cheese.

She drove behind Cicely onto the ferry and parked two cars across, paying for her ticket when a SeaLink employee came to the window. The ramp was raised, and the ferry glided away from the wharf into the D'Entrecasteaux Channel. Cicely got out of her car and leaned against the railing, cleansing her lungs with the fresh sea air. Ted would have loved to do the same, but she decided it was safer to stay inside the Camry.

The trip was only fifteen minutes, so they were soon disgorging off the ferry onto uninhabited Roberts Point towards the northern end of Bruny Island. Fortuitously, there was only one road heading south, so Ted was able to disappear in the line of cars. She was electric with anticipation as she tailed Cicely for thirty minutes to Alonnah, a tiny and picturesque seaside township. Was this where Duncan and Michael were hiding?

But Cicely drove straight through Alonnah and travelled for another seven or eight minutes, before finally turning off the road and driving through a gate and down a driveway framed by clumps of trees. There was a large 'for sale' sign at the gate. Ted swerved off the road and parked the Camry under a tree. She grabbed her phone and sprinted through the gate, disappearing into the greenery so she could see down the driveway undetected.

Cicely had just pulled up beside a shiny black BMW with 'Kettering Real Estate' signage, outside a rammed-earth house with leadlight windows and a large studio off to the left. As she alighted from her car, two men emerged from the house. One was a typical real-estate type with greased-back hair and a natty suit, and the other was tall, blond and much more prosaically attired in a T-shirt and board shorts. Duncan Bunting!!

Gotcha, fraudsters! Ted scooped up her phone to snap Cicely meeting up with her late husband – only to realise she had it wrong. At second glance, the blond guy wasn't Duncan Bunting, he was Michael Wall. It was a body blow, and Ted wondered why it hadn't occurred to her before that Duncan and Michael looked so alike, they could almost be brothers. But where was Duncan? Inside the house?

The real estate guy led Cicely and Michael back inside, and Ted checked out the sign at the gate. The house looked awesome – the rooms pictured on the sign were big, but still kind of earthy and cosy. The blurb waxed lyrical about how the architect-designed house was secluded in trees but just five minutes' walk from the beach, with a purpose-built art studio. *Huh!* Ted thought. *The ideal home for knitting and sewing in splendid isolation after you've betrayed Bob Bristol's friendship and played everyone else for a fool, including Ted Bristol PI, and defrauded ANM of 1.5 million dollars!*

Ted's organs flamed with rage again. Cicely thought she'd fooled her. Well, she'd soon find out different. She logged into realestate.com.au and discovered the house was on sale for exactly one million dollars. Perfect, she thought caustically. So, Cicely and Duncan could buy the house, and Michael would still get a third share of the payout. Which he'd probably lose to the former client who was suing him. Unless he was planning to do a runner before that happened.

Ted melted back into the trees. After a few minutes, Cicely, Michael and the real estate dude emerged from the house, and there was a lot of chummy handshaking. The real estate dude climbed into his car and drove past Ted and out the front gate. She made a mental note to ring Kettering Real Estate and advise them that the funds Cicely and Duncan Bunting were planning to use to pay for the house were the proceeds of crime. Then she turned to look back down the drive – only to witness Michael pulling Cicely into a passionate kiss!

Ted's eyes boggled. So, Cicely and Michael were on together. Did Duncan know? Maybe he did, and the three of them had some kind of pseudo-sophisticated 'arrangement'? *Ergh.* Or maybe Cicely and Duncan had agreed to part ways and split the money? Did that mean Duncan wasn't here on Bruny after all? That prospect felt like a blow, because on their own, Cicely and Michael didn't prove anything. Where the hell was Duncan Bunting? Ted still had no idea where he'd been hiding out since he and Cicely were photographed at the Peninsula Festival Market three days after he wrote his fake suicide note.

Michael and Cicely finally stopped sucking face, and Michael grabbed a backpack and a fold-up beach chair that were sitting near the house's front porch. They climbed into Cicely's rented SUV. Ted sprinted back to the Camry, and when Cicely turned out of the driveway, she waited a decent interval and followed. The SUV travelled back through Alonnah and headed east past verdant farmland, then arced south along a spectacular coastline, and soon afterwards they arrived at Adventure Bay Beach, a gorgeous crescent of white sand and turquoise water framed by coastal trees and scrub.

Ted felt her eyes light up when she saw a few cars in the carpark with surfboard racks. Of course, Duncan Bunting was a surfer! Maybe Michael and Cicely were meeting him here. With renewed hope, she grabbed her tote and followed Michael and Cicely at a distance down the long winding staircase to the beach. But when she stepped onto the sand, there were no surfers 'out the back', just a few guys with boards comparing notes on the beach. Ted felt the sting of disappointment as she realised the ever-elusive Duncan wasn't among them.

She removed her heels and tossed them into her bag, feigning a casual stroll on the sand. In her peripheral vision, Michael

Wall unfolded the beach chair for Cicely, and Cicely sat and took out the knitting Ted had seen at the airport. If it was anyone else, knitting would have seemed like an odd choice at the beach, but Ted knew from surveillance that Cicely's many hobbies didn't extend to swimming or walking.

Michael leaned down to give Cicely a kiss, and then he threw off his T-shirt and dropped it on the ground along with his towel. Ted felt a visceral chill. It was only twenty degrees, and the Tasman Sea would be freezing. It seemed that Michael was one of those hardy types who swam all year around, like a Bondi Iceberg. He started heading across the pristine sand towards the water, and Cicely turned her attention to the sock on her knitting needle.

Ted felt deflated about the continuing dearth of Duncan, but hopefully if she followed Cicely and Michael for the rest of the day, they might lead her to him. She was contemplating going back to the Camry to wait, when she was arrested by the sight of Michael pausing in the shallows and looking out to sea. Ted frowned. His silent stance was ringing some distant bell in her brain. And then she realised she was being reminded of the photo that Don Swift had taken of Duncan Bunting on the day Duncan had allegedly disappeared.

Ted pulled up Don Swift's pic on her phone and compared it to Michael standing at the water's edge. He had the same wavy blond hair, the same broad tanned shoulders, the same confident pose as Duncan, but did that mean anything? She'd already realised they could be brothers. But then, out of nowhere, she was assailed by a thought so crazy that it made complete sense – and she knew she had to see Michael's back before he disappeared under the waves. But there was a vast expanse of sand between them, she'd never get there fast enough. She reached into her tote for her binoculars, but she caught Cicely glancing in her direction. If she trained her binoculars on Michael, she risked giving the game away. Dammit!

And then she remembered Cody Venables's ridiculous Coke-bottle eyeglass binoculars. She had nothing to lose. She took them out and slipped them on, and Cicely returned to her knitting. Ted trained the eyeglass binoculars on Michael, and his back came into crystal focus. She heard herself gasp above the roar of the sea. She looked down at Don Swift's photo of Duncan, and then back at Michael – and there it was, the exact same birthmark shaped like the South Island of New Zealand.

Don Swift hadn't taken a photo of Duncan Bunting that day, he'd taken a photo of Michael Wall!

Chapter Thirty-Eight

On the 7 pm flight back to Melbourne, Ted's head was spinning with questions.

She knew from the GPS data on Duncan's Apple Watch that he'd set up the secret camp in Point Nepean National Park in preparation for his disappearance. So why had it been Michael Wall on Cheviot Beach that day, and not Duncan? Had Duncan been prepping the camp for Michael? But that didn't make sense, because Michael Wall had been working as normal out of his North Melbourne office in the twelve months since Duncan's disappearance.

A trolley rattled to a stop at Ted's row, and she declined the offer of a dank frittata. Beside her, a manspreader forced her arm off the armrest. Ted pushed his arm back, and he looked baffled.

What if Michael Wall had staged Duncan's disappearance to cover his tracks? What if he'd done it because he knew that Duncan Bunting was already dead? Because he'd killed him, or Cicely had? Oh my God! But that didn't stack up, because Duncan had been pictured with Cicely at the market in Sorrento, three days after he wrote the note.

A lightning bolt shot through Ted. Or had he?

Her heart was racing like a getaway car as she grabbed her phone and brought up the shot of Duncan at the market, his face partly obscured by his wide-brimmed hat. Ted enlarged the image with her fingers, and realised with a jolt that the tall blond man with Cicely could just as easily be Michael Wall! Which meant that Duncan could feasibly have been dead by then.

Holy shit! Ted felt chilled and thrilled all at once. Was she on the trail of her *third* murder? This was way beyond EBI's business projections! But she told herself to pull her head in. A man might have been murdered in cold blood, and that horrendous reality was way more important than EBI's expansion planning.

The plane made a sudden drop, and the manspreader screamed. Ted's heart plummeted with the plane as it buffeted around in extreme turbulence, and she found herself thinking, *Please don't let me die before I see Spike.* After a few minutes the turbulence dissipated outside the plane, but it seemed to have rehomed itself in Ted's stomach. It was a shock to realise that even in the face of a potential murder, when mortality beckoned, her brain took a direct route back to Spike.

She stared out the window as the plane streaked through the nascent darkness, and she felt a delicious kind of sick. Spike's Magistrate's Court hearing would be well and truly over. She wondered if he'd tried to call her the second he was set free. She pictured him barging his way through well-wishers in the courtroom to FaceTime her and declare his love.

It was almost 8.30 pm when they commenced their bumpy descent into Melbourne. How many times had Spike tried to reach her? As soon as the plane's wheels hit the ground, Ted turned off Aeroplane Mode. She waited for the *cheep* of a message, or preferably several *cheeps* from several messages, but after a few minutes there were still no *cheeps,* and the only missed call was from Bob.

Ted was crushed.

Sit with that feeling, she told herself. Wasn't that what emotionally mature people did? But she quickly realised there was no need to sit with anything, because this was actually a godsend. She'd been deluding herself, things would never work between her and Spike. And, besides, she couldn't be expected to overcome her fear about kids so quickly, there was such a thing as too much emotional growth too soon. Plus, she now had too much on her plate with Duncan Bunting's possible murder. So, Spike had done her a favour by not bothering to call.

Phew.

Ted filed out of the plane with the rest of the cattle and into the tunnel that led to the gate. She'd go straight from the airport to pick up Miss Marple, and they'd resume their lives as two unencumbered, crime-fighting females. Just how she liked it.

She stepped out through the arrivals gate – where Spike was waiting with a bunch of flowers three times the size of his stupid great head.

Ted was annoyed. She'd just rearranged her brain. But before she could say, 'What are you doing here? Things will never work between us,' Spike was throwing his huge hairy arms around her and saying, 'Thank you for clearing my name, Ted. I love you.'

And before she could object, he was kissing her passionately and she was transported to a place she'd never been before, a place where she felt simultaneously safe and ecstatic. And then he briefly pulled away to present her with the ginormous bunch of flowers. And because there was so much going on in her heart, all she could muster was a smart-arse remark.

'I hope these flowers were sourced sustainably.'

'What?'

And then she heard herself burst into tears.

'Thank you. I love you too.'

The next morning, as Ted lay curled up in the crook of Spike's hairy armpit, sunlight spilled through his bedroom window and seemed to wrap them both in a halo.

'I won't let Maven get away with it twice,' Spike said, stroking Ted's arm with a finger so lightly that it made her tingle with pleasure. 'If he won't acknowledge EBI for nailing Niarchos for Mitch's murder, I'll shout it from the rooftops myself.'

'You'd better,' Ted said cheekily.

For at least the tenth time, she found herself tempted to confide in Spike that she was on the trail of a potential third murder. But just as she had last night, she kept schtum. Spike didn't want to hear about murders when he'd just been wrongfully imprisoned for one. Plus she wasn't sure what she was dealing with yet, and she wanted to work that out alone before she brought anyone, even Spike, into the loop.

'I promise,' Spike was whispering.

Seriously, who would have thought the prosaic words 'I promise' could sound so unbelievably sexy? Ted leaned up to kiss him, and they drank each other in again. It occurred to her that everything about Spike was irresistible, even the things that weren't. As their lips parted, she smiled up at him and whispered softly, 'Your morning breath smells like a bin the garbos forgot to empty.'

Spike laughed. 'Yeah? Yours smells like a kitty litter tray.'

Ha!

Ted lay back against the pillows and let her eyes roam the room. She saw things she hadn't noticed in the delicious urgency of last night, like a fairy wand and a couple of books called *Forgotten Fairy Tales of Brave and Brilliant Girls* and *Girls Who Changed the World*. A mini cricket bat was lying on a chair. Ted's eyes came to rest on the bat, and memories started coming in fragments … memories of her own tiny cricket bat when she was three … and her brothers refusing to let her play because she was too small … and her mummy wiping a tennis ball on her apron and saying, 'Here it comes, Teddy,' because her mummy would *always* play with her.

She felt her organs clench. How did anyone find the courage to have kids, when they risked dying when the kids were little? She had no idea. But then it occurred to her that she'd taken that risk with Miss Marple. And courage had had nothing to do with it, she'd just yearned for a dog. She threw back the doona and climbed out of bed.

'I've got to pick up Miss Marple. Can I have a shower?'

'Sure. Why don't I join you?'

'You're not invited.'

Spike laughed. Ted was halfway across the room before she realised she didn't feel self-conscious being naked in front of him; she felt like a confident, powerful woman. But then Spike got out of bed, and looking at his tall, broad-shouldered body made her morph from powerful woman into lovesick teen.

'Why don't I make pancakes?' he suggested. 'Isn't that what you do in these situations?'

'I don't know, is it?'

They laughed.

'Or I could give you a bus ticket and throw you out?'

'Make me the pancakes first.'

Spike threw on sweat pants and an old T-shirt and headed to the kitchen. Ted showered in the ensuite and put on the maxi-dress she'd worn to Tassie – she hadn't made it home last night to get her real clothes. It felt weird wearing the dress out of context, but at least she was make-up free. And she'd managed to shed the false eyelashes, that were now lying forlornly on the shower floor. Ted picked them up and chucked them into the bin, and then she wandered out to the kitchen and found Spike rustling up pancakes with mixed berries.

'Yum, this looks great.'

'Kids, remember? I'm the pancake king.' Spike removed a plastic tiara from a dining chair. 'Take a seat.'

'Thanks.'

Ted sat. The pancakes were great, but she was missing Miss Marple more with every passing minute. Plus, she had to be home in time to get ready for Blooming Beautiful's relaunch party this afternoon, and she needed to start thinking about her next steps in Duncan Bunting's possible murder case.

As soon as she'd finished her breakfast, she pushed her chair away from the table.

'Thanks. That was delicious, but I'd better get going.'

The doorbell rang.

'Give me a sec,' Spike said.

He disappeared to answer the door, and soon afterwards Ted heard an excited babble of little girls' voices.

'Dad!'

'Daddy!'

'You're home!'

'We missed you!'

It was an unexpected development, and Ted felt herself tense up again. But she couldn't avoid Spike's daughters forever.

She straightened in her chair and arranged her features into a friendly smile. She assumed Giselle had dropped the kids and headed off, but when the three little girls charged into the kitchen, Giselle was right on their heels.

The girls came to a grinding halt when they saw Ted, and their small faces darkened with indignation. Giselle looked unpleasantly surprised. Despite her graciousness about Ted and Spike, it seemed that their kids finding Ted in Spike's house first thing in the morning was a bridge too far.

Ted tried to affect normality. 'Hey, Giselle.'

'Hello, Ted,' Giselle said with pursed lips.

Spike reappeared. Hallelujah.

'Girls, this is my friend, Ted. Ted, this is Maisy, Ava and Romy.'

'Hi, girls,' Ted said, trying to effect the kind of smile an early-childhood educator like Fleur might use. 'It's lovely to meet you.'

The photos hadn't lied, Spike's kids were beautiful. Maisy and Ava were wearing floaty dresses that must have been curated by Giselle. Maisy, the oldest, was also sporting a handbag and sparkling silver polish on her fingernails. Ted noticed that every one of her toenails was painted a different colour. The smallest, four-year-old Romy, was in jeans and a T-shirt, and she had a defiant spark in her eye that reminded Ted of photos she'd seen of herself at that age.

'*Ted?* That's a boy's name,' Romy said with a curled lip.

'It's a girl's name too,' Spike said. He added pleasantly to Giselle, 'You were supposed to be dropping them off at eleven.'

'No, we agreed on ten,' Giselle said through a smile so thin you could slice a sandwich with it.

'No,' Spike said amicably, 'eleven. I watched you put it in your phone. Will we have a quick word?'

'Yes. Let's.'

Spike threw Ted an apologetic look. He said to the girls, 'We'll just be a minute,' and then he left Ted to his daughters' mercy.

Maisy was glaring at her with narrowed eyes and folded arms, and the younger two looked even more hostile. Ted tried to channel Fleur again.

'Are you going to spend the day with your dad? That'll be nice.'

'You need to go,' Maisy said. 'This isn't *appropriate*.'

Not appropriate? Maisy seemed frighteningly grown-up for a ten-year-old. Ted wondered if she'd even heard the word 'appropriate' when she was ten, let alone known how to use it. Ava and Romy seemed to be looking to Maisy for cues. She had the superior air of the oldest child who knows she's the boss of the offspring.

'It's not *appropriate* for you to sleep here.'

Woah.

'I was just about to leave,' Ted said.

'Daddy doesn't want you,' Ava spat nastily.

Ted would have been surprised by Ava's venom if she hadn't heard her sisters-in-law bemoaning the fact that eight was a 'nightmare age' for girls these days.

'Dad loves Mum,' Ava said. 'He doesn't love *you*.'

Ted just smiled and kept her trap shut because she was the most mature person in the conversation. Arguably. Little Romy moved close and jutted her head back, staring up at Ted defiantly.

'Go home or I'll hit you.'

It was like listening to herself as a kid, and Ted felt her buttons being pushed again. Spike and Giselle finally reappeared. Giselle kissed the girls goodbye and gave Ted a cool nod. As she wafted towards the door, Ted wanted to ask if she could come too. The little girls' demeanours transformed in front of Spike, and they adoringly clutched his hands and hugged him. Spike tickled Ava and Romy, and they squealed and giggled. Maisy said she was too old for tickling, but when Spike refrained she looked disappointed, so he tickled her too, and she giggled the loudest. Spike beamed at Ted as though to say, *Aren't they cute?* Ted was astonished by how oblivious he seemed to the hostile undercurrents.

'How are you getting on with my little monsters?' he asked.

'Your words, not mine,' Ted said.

Spike laughed because they both knew she was joking.

Yeah, right!

Chapter Thirty-Nine

Bob was radiating joy as she wove her way through the chaos of Bristols to give Ted and Chantal a guided tour of the new Blooming Beautiful Sustainable Floristry Store and School. The space was even more awesome than Ted had imagined. It was huge compared to Bob's former shop, and every centimetre reflected her warm, eclectic style – and Cicely's, Ted was forced to admit, if you counted the handwoven rug. Bob paused at her new counter to top up their glasses, and she couldn't keep the smile off her face.

'So, what do you think?'

'I love it!' Ted said.

'It's beautiful!' Chantal declared, raising her glass in a toast.

Ted watched Bob beam as she downed her bubbles. She felt stoked for her big sister, but it was hard staying focused on the relaunch party when Duncan Bunting was top of mind.

What had happened to Cicely's husband? Had Cicely and/or Michael Wall killed him? And if she/he/they had, where was Duncan's body? Ted had deliberately kept things vague with Bob and Raj, briefing them about the house on Bruny Island, but not about Michael impersonating Duncan. There was nothing concrete to report yet, and she didn't want to detract from Bob's big moment.

It was a bummer that Cicely's flight was late – according to Bob, she wouldn't be here for at least another forty-five minutes. Ted was hoping to corner her and conduct a discreet interrogation. Something was niggling at her; tiny fragments at different points in space, waiting to be fitted together to form one cohesive shape.

Beside Ted, Chantal was raising her glass again.

'Another toast! To the Bristol women finding love.'

Bob and Chantal sipped, but Ted snorted.

'Let's see if me and Spike make it past five o'clock. I'm meeting him and the evil triplets at his place for a backyard picnic.'

Chantal laughed that earthy chuckle of hers, and Ted gave Bob a discreet thumbs-up. Chantal had turned up in purple velvet flares and a flowy, multi-coloured top, and declared, 'I'm off the clock,' and now her earthy laugh was proving her outfit was no anomaly. It seemed the OG Chantal was finding her way back up to the surface, and Ted thought that was awesome.

She noticed little tufts of Miss Marple's grey-and-white fur caught on Chantal's flares. Chantal had given her a shampoo, brush and blow-dry when she'd minded her overnight, and now Miss Marple was devouring a pig's ear out in Ted's car, looking like a million bucks.

'Top-up, ladies?'

Raj appeared from the chaos of Bristols with a fresh bottle of bubbles, and he and Bob exchanged sweet looks. Ted thought how unrecognisable Bob was from her sister of a few weeks ago, who'd been bereft about the loss of her pregnancies, and trying to come to terms with the fact that she'd fallen for an internet scam.

'We've just topped up, but why not?' Bob said, holding out

her glass. 'Make mine a big one, I might need to do a few takes for TikTok.'

'You'll kill it, babe,' Raj said encouragingly. 'You'll get it in one.'

Bob mouthed a kiss. As Raj moved on, Chantal gave Bob a sly smile.

'He's gorgeous, Bob.'

Bob's face turned almost as pink as the cerise pedal-pushers she was wearing with a vintage slip.

'Thanks, Chantal. *I* think so.'

'We *all* think so,' Ted said, feeling like a huge, albeit self-imposed, weight had been lifted from her shoulders. 'Raj is awesome,' she told Chantal. 'For the first time ever, I feel like I don't have to worry about Bob.'

'Thank God for that,' Bob joked, 'or *I* might've been charged with murder too.'

It just took that one little quip to send Ted's brain rocketing back to Duncan Bunting. The key to everything was finding him. But how would she know where to look? And would she find him alive or dead?

Ted's dad, Cal, appeared by her side with Kerry. Ted gave her father a peck on the cheek.

'Hi, Dad.'

'What's this I hear about a new fella?' Cal teased.

'Yeah,' said Kerry. 'Who *is* the poor bloke?'

'Hilarious.'

Chuck emerged from the crowd behind them.

'Hey, Aunty Ted.'

'Hey, Chuck.' Like Bob and Raj, Ted had kept Chuck on a need-to-know basis about the Tassie trip. She felt the same kind of protectiveness for Chuck that she'd felt over Mitch Prowse's case. Her niece was too young to be embroiled in a murder investigation – if that's what this turned out to be.

'Guess what,' Chuck announced. 'I almost forgot to tell you guys – I got 83 per cent for my *Macbeth* essay.'

'That's wonderful sweetie!' Bob said.

Ted was so astounded she spilled her champagne. 'You got 83 per cent for *Macbeth?* Did you even read it?'

'Does it matter?' Kerry said. 'She got 83 per cent!'

Ted snorted. 'Way to go with the parenting.'

'Are you ready?' Chuck asked Bob. 'The place looks sooooo beautiful, and everyone's here. Let's film the TikTok, now.'

'Okay,' Bob said.

Chuck put two fingers between her lips and did one of those piercing whistles. Then two more. It took forever, but, eventually, the baying mob settled into something that vaguely resembled silence.

'Okay, cool,' Chuck yelled authoritatively. 'We're filming the TikTok now. So, Aunty Bob's going to talk about the new store and floristry school and stuff, and then she's going to raise her glass and I'm going to turn the camera on you guys, and you're all going to raise your glasses and say, "To the Blooming Beautiful Sustainable Floristry Store and School." So, let's practise! Say it now!'

A jumbled mess of gobbledygook ensued.

'That was crap!' Chuck said and threw her hands in the air.

Bob sighed resignedly. Ted knew why. Trying to wrangle a chaos of Bristols into one cohesive sentence was a fool's errand.

'It's okay,' Bob shouted. 'Why don't you all just raise your glasses?'

But someone was loudly clearing their throat. It turned out to be Raj, who was standing on top of an upturned flower bucket.

'Er, could we try that again?' he shouted in a squeaky voice, looking shy and flustered. 'In unison, for Bob's sake?'

There was an astonished silence, and then everyone repeated the toast, and this time it was almost perfect.

'Sweet! That's more like it!' Chuck said.

'Thanks, Raj,' Bob said gratefully.

Ted turned to Chantal. 'How cool was that? Raj is the best.'

But, bizarrely, Chantal's soft face had assumed a pinched look, and her round blue eyes were signalling something that Ted couldn't quite decipher.

'Chantal? Are you okay?'

'Yes, yes, I'm fine,' Chantal said unconvincingly. 'To tell the truth, I've got a headache. I think I should go.'

'Now? But we're about to film the TikTok—'

'I know, I'm sorry, but I think it might be the start of a migraine. I'd better get home. Can you apologise to Bob for me?'

'Of course. Can I do anything?'

'No, I just need to get home,' Chantal said.

'Well, thanks again for minding Miss Marple—'

But Chantal had already disappeared into the crowd.

Ted didn't have time to dwell on Chantal, because her eye was caught by Lee and Marco positioning the upturned flower bucket on Cicely's handwoven rug, right in front of the large cabinet that was displaying Cicely's handicrafts and accessories like crochet hooks, tapestry patterns and knitting needles. A folded quilt for a baby's cot took pride of place on a shelf, and an image flashed into Ted's mind – Cicely's famed ballerina quilt that used to occupy the wall that the cabinet now stood against. One of the disparate fragments in her mind was magnetically drawn to another fragment, and the two melded.

As Bob passed, Ted grabbed her arm.

'Hey, Bob. You know the quilt Cicely took off the wall because of the biro mark?'

Bob nodded vaguely. 'Yeah?'

'Did you see the biro mark yourself, or did Cicely just tell you about it?'

'She told me about it. Why?'

Chuck reappeared with a bossy air.

'Come on, Aunty Bob, we're up.'

Chuck led her away, and the crowd parted like the Red Sea for the universally beloved Bob. Ted tried to give her sister her full attention as Bob climbed up onto the upturned bucket and looked emotionally at the hordes, dabbing at her eyes.

'Thank you all for coming to celebrate with me, it means so much.'

'Ready?' Chuck called. 'Action!'

And that was the last thing Ted heard, because her brain was too crowded with that missing quilt. Cicely's financial situation was dire, so why would she give away a quilt she'd been offered thousands of dollars for? And sure, she was a perfectionist, but she was also a whiz at anything crafty. Couldn't she have found a way to remove the biro mark, instead of taking the quilt off the wall? That's if the biro mark even existed!

Ted's pixie cut stood on end.

She was only vaguely aware of Bob fluffing her lines and starting again, and her family waiting with their glasses poised for the toast. All the remaining fragments in her brain were now flying around and colliding, and a series of images flashed through her mind like an overly edited Insta reel: the replacement floorboards put down in Sew Darn Crafty last year ... the new carpet laid on top of them ... the rug that Cicely wove and insisted on covering those same floorboards with, after Bob had ripped up the carpet and exposed them ... the way Cicely had persuaded Bob to put the large cabinet on top of the brand new rug ... and the way the cabinet was sitting flush against the wall where Cicely's ballerina quilt used to hang, until it mysteriously disappeared.

The fragments were fusing into one blob now, and Ted was starting to make out its single, ghastly shape. Something reached inside and scooped out her organs as all around her the family watched Bob's TikTok spiel.

Suddenly, she knew what she had to do. She was loathe to ruin Bob's big day, but, sadly, there was no other way. Bob finished her monologue and raised her glass, and the chaos of Bristols raised theirs, and thirty-three voices said in perfect unison, 'To the Blooming Beautiful Sustainable Floristry Store and School!'

Chuck clapped. 'Elite! That's a wrap.'

All the Bristols cheered except for Ted. She was too busy yelling at the top of her lungs in a voice more commanding than she'd known she could muster.

'Everyone's got to get out of here, *now*!'

Chapter Forty

Miss Marple's coiffed fur was standing on end as she urgently ran her snout along Cicely's floorboards. Her eyes shot up to Ted's as if to say, *I'm afraid you were right,* and she started issuing a blood-curdling bark. Ted's legs nearly collapsed beneath her, but she urged herself to stay in control.

'Thank you, Miss Marple. Excellent work.' Ted turned to Raj, who was standing in a stunned tableau with Bob. 'We'll need crowbars, and probably shovels too.' Raj nodded speechlessly, and Ted shifted her gaze up to her sister's ashen face. 'I'm so sorry, Bob.'

Bob gestured helplessly, shaking her head.

'But he couldn't be ... She wouldn't ...'

'We'll see,' Ted said grimly.

Miss Marple's bark was now devolving into a deep growl at the back of her throat. Every fibre of her little body was taut as she stood rooted to the floorboards like a neon sign: 'Look here!' She was a deadset legend, and yet, Ted knew she'd have to remove her from the scene. As extraordinary as Miss Marple might be, she was still a dog, and if they unearthed anything, she might be unable to resist nosing at the evidence and contaminating it.

Ted took her outside and tied her to a wrought-iron pillar in the sightline of the shop.

Miss Marple looked up at her as if to say, *This is how you thank me?*

Ted winced apologetically. 'I'm sorry. You were awesome. This is just in case ...' But she was too preoccupied to finish the sentence. She hurried back into Blooming Beautiful, closing the door behind her. She and Raj took two crowbars that he'd grabbed from his garage and his next-door neighbour, while Bob readied her phone torch. Words seemed superfluous, which was just as well, because Ted wasn't sure she could find any.

Ted and Raj bashed away at the floorboards that had been hidden under Cicely's rug and the cabinet, trying to loosen the nails from the bearers beneath. It was tough work, but soon they could each fit the top of their crowbars under a board.

Ted could hear her jagged breath as she strained to prise the floorboard up. She finally lifted it back and squinted gingerly into the darkness beneath. Bob shone her torch down into the void. In the glare of its beam, they saw that a large section of soil had been disturbed.

'Shit.'

Raj prised up a second floorboard, and then Ted another, and so it went until they'd removed nine boards, and the cavity in the floor was big enough to swap their crowbars for shovels and lower themselves down into the space between the bearers. They started digging at the disturbed soil in Bob's torchlight. Soon Ted's shovel encountered something soft, and she felt a quiver of terror.

'I think I've got something ...'

She worried at the spot with her shovel until the soft thing emerged in the dirt, and Bob focused her torch on Ted's find – a corner of Cicely's signature quilt, stained with blood.

Nobody spoke.

Ted started yanking at the fabric, half-expecting it to be an offcut, but it soon became clear it was still attached to the rest of the quilt, which was buried under the dirt. Everything was a blur after that. At some point, Bob found a small shovel she used for repotting and helped dig with one hand, while holding her torch in the other. They all dug hard, following the trail of the blood-stained quilt, and sending soil flying up through the hole in the floor. Suddenly, Ted felt something malleable under her feet. She recoiled.

'Here!'

Bob directed her torch's beam at the spot. Ted swallowed dread as she and Raj shovelled away the last of the dirt to unearth the quilt in its entirety. It was wrapped around a large human-sized shape, and there were blond waves matted with blood poking out of one end.

Duncan Bunting!

Ted couldn't swear to what happened next, but she and Raj must have scrambled out of Duncan's grave with Bob's help, and they must have all clambered up out of the cavity between the bearings, because the next thing she knew they were back in the shop, staring at each other in horror. Ted's heart was pounding in her chest, and Bob looked like she might pass out.

'Oh my God, oh my God, poor Duncan …' Bob started dry-retching.

Ted forced herself to rally. She instructed Raj to take Bob home, but Bob was reluctant to leave Ted alone with the body. Ted assured Bob she'd be fine, which she privately doubted, but really, did she have any choice? She couldn't leave Duncan here alone.

Raj, who hadn't uttered a word and was still looking green around the gills, somehow managed to pull himself together to lead Bob out the back door.

The grimmest of silences descended, and Ted couldn't help thinking how, just ninety minutes ago, this beautifully renovated space had been filled with hope and laughter. But now, her sister's warm, inviting domain had taken on a sinister air. Would Blooming Beautiful forever be tainted by Duncan's killing?

She dialled 000 to report a murder, then she was drawn back to their ghastly find. It looked as if Duncan had died from a blow to the head. Ted felt the acid of bile rise in her throat, and it was all she could do to hold back her vomit. It was all very well to fantasise about the 'glamour' of solving murders, but the reality was brutal beyond the imagination. No-one deserved this fate. She thought of Duncan's poor family learning the shattering news, and how that same family had embraced Cicely as his wife. It was the ultimate betrayal, even worse than what Cicely had done to Bob.

Duncan was a big guy, and Ted doubted that Cicely would've been physically capable of disposing of the body by herself. Her secret boyfriend, Michael Wall, must have helped her bury her husband under the shop. And then Cicely had simply replaced the floorboards and gone about her business, selling bloody buttons and ribbons! Ted was incensed. She'd been right. Cicely Bunting was a sociopath – and so was Michael Wall.

A small bark permeated her consciousness, and Ted realised she'd forgotten about Miss Marple, possibly for the first time ever. She turned to the window, only to realise Miss Marple's bark had been a warning – Cicely Bunting was approaching the shop!

Ted froze. They'd assumed Cicely was no longer coming, but here she was hurrying towards Blooming Beautiful as though a delayed plane was her only worry in the world. *Well guess what,* Ted thought, *you're about to walk into your worst nightmare.* She drew herself up to her full height, which admittedly wasn't high at all, and her eyes greeted Cicely like lasers as she entered.

'Sorry I'm so late,' Cicely said, sounding flustered. 'Mechanical fault, and then we had to wait for another plane. Is Bob still—' But she stopped mid-sentence as she registered the large hole in the floor.

In the second it took Cicely to absorb the full nightmare, Ted sprinted to stand between her and the door. Cicely's eyes were blue orbs of panic as they shot between Duncan's body and Ted. Ted could've sworn she could see the machinations in Cicely's brain as she tried to work out how to turn this catastrophic development to her advantage.

'Oh my God! Is that Dunc? My poor Dunc! How on earth?'

'Give me a break,' Ted spat contemptuously. 'You and Michael Wall put him there.'

Cicely's face turned the colour of milk.

'What? I don't know what you're talking about. I thought Dunc was alive. I hired you to—'

'Enough of your bullshit.'

Cicely's eyes flared, and before Ted could react, Cicely suddenly lunged forward. She snatched a sharp knitting needle from the display cabinet, advancing on Ted with the needle raised high.

Ted threw up her arms to defend herself, but Cicely was coming at her hard, and she was surprisingly strong. Within moments Cicely had Ted baled up against a wall, and all Ted could see was the pointy end of the knitting needle, headed straight for her right retina. Would it be the last thing she'd ever see out of that eye?

'Don't ... make ... things ... worse ... for ... yourself!' Ted panted. She was vaguely aware of Miss Marple barking like a banshee outside.

A further struggle ensued, and she finally managed to grab hold of Cicely's wrist. But keeping her at bay was taking all Ted's strength, and now they'd fallen, and they were rolling around on the floor like female wrestlers minus the mud. Ted realised with horror that they were in danger of toppling into the abyss that housed Duncan's body. The prospect was so abhorrent that it gave her the injection of fuel she needed to get her arms around Cicely's neck and perform a jujitsu rear naked choke. Cicely's hands flew up to try to dislodge Ted's arm from around her neck, and the knitting needle fell to the floor and bounced down into the hole with Duncan, just as a voice yelled, 'Hey, that's enough!'

Enzo Finelli and a female detective were barging into the shop. Thank God! Enzo's eyes flashed with surprise as he took in Ted and Cicely locked in their hostile embrace on the floor. Ted could tell he'd recognised her, but regardless he flashed his yellow badge.

'Senior Detectives Enzo Finelli and Sally Bland. Let this woman go.'

But Ted had no intention of releasing Cicely until she was certain she'd be restrained by other means.

'Under ... the floorboards!' she gasped.

Enzo and Sally sprinted to the cavity and jumped down to assess Ted's dreadful find. Ted eased her chokehold on Cicely's neck, but she kept a vice-like grip on her captive's arm as she scrambled to her feet and dragged Cicely with her. Cicely struggled vainly against Ted's grasp.

'The deceased's name is Duncan Bunting,' Ted informed the cops, 'and he allegedly disappeared while surfing off Cheviot Beach a year ago.'

Sally pulled out her phone and called for forensic backup, while Enzo took in Cicely and Ted.

'I said to let her go.'

'But she's ... your murderer,' Ted said, still panting. She shoved Cicely forward without loosening her grip. 'This is ... Duncan's wife, Cicely.'

'It wasn't murder!' Cicely shrieked. She seemed to realise that her powers of manipulation had reached their use-by date, and the truth finally spewed out. 'I had a bad feeling, so I followed Dunc. He was going to fake his death and leave me with all the debts. We had a fight, I threw my sewing box at him – but he bent to avoid it, and it hit his head. I wasn't trying to kill him!'

The cops considered her coolly.

'I swear that's true.'

'Then why didn't you call the police?' Sally asked.

'Because she called her lover, Michael Wall, instead,' Ted revealed, like a badarse Hercule Poirot. 'And Michael helped her bury Duncan's body under the shop and replace the floorboards.'

Cicely looked febrile with panic. She pulled vainly against Ted's grip as her eyes darted between the two cops.

'Okay, he helped me,' she said beseechingly to Sally, who seemed to be wearing a home-made blouse. Ted wondered if Cicely had sold her the buttons, and she suspected Cicely was wondering too. 'But Michael wasn't my lover then, I was completely committed to Dunc, I swear. But I panicked, and I knew Michael was in love with me.'

Ted snorted. 'There's no accounting for taste.'

Enzo shot Ted a dirty look. 'Let her go, or I'll charge you with assault.'

Ted thought that was pretty rich, but Sally had just pulled out handcuffs, so she finally released her captive. Sally slapped handcuffs over Cicely's cardigan sleeves and advised her of her rights.

Enzo turned his focus back to Ted. 'What is it with you and murder victims?'

'Just doing my job. Shame I can't say the same for your boss.'

Enzo coloured. Ted had him there, and he knew it. Meanwhile, Cicely was ignoring the use-by date and giving her powers of manipulation one more red-hot go.

'That's a beautiful blouse,' she said to Sally. 'Did I sell you the buttons?'

'No, you didn't.'

Sally took Cicely's arm to march her out.

'You have to believe me,' Cicely wailed. 'It all just happened in the spur of the moment. It wasn't premeditated.'

'Maybe the first bit wasn't,' Ted said, channelling Poirot again. 'But her lover, Michael Wall, looks a lot like Duncan. They conspired for Michael to fake Duncan's disappearance, and then they wrote a fraudulent suicide note, even though they knew he was already dead, so they could claim 1.5 million bucks in life insurance.'

Somehow, it always came down to money. A pall fell over the room as they all looked down at what remained of Duncan Bunting and felt the utter futility of it. Cicely's head drooped onto her hand-sewn dress, as though she were hoping to escape into one of its pockets. She seemed to have finally accepted defeat, and Ted decided to push it.

'You know what I don't get? Why did you and Michael go to all the trouble of staging Duncan's disappearance and then writing a suicide note a month later? It was so overly elaborate – why didn't Michael just stage his suicide that day at the beach?'

Cicely was silent for a moment, and then she sighed.

'I didn't know you had to wait seven years before you could get the money if someone was missing. When Michael told me a month later, we wrote the note.'

It was a surprisingly banal explanation, but in Ted's experience, they often were. Enzo regarded Cicely in silence for a moment and then he took out his notepad.

'Where can I find this Michael Wall?'

Chapter Forty-One

When Ted pulled up outside Spike's house at 5.02 pm, she was talking to Cody Venables. She'd figured the least she could do was call the kid and let him know that his eyeglass binoculars had been instrumental in solving a murder. Needless to say, Cody was frothing.

'Sweet! Does that mean you'll give me another gig? How about tomorrow? I'm supposed to have knee surgery, but I can cancel—'

'No, don't cancel your surgery,' Ted said quickly. 'There's nothing going on tomorrow, but I'll be in touch.' She hoped that sounded vague enough.

Ironically, she'd been full of good news this afternoon, despite the day's ghastly events. Enzo Finelli had promised not to tell the media where Duncan Bunting's body had been found. It turned out he was still feeling guilty about Spike's arrest, so he'd acceded to Ted's request (some might say order) to simply say that the body was discovered in premises on the north side of the city. Bob had been speechless with relief when Ted had called to tell her, and Ted was stoked that the Blooming Beautiful Sustainable Floristry Store and School would be spared the negative publicity.

So, there it was. Good news coexisting with bad. And another day, another murder. EBI had added to its already impressive tally, and now Ted was waiting a respectful amount of time before she posted about solving her second *and* third murders. Count them: *three!*

#ebi #multiplemurderssolved

She started mentally composing an Insta post, but halfway through she lost her thread. She couldn't keep her socials top of mind. More than anything, she wanted to tell Spike, but she couldn't do that with his kids around.

Butterflies materialised in her chest, and Ted realised to her horror that even after engaging in hand-to-hand combat with two killers, she was still terrified of Spike's little girls. It was a galling admission, to say the least. Ted told herself to get a grip, they were just kids. And, besides, she'd brought her secret weapon.

She alighted and opened the rear door, and Miss Marple leaped out looking so glamorous that she might as well have been in slow motion. Despite her cadaver-dog work this afternoon, Chantal's coiffure remained uncompromised, and in Ted's opinion, her dog looked drop-dead gorgeous. Miss Marple seemed to agree – Ted could have sworn she'd seen her checking herself out in the rear-vision mirror. She looked so fluffy and adorable that Ted felt reassured all would be fine. Little girls loved dogs, and Miss Marple would pile on the cuteness for them. Sure, she was aloof by nature, but there was nothing she liked more than a challenge.

'Think of this as an important mission,' Ted instructed her. 'I need you to act like a friendly fluffball.'

Miss Marple looked up at her as if to say, *Mission accepted.* She had such a Tom Cruise vibe going on that she should have been wearing aviators.

Ted opened the boot and took out the picnic basket she'd bought at Ikea half an hour ago. There were definite advantages to living across the road from the global behemoth. She'd grabbed a cake and some sandwiches from a deli in the Victoria Gardens Shopping Centre, so she was good to go.

As she stepped into Spike's small front garden, she could hear Maisy, Ava and Romy giggling in the backyard. Children's laughter was one of the most beautiful sounds in the world, even Ted knew that, but still, her grip on Miss Marple's lead tightened. Miss Marple looked up at her as if to say, *What are you so tense about?* And Ted looked back at her as if to say, *I don't know.* It was the first time she'd ever lied to Miss Marple, even though nothing verbal had passed between them. Ted knew exactly why she was so tense. How could she take on three little kids when she'd only just realised why she'd never wanted kids in the first place? What if she died and caused them the kind of pain that can ripple through decades? It wasn't worth the risk.

But then a bolt of clarity hit her like lightning. Hadn't it been worth the risk with Miss Marple, a hundred times over? If she'd decided not to go to the RSPCA in case she died and left her adopted dog an orphan, she would have missed out on knowing Miss Marple, and that felt worse than she could imagine. Surely the same applied with kids. She'd been an idiot – *of course* it was worth the risk.

'I can do this,' she said to Miss Marple, and Miss Marple looked at her as if to say, *Duh.*

They headed around the side of the house, and Spike and the girls came into view. Spike was sitting on a large picnic rug with Ava, and there was rudimentary Dad-style picnic food spread out in front of them. Maisy was taking it upon herself to set out the plastic plates and cutlery. Spike was saying something funny with his goofy smile, and Maisy and Ava were giggling. Nearby, little Romy was kicking a small soccer ball around the rectangular backyard. She aimed it at Spike, and he reached up and caught it effortlessly in his huge paws. It was an idyllic scene, and Ted couldn't deny that Spike's gentleness with his daughters touched her. She assured herself she'd win them over. She had the world's cutest dog with her, after all.

'Hi, you guys!' she called. 'We're here!'

They all turned, but Ava inexplicably started screaming and hurled herself into Spike's arms.

'Aggh! Daddy!'

Spike wrapped his beefy arms around Ava and turned his body away from Ted and Miss Marple. Ted was stonkered. *What the hell?*

'Ava's scared of dogs,' Spike said.

Oh, was that all? It was no biggie. Ted had encountered scared kids before, and it was usually an easy fix. She put her basket down on the grass and took Miss Marple over to the picnic rug on her lead.

'You don't have to be scared, Ava,' she said softly. 'Miss Marple's very gentle. Would you like to pat her?'

She could sense Miss Marple instinctively going into docile mode (what a star), but Ava just screamed louder and burrowed herself deeper into Spike's shoulder. Spike threw Ted a harried look.

'That won't work, it's a phobia.'

'Yeah, it's a *phobie*!' Romy yelled at Ted.

'Don't you know what *phobia* means?' Maisy said with a superior sneer. 'You need to get it away from her.'

So, they were going full evil triplets again. And referring to Miss Marple as 'it'? Ted bit back a rebuke as she retreated, putting distance between Ava and Miss Marple. Spike met her eyes over Ava's head.

'You didn't tell me you were bringing her.'

He sounded a tad too accusatory for Ted's tastes.

'You didn't tell me not to.'

'Well, that was my bad,' Spike said, stroking Ava's back soothingly.

She was still crying and carrying on like a pork chop. 'Daddy, make it go away!'

'Sorry,' Spike said. 'Would you mind putting her in the car?'

Frankly, yes, she *would* mind. But keeping Miss Marple here clearly wasn't tenable with Ava going bananas. So Ted graciously acquiesced, when what she really wanted to do was spit the dummy and leave altogether. Finding Duncan's body had taken it out of her, maybe she should have bailed on the picnic. She took Miss Marple out to the car and left her on the back seat, after lowering the windows for air. Miss Marple was *not* happy.

'I'm sorry,' Ted said guiltily. 'The kid's got a phobia. I promise I'll take you for a long walk later.' She locked Miss Marple in the car and returned to the picnic.

Ava had stopped crying, and she said politely, 'Thank you for putting Miss Marple in the car, Ted.'

Ted could tell she'd been coached by Spike, but at least it was some kind of concession. 'That's okay,' she said with an apologetic smile. 'I'm sorry you were frightened.'

And she *was* sorry. Nobody wanted to see a kid in that kind of distress. Spike made room for Ted on the rug, and Maisy instructed them all on what they were allowed to eat, and in what order. The girls seemed more tolerant of Ted than they'd been this morning. She suspected that was also down to coaching from Spike, but she didn't care – they were being civil, and that was all that counted. They talked about stuff like YouTube and TikTok and birthday parties, because what else do you talk about with kids? It turned out that Maisy watched some of the same TikTok make-up tutorials as Chuck, which seemed to freak Spike out. Ha! Ted kicked the ball around the yard with little Romy, and she could tell that Spike was stoked.

She loved that she was making him happy, but her mind kept flying back to Miss Marple, reviled and exiled, all alone in the car. Miss Marple was her constant companion and her most loyal friend, and she'd always had Ted's back. In the last forty-eight hours alone she'd saved Ted's life and pinpointed the location of Duncan's body, and Ted had repaid her by dumping her in the car and excluding her from the social gathering. Was that supposed to become a habit? Sure, some people would say, 'So what? She's only a dog,' but what did 'only a dog' mean, really? Except for Bob, Miss Marple was the number-one person in Ted's life. Ted felt an urgent need to be with her, so after an hour she said she should go.

Spike blew her a kiss above the kids' heads and Ted's knees turned gelatinous. And she realised with a surge of relief that this situation wasn't as bad as it had first appeared. Obviously, it was a shame for poor Ava that she had a phobia of dogs, but this meant that Ted and Spike would have to spend the bulk of their time together when the girls were with Giselle. That would spare Ava from having to confront her phobia again and, handily, it would also spare Ted from having to confront her phobia of getting to know the kids too well. Part of her suspected things wouldn't be that simple, but she chose to ignore that part.

She blew Spike a kiss in return and headed around the side of his house and out to the front where her car was parked.

She reunited with Miss Marple and drove to Mordialloc Beach, where they took a long walk. Miss Marple chased a flock of seagulls, and her good humour was restored. When they got back in the car, Ted decided to go to the office. She needed to catch up on some report writing that she'd put on the back burner while she'd been focusing on the Buntings and Mitch's murder. On the way, she heard over the radio that Stelios Niarchos had been formally charged with Mitch's murder (finally!) and that a man's body had been found in premises on the north side of the city, and a woman and man in their forties were 'helping police with their enquiries'.

'Those three arrests are down to us,' she said to Miss Marple, and Miss Marple looked back at her from the rear seat as if to say, *We're awesome*. Ted could only agree, but she had to admit she was feeling exhausted. For all the week's success it had been incredibly intense, and she was looking forward to spending the next few days on harmless, low-stakes cases.

It was a Sunday evening, so they found a park right outside EBI. As Ted unlocked the office door, Chantal appeared behind her.

'Ted! I saw your car pull up.'

'Oh, hey, Chantal.'

Woof! Woof!

Miss Marple gave Chantal a standing ovation that lasted even longer than usual. Ted felt badly for her dog. Was she seeking extra affirmation after being rejected by Spike and the girls? Luckily Chantal always obliged. She gave Miss Marple lots of pats, but Ted could see that Chantel still wasn't herself, and figured it must be the migraine that had forced her to leave Bob's party earlier. Ted decided to spare Chantal the news about Duncan for now in case it set off another headache.

'How are you feeling?' she asked. 'Any better?'

'Not really,' Chantal said. 'I need to tell you something.'

'What?'

Chantal hesitated.

'I don't know how to say this ...'

Ted felt a prick of alarm.

'Just tell me. What is it?'

Chantal sighed. 'I'm afraid I've had another vision, and it was pretty disturbing.'

Now Ted was officially panicking.

'What do you mean, disturbing?'

'Before I share it with you, I want to be clear that it wasn't Bob.'

Ted freaked.

'What wasn't Bob?'

'It's a short woman with wavy red hair. So definitely not Bob, okay?'

Where the hell was Chantal going with this?

'Okay, okay, it wasn't Bob. But what did you see?'

Chantal sighed again. 'I saw Raj.'

'Oh no. Is Raj going to die?'

'It's worse than that.'

Ted was confounded. What could be worse?

Chantal took a deep breath. 'It's hard to even say this ... When I was at the party, I felt a sudden tightness around my neck. It was like I couldn't breathe. And then ...'

'And then *what*?'

'I can still barely believe it, but ... I sensed Raj strangling a woman to death.'

Join Ted Bristol and Miss Marple for another delightfully sharp and clever murder mystery

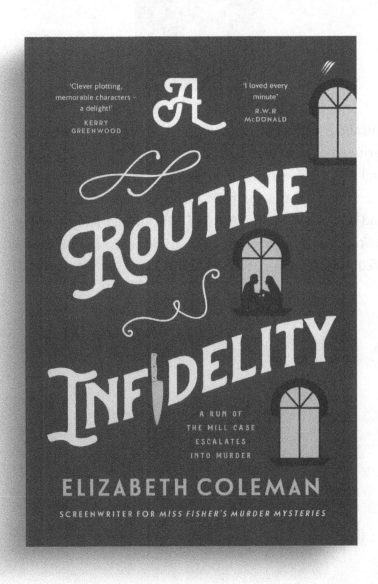

Elizabeth Coleman is a successful screenwriter who has written on every season of *Miss Fisher's Murder Mysteries* and *Miss Fisher's Modern Murder Mysteries*. She is also the author of the hit play *Secret Bridesmaids Business* and co-created the much-loved ABC drama *Bed of Roses*. *A Routine Infidelity*, her first novel featuring PI Edwina 'Ted' Bristol, was published in 2023.